The Age
of Miracles

By the Same Author

The Age
of Miracles

STORIES

ℰ

Ellen Gilchrist

BLOOMSBURY

First published in Great Britain 1995

Copyright © 1995 by Ellen Gilchrist

The moral right of the author has been asserted
Bloomsbury Publishing Plc,
2 Soho Square, London W1V 6HB

The author is grateful for permission to include the
following previously copyrighted material: "Begin the
Beguine" by Cole Porter. Copyright © 1935 by
Warner Bros., Inc. (renewed). All rights reserved.
Made in the U.S.A. Used by permission of
Warner Bros. Publications, Inc.

A CIP catalogue record for this book is available
from the British Library

ISBN 0 7475 2155 7

Printed in Great Britain by Clays Ltd, St Ives plc

For Pierre

"It cannot be love, for at your age
the torment in the blood is quiet.
It waits upon the reason."

William Shakespeare

Contents

The Age
of Miracles

A Statue of Aphrodite

IN NINETEEN EIGHTY-SIX I was going through a drought. I was living like a nun. I was so afraid of catching AIDS I wouldn't sleep with anyone, not even the good-looking baseball scout my brothers ran in one weekend to see if they couldn't get me "back into the swing of things." My brothers love me. They couldn't stand to watch me sit out the game.

My name is Rhoda Manning, by the way. I write for magazines. I've lived in a lot of different places but mostly I live in the Ozark Mountains in a little town called Fayetteville. "I live in a small city, and I prefer to dwell there that it may not become smaller still." Plutarch.

During nineteen eighty-six and nineteen eighty-seven, however, I lived in Jackson, Mississippi, in the bosom of my family. I had gotten bored with the Ozarks and I wanted to make my peace with my old man. "The finest man I've ever known," as I wrote in the dedication to a book of poems. I don't think he ever read them. Or, if he did, he didn't read them very hard. He reads the *Kiplinger Newsletter* and *Newsweek* and *Time* and books he orders from the conservative wing of the Republican Party. He has large autographed photographs of Barbara and George Bush and Nancy and Ronald Reagan and flies an American flag in the front yard. You get the picture. Anyway, I admire him extravagantly and I was riding out the AIDS scare by being an old maid and eating dinner nearly every night with my parents.

Then this doctor in Atlanta fell in love with me and started writing me letters. He fell in love with a piece I did for *Southern Living* magazine. It was all about how we used to sit on porches at night and tell stories and the lights would go out when it stormed and we would light candles and coal-oil lamps until the power company could get the lines repaired. One of those cute, cuddly "those were the good old days" pieces that you mean while you are writing them. Later, you remember that you left out mosquitoes and flies and how worried we were that it wouldn't rain and make the cotton or that it would rain at cotton-picking time. The reason I leave that out is that I was a child at that time and thought the world was made of gold. It was made of gold and my daddy came home from the war unscathed and mostly we were able to pick the cotton and the black people on Hopedale Plantation were not miserable or unhappy and were treated with love and respect by my deeply religious family. I will never quit saying and writing that no matter how much people who were not there want to rewrite my personal history.

Anyway, this doctor was recently widowed. He was the head of obstetrics for Emory University Hospital and he fell in love with my article and the airbrushed photograph of myself I was putting into magazines at that time. I guess I was still having a hard time admitting I was pushing the envelope of the senior citizen category. Anyway, I kept putting this soft, romantic photograph into magazines and I still think it was that goddamn photograph that caused all the trouble and cost me all that money. I figured up the other day what my affair with the widowed physician cost me and it is upwards of ten thousand dollars. Do you know how many articles I have to write for magazines to make ten thousand dollars?

Back to the letters from the doctor. They were full of praise for my writing and "an intense desire to have you come and speak at our hospital enrichment program. We are very interested in keeping our staff in touch with the finer things in life and have a series of programs featuring writers and painters and musicians. We could pay you two thousand dollars and all your expenses and would take good care of you and see to it that we don't waste too much of your valuable time. Anytime in April or May would be fine with us. If you are at all interested in coming to light up our lives with a short reading or lecture please call collect or write to me at the above address. You could read the fine piece from *Southern Living*. And perhaps answer a few questions from the audience. Yours most sincerely, Carter Brevard, M.D."

Can you imagine any fifty-year-old woman turning that down? I could read between the lines. I knew he was in love with me before I even got to the second paragraph. I've fallen in love with writers through their work. And here's the strangest thing. You don't care what they turn out to be. If you fall in love with the words on the page, you are hooked. They can be older than you thought they were, or messily dressed or live in a hovel. When their eyes meet yours all you hear is the siren song that lured you in.

Of course this doesn't work for romance or mystery writers or people whose main objective is to get on the *New York Times* bestseller lists. This only works for writers when they are singing the song the muse gives them. I don't sing it all the time, like my cousin Anna did, but sometimes I do. Sometimes I trust myself enough to "know the truth and to be able to tell the truth past all the things which pass for facts," and when I do, people who read it fall in love. Re: Carter Brevard, M.D. Actually, if you subtract the two thousand dollars he paid me, I guess he only cost me eight thousand dollars. Which isn't all that much, considering the fact that I was living in an apartment and eating dinner with my parents every night. I guess I could afford eight thousand dollars to remember how nice it is to come. Have an orgasm, I suppose I should say, since this might make it into a magazine. But not *Southern Living*. They don't publish anything about what happens after people leave the porches and go to bed. It's a family magazine.

So I gave Doctor Brevard a date in April and his secretary called and made travel plans and sent me a first-class airline ticket, which is an absurd waste of money between Jackson, Mississippi, and Atlanta,

Georgia, and made me a reservation for a suite of rooms at a four-star hotel and in short behaved as though I were the queen of England coming to pay a visit to the provinces. It was "Doctor Brevard wants to be sure you're comfortable," and "Doctor Brevard will meet your plane," and "Oh, no, Doctor Brevard wouldn't hear of you taking a taxi."

So now there are two people in love. Doctor Carter Brevard in love with an airbrushed photograph and a thousand-word essay on porches and yours truly in love with being treated like a queen.

My parents were very interested in this visit to Atlanta. "You ought to be thinking about getting married, Sister," my father kept saying. "It would be more respectable."

"It's against the law for me to get married," I would answer, wondering how much money someone made for being the head of obstetrics for Emory University Hospital. "I have used up my allotment of marriages."

February and March went by and unfortunately I had gained several pounds by the time April came. I trudged down to Maison Weiss and bought a sophisticated black three-piece evening suit to hide the pounds and an even more sophisticated beige Donna Karan to wear on the plane. I was traveling on Friday, April the sixth, leaving Jackson in the middle of the morning and scheduled to speak that night to the physicians of Emory University and their significant others. I was an envoy from the arts, come to pay my respects to applied science. I put on the beige outfit and high-heeled wedge shoes and got on the plane and read Denise Levertov as we sailed through the clouds. "The world is too much with us . . . Oh, taste and see. . . ."

He was waiting at the gate. A medium-sized white-haired man with nice eyes and a way about him of someone who never took an order and certainly almost never met planes. I could tell I was not exactly what he had ordered, but by the time we had collected my luggage and found a skycap and started to the car he was taking a second look. Letters can always win out over science. Letters can articulate itself, can charm, intice, beguile. Science is always having to apologize, is hidden in formulas, statistics, inexact results, closed systems. An obstetrician can hardly say, "I saw a lot of blood this morning. Pulled a screaming baby from its mother's stretched and tortured vagina and wondered once again if there isn't a better way."

He tried. "I did three emergency C-sections in the middle of the night. I'm going crazy with this AIDS thing. I'm trying to protect an entire operating room and I'm not even allowed to test the patient. It's the charity cases that scare me. Fourteen- and fifteen-year-old drug addicts. My sons are doctors. I was covering for one of them last night. Sorry if I don't seem up to par." He opened the door to a Lincoln town car and helped me in.

"I know what you mean," I answered. "I haven't been laid in fourteen months I'm so afraid of this thing. My friends call from all over the United States to talk about it. We're all scared to death. I don't think there's anyone in the world I would trust enough to fuck." Except maybe a physician, I was thinking. I don't suppose a doctor would lie to me. He got behind the wheel and started driving, looking straight ahead. "My wife died last year," he said.

"That's too bad. What did she die of?"

He took a deep breath. He went down a ramp and out onto an expressway. "She died of lung cancer. You don't smoke, do you?"

"I haven't smoked since the day Alton Ochsner told my mother it caused cancer. She was visiting them one summer and came home and told us of his findings. I don't do things that are bad for me. I'm too self-protective. I'm the healthiest person my age I know and I'm going to stay that way. I can't stand to be sick. If I got cancer I'd shoot myself." There, that should do it, five or six birds with one paragraph.

"I hope you enjoy the evening. It's at the University Club. The staff will be there and the resident physicians and their wives. They're all very eager to meet you."

"I hope I won't disappoint them."

"Oh, I don't see how that could happen."

He delivered me to the hotel and three hours later picked me up. He was wearing a tuxedo and looked very handsome. I began to forget he was of medium height. In the last few years I have decided such concerns limit the field too much for the pushing the senior citizen category. After all, I don't want to breed with the man.

The dinner and reading went well but there were two incidents that in retrospect seem worth nothing. Two things I did not give enough weight to when they occurred. There was a woman with him when he picked me up. A thin, quasi-mousy woman about my age who introduced herself as his interior decorator. "I'm doing his country house in English antiques," she told me.

"I used to have a house full of antiques," I answered. "Then one day I hired a van and sent them all back to my mother. I couldn't face another Jackson press or bearclaw chair leg. I like simple, contemporary things."

"He likes antiques," the woman said. "In furniture, that is." She and Doctor Carter Brevard laughed and looked at each other with shy understanding and I felt left out. Later, in the ladies room at The University Club she made certain to tell me that they were not "lovers." Did he tell her to tell me that, I wondered. Or did she think it up for herself.

Later, while we were drinking wine and eating dinner I was telling the people on my right about my father. "He's a heroic figure," I was saying. "He has never told a lie. He's too stuck up to lie to anyone. And he's very funny. When he was about seventy-five he decided he was getting impotent. He told everyone about it. He told my brothers the minute that he noticed it. They said he came down to the office that morning shaking his head and laughing about it. 'I can't do it anymore,' he told them. 'Imagine that.' "

"What?" Doctor Brevard said, turning fiercely toward me. "He told your brothers that? He thought that was funny?"

"He's a great man," I answered. "He doesn't have to worry about his masculinity. It's grounded in stuff much more imperishable than whether he can get it up or not." I was laughing as I said it but Doctor Carter Brevard was not laughing. Maybe this is Atlanta society, I decided. Or what happens when people climb into society on their medical degrees.

★　★　★

So that sort of soured the evening, although I partially made up for it by making the doctors laugh by reading them a story about a woman who tries to stop drinking by going to live in the woods in a tent. It's a really funny story, a lot funnier than you'd imagine just to hear me tell about it.

Anyway, after the reading the doctor and his quasi-mousy interior decorator friend drove me back to the hotel and he walked me through the lobby to the elevator and stood a long time holding my hand and looking sort of half-discouraged and half-sweetly into my eyes. Then, suddenly, he pulled me to him and gave me a more than friendly hug. "I have a check for you in my pocket but I'm embar-rassed to give it to you."

"Give it here. I'm embarrassed to take it, but what the hell, I have to work for a living like everybody else." I kept on holding his hand until he withdrew it and reached into his tuxedo pocket and took out the check and handed it to me. "You were marvelous," he said. "Everyone was so pleased. I wish we could have paid you more."

"This is fine. It was a nice night. You were nice to want me here."

"Maybe I'll come and visit you sometime. I'd like to see where you live."

"Come sit on the porch. I'll take you to meet my parents."

"Your father really said that to your brothers?"

"He did indeed. Well, I guess I better go upstairs. Linda is waiting in the car."

"She's only a friend. She's my decorator."

"So she said." I left him then and went up to my suite and turned on CNN and C-Span. Then I took a Xanax and went to sleep. What a prick-teaser, I was thinking. Is this what I've come down to now? Flying around the country letting aging doctors flirt with me and give me terrified hugs in hotel corridors? I stuck my retainer in my mouth to keep my capped teeth in place and went off to sleep in Xanax heaven. I only take sleeping potions when I'm traveling. When I'm at home I don't need anything to make me sleep.

* * *

Well, I didn't forget about it. When you haven't been laid in fourteen months and a reasonably good-looking doctor who makes at least two hundred and fifty thousand dollars a year hugs you by the elevator, you don't forget it. You mull it, fantasize it, angelize it. Was it him? Was it me? Am I still cute or not? Could you get AIDS from a doctor? Maybe and maybe not. All that blood. All those C-sections on fourteen-year-old girls. There is always nonoxynol-9 and condoms, not that anyone of my generation can take that seriously.

So I was mind-fucking along like that and five or six days went by and I was back to my usual life. Writing an article on Natchez, Mississippi, for a travel magazine, exercising all afternoon, eating dinner with my parents. Then, one afternoon, just as I was putting on my bicycle shorts, the phone rang and it was Carter calling me from his office.

"I've been thinking about you. How are you? Are you all right?"

"Sure. I'm fine."

"You were a big hit. You did the series a lot of good. Several people told me they'd attend more of the events if all the speakers were as entertaining as you were."

"That's nice to hear. That cheers me up and makes my work seem worthwhile."

"I don't suppose you'd like to come and visit me. I mean, visit in the country at my country house. It's very nice. I think you'd like it."

"The one with the antiques?"

"Oh, you really don't like them?"

"I don't care if you like them. I just don't want to have to dust them."

"Oh, I see." Was I actually having this scintillating conversation? Was I actually going to buy an airline ticket to go see this guy and have conversations like that for three days when I could pick up the phone in Jackson, Mississippi, and talk to writers, actresses, actors, television personalities, National Public Radio disc jockeys, either of my brothers, any of my nine nieces and plenty of other people who would have talked true to me and gotten down and dirty and done service to the language bequeathed to us by William Shakespeare and William Faulkner and Eudora Welty.

You bet I was and that was not the worst of it. I was going to a wedding. "I'll tell you what," he proposed. "I'm having a wedding for my daughter in June. Would you come and be the hostess? She's a lovely girl. I have four children. Two are my wife's from a previous marriage. Two are my own, also from a previous marriage. It's going to be a garden wedding in my country house."

"With the antiques?"

"Very old-fashioned. The girls will all wear garden hats. The gardens will be in bloom. Some other famous people are coming. You won't be the only famous person there."

"I'm not famous."

"Yes, you are. Everyone here has heard of you."

"Well, why not. Okay, I'll come and be your hostess. I won't have to do anything, will I?"

"No, just be here. Be my date."

"Your date?" I started getting horny. Can you believe it? Talking to this man I barely knew on the phone I started wanting to fuck him?

Oh, yes. After the wedding, after the guests went away singing my praises, we would go upstairs and with his obstetrical skills he would make me come. Oh, life, oh, joy, oh, fecund and beautiful old world, oh, sexy, sexy world. "With everything either concave or convex, whatever we do will be something with sex."

The next morning two dozen yellow roses arrived with a note.

I tried to lose a little weight. Every time he would call and do his husky can't-wait-to-see-you thing on the phone I would not eat for hours. Remember, it was late spring and the world was blooming, blooming, blooming, "stirring dull roots with spring rain."

I had my white silk shantung suit cleaned and bought some new shoes. It is a very severe white suit with a mandarin jacket and I wear it with no jewelry except tiny pearl earrings and my hair pulled back in a bun like a dancer's.

"I want you to have gorgeous flowers," he said on the phone one afternoon. It was raining outside. I was sprawled on a satin comforter flirting with him on the phone. "What are you going to wear?"

"A severe white suit with my hair in a bun. All I could possibly wear would be a gardenia for my hair and I'm not sure I'll wear that."

"Oh, I thought you might wear a dress."

"I don't like dresses. I like sophisticated suits. I might wear a Donna Karan pantsuit. Listen, Carter, I know what looks good on me."

"I thought you might like something like a Laura Ashley. I'd like to buy you one. Let me send you some dresses. What size do you wear?"

"Those tacky little-girl clothes? No grown woman would wear anything like that. You've got to be kidding."

"I thought. That picture in that magazine."

"In that off-the-shoulder blouse? I only had that on because I was in New Orleans and it was hot as hell. Then that photographer caught up with me. It was the year I was famous, God forbid."

"I wish you'd wear a flowered dress from Laura Ashley. I'll have them send you some. I know the woman who runs the store here. She's a good friend of mine."

Wouldn't you think I would have heard that gong? Wouldn't you think that someone with my intelligence and intuition would have stopped to think? Don't you think I knew he was talking about his dead wife? A size six or eight from smoking who let him go down to Laura Ashley and buy her flowered dresses with full skirts and probably even sheets and pillowcases and dust ruffles to go on the antique beds and said, Oh, Daddy, what can I do to thank you for all this flowered cotton?

Listen, was I that lonely? Was I that horny? Right there in Jackson, Mississippi, with half the old boyfriends in my life a phone call away and plenty more where they came from if only I could conquer my fear of AIDS and quit eating dinner every night with my parents.

"All right," I said. "Send me one or two. A ten will do. I can take it up if it's too big."

So then I really had to go on a diet. Had to starve myself morning, night, and noon and add three miles a day to the miles I ran and go up to six aerobic classes a week.

By the time the dress arrived I was a ten. Almost. It was blue and pink and green and flowered. It came down to my ankles. Its full skirt covered up the only thin part of my body. Its coy little neckline made my strong shoulders and arms look absurd. Worst of all, there was a see-through garden hat trimmed in flowers.

Was I actually going to wear this out in public? I had the hots for a guy who had to have everything I take for granted explained to him. In exchange for which he had given me a dead wife, three C-sections performed in the middle of the night wearing double gloves, two dozen roses, a check for two thousand dollars, and one long slow hug by the elevator. You figure it out. Women and their desire to please wealthy, self-made men. Think about that sometime if you get stuck in traffic in the rain.

I found a Chinese seamstress and we managed to make the dress fit me by taking material out of the seams and adding it to the waist. We undid the elastic in the sleeves and lengthened them with part of the band on the hat. I found an old Merry Widow in my mother's cedar chest. Strapped into that I managed to look like a tennis player masquerading as a shepherdess.

In the end I packed two suitcases. One with the Laura Ashley special and its accoutrements. The other with my white shantung suit and some extremely high platform shoes, to make me as tall as he was.

I left Jackson with the two suitcases, two hatboxes, and a cosmetic kit. An extra carry-on contained my retainer, my Xanax, a package of rubbers and a tube of contraceptive jelly containing nonoxynol-9, and a book of poems by Anne Sexton.

He was waiting at the gate, wearing a seersucker suit and an open shirt. He was taking the weekend off. We went to his town house first and he showed me all around it, telling me about the antiques and where he and his wife had bought them. "My first wife will be at the wedding," he said at last. "Don't worry about it. She's very nice. She's the bride's mother."

"How many wives have you had?"

"Just those two. You don't mind, do you? There's a guest cottage at the country house. She and her husband are staying there."

"Oh, sure. I mean, that's fine. Why would that matter to me?"

"You won't have to see her if you don't want to. I thought we'd stay in town tonight and go out there tomorrow morning. The wedding is in the afternoon. Everything's done. The caterer is taking care of everything, and Donna is there to oversee him."

"Donna?"

"The bride's mother."

"And I'm your date."

"If you don't mind. I thought we'd go downtown and hear jazz tonight. There's a good group playing at the Meridien."

My antennae were going up, up, up. This was turning into a minefield. I had starved myself for two weeks to show off for his ex-wife and tiptoe around this minefield? I could have been in New Orleans with my cousins. I could have been in New York City seeing the American Ballet Theatre. I could have been in San Francisco visiting Lydia. I could have gone to Belize to go scuba-diving. I could have driven to the Grand Canyon.

"I can't wait to see the country house," I said. "Since you've told me so much about it." But that was a thrill postponed. We went first to his town house.

He showed me to my room. A Laura Ashley special. Enough chintz to start an empire. So many ruffles, so many little oblong mirrors and dainty painted chairs.

"You want me to sleep in here?" I asked. "Where do you sleep?"

"You can sleep wherever you like. I just thought you'd like your own room. Would you like to see the other ones? To see if there is one you might like better?"

Always play your own game, my old man had taught me. Never play someone else's game. "The room's fine. I mean, aren't you going to sleep with me? I'm a grown woman, Carter. I didn't come down here to dress up like a shepherdess and let you show me off to your friends. I thought you wanted to make love to me. What was all that talk on the phone? I mean, what are we doing here?" I sat back on the chintz bed. It was not the sort of atmosphere in which a fifty-year-old woman can feel sexy, but I tried.

"I wanted to take you to dinner first. Then to hear some jazz."

"What's wrong with now? We are alone, aren't we?"

"Now?" He stood very still. I could see the receding hairline and the bags under his eyes and there was no spark, no tinder, sulfur, or electricity.

"Never mind," I said. "Well, if you'll leave me, I'll unpack. I wouldn't want my wedding clothes to be wrinkled."

"If you really want to . . ."

"Never mind. I just wanted to know what was going on. Go on, I'll unpack and freshen up and we can go out to dinner."

"I have reservations at the club at eight."

"Fine. I'll be ready."

I patted him on the arm and he turned and left the room. I opened the suitcases and hung up the dress and suit. I took a bath and put on a black silk Donna Karan with small pearl earrings and went downstairs and waited in the overstuffed living room. In a while he joined me and we went out and had dinner and he got drunk and then we heard some jazz and he got drunker and then we went home and he got into the chintz-covered bed with me and made me come with his fingers. I'll say this for him, he lived up to my expectations in that corner. He knew how to use his fingers. In maybe two minutes he made me have an incredible orgasm and he had done it with his fingers. "I can't make love," he moaned into my shoulder after it was over. "I can't desire women I admire. I can only desire young girls that I can't stand to talk to. I don't know what's wrong with me."

"It's okay," I said. "Go to sleep. Go on to sleep."

I woke up in a really good mood. An orgasm is an orgasm and it's a hell of a lot better than Xanax. By nine o'clock we were in the Lincoln headed for the country house. I had one suitcase in the trunk. The one with the white suit and extremely high platform heels.

The country house was very nice. Most of the chintz and printed cotton was green and white and there were plants everywhere and plenty going on in every room. His interior decorator was there and his first wife and her husband and all four of the children and their wives and husbands. The bride-to-be and the groom-to-be were busting around fixing flowers and watching the caterers set up the tents and the bandstand. The children were all loudly and publicly fighting over a diamond ring the bride-to-be was wearing. It had belonged to wife number two and her children claimed it and were angry that Carter had given it to his daughter. Since he had given it to wife number two Carter thought it was his to bestow and he had given it to the bride because her impecunious bridegroom couldn't afford one yet. "She'll give it back to you in time," he told the stepchildren. "Don't spoil her wedding day."

But it was being spoiled so there was no chance of my being bored that morning. The hostility rose to fever pitch now that Carter was there to suffer it and I sat at the kitchen table with wife number one, who was sipping rum and tonic, and I thought, it's true I could be somewhere where the natives speak my language, still, nothing is ever lost on a writer. Notice everything, the older stepdaughter washing dishes in a fury. The grandchildren, the first wife smoking, the pool cleaners trying to clean the pool, the striped tent being raised, the lobster salad, the uncomfortable sofas, the yard full of BMWs, the permanent waves, the eyelash liner, the way the ring has taken the heat off my being Daddy's date. "I have ten grandchildren," I told Donna and her dishwashing daughter. "Things won't always be this hectic in your family. It will settle down when you reach my age."

"How old are you?" they asked.

"I'm pushing sixty," I told them. "The older you get the better."

The day went from bad to worse. It got hot and hotter. The air conditioning couldn't deal with the doors being opened and slammed as the hour for the wedding drew near and the two-carat diamond ring belonging to the dead wife's children was still on the bride-to-be's hand.

I went upstairs and put on the white suit and heels. The guests arrived. An anorexic internist cornered me in the hall and told me about his addiction to running. Two of his colleagues joined the conversation, praising him for looking fatter. I talked to the interior decorator. I talked to the husband of the mother of the bride, who was getting drunk enough to be jolly.

The wedding party gathered. We all pressed around. A minister read the ceremony. Video cameras were everywhere. I hid behind a group of pedestals holding potted ferns. The guests went out to the tent and began to eat and drink and listen to the music. I went upstairs and lay down on a bed and read medical journals and a bestseller on the doctor's bedside table. I read his little black book, which was beside it. There was a list of women with their names checked off. Mine was at the bottom. I went back to the novel, *Russia House*.

After a long time Carter came upstairs to find me. "What's wrong?" he said drunkenly. "Aren't you having a good time?"

"Are you going to make me come again or not?" I asked. "I'm tired of waiting."

"Well, not right now," he said.

"Why not? What's wrong with now?"

"I don't know, Rhoda. I don't think this is working out, do you?"

"No. As a matter of fact I was thinking of catching an earlier plane. I mean, now that we have them married and everything. There's a plane that leaves at nine. Could someone take me there? Or perhaps you could lend me a car." I got up off the bed. "You can mail the things I left at your house. Especially that nifty dress you bought me. Someday I might want it to wear to a Halloween party."

"I don't understand," he said. "What have I done wrong?"

"It's a class thing," I answered. "Your M.D. doesn't make up for the chintz."

Well, that isn't exactly what I said. I said something more subtle than that but probably equally mean. He didn't answer for a long time. Then he handed me the keys to the Lincoln and offered to have his son drive me to the airport but I refused. The band was playing Beatles' songs. I sneaked out the kitchen door and got into the Lincoln and drove myself to the Atlanta airport and flew on home.

★ ★ ★

Where did the rest of the ten thousand dollars come in? you might well ask. Well, that's what it cost to call up my old boyfriend in Fayetteville, Arkansas, and get him to fly down to Jackson and take me to New Orleans to make love and eat oysters and beignets. That's what it cost to spend a week at the Windsor Court getting nonoxynol-9 all over the sheets and then fly back to Fayetteville, Arkansas, with him and make a down payment on a house on the mountain.

In a small city that needed me back so it wouldn't be smaller still. In a small, free city where no one I am kin to lives and where being respectable means getting your yard cut every two weeks in the summer and not smoking dope or getting your hair dyed blue.

Plus, three hundred and fifteen dollars for a reproduction of a statue of Aphrodite, which I belatedly mailed the bride and groom for a wedding present.

Madison at 69th, a Fable

⌒ℐ

THERE WERE FOUR PEOPLE in on the kidnapping, although
only three of them were kin to the victim and the fourth really
shouldn't be held accountable since she was in love. The fourth is me.

Maybe no one should be held accountable. After all, Edwina is
their mother. It's not like they set out to kidnap some total stranger.
Which is why it was so easy. She was staying at the Westbury, on
Madison at 69th. We thought about doing it there. Then Arthur fell
heir to a house in Brooklyn. Fate was running with us. The tide of
fate carried us along.

Actually, no one is to blame but Edwina herself. You shouldn't
tell your kids you are going to get a face-lift, especially if two of them
are medical students. You shouldn't go all the way up to New York
City to have it done when there are plenty of good doctors right here
in Memphis, Tennessee, where we live.

The middle child, Arthur, is the one I love. He's just finished his
first year in medical school at Vanderbilt. The other two are women:
Cary, age twenty-two and floundering, and Kathleen, in her second
year in med at Ohio State. So Edwina invites them all up to New
York for four days in June to help her get ready for the surgery. Then
Arthur invites me to come along and the first thing I know we are at
the Westbury signing Edwina's name to chits. Later that night we

went down to SoHo to go barhopping and Cary brought it up. "We're accomplices to a crime. She doesn't need a face-lift. What's she doing this for?"

"Because she broke up with your dad. Elemental."

"She wanted the divorce. He's the one with the broken heart."

"They take your face off and lay it on your chest." This from Arthur. "It's nuts."

"She left him because he had to take blood pressure pills. She doesn't have any sympathy for him."

"So what are we doing here? Taking bribes." This from Cary. There hadn't been a word out of Kathleen. She's a goddess. She's five eleven and she has this way of staying completely still for long periods of time and letting everyone have their say. It's one of the most beautiful things I've ever seen. Sometimes I try to do it at parties, but it never works for me. I'm not the type for it. Too manic and too short.

I guess I better stop here and tell you about myself. I'm Sara Garth from Courtland, Alabama. I play tennis for Vanderbilt and I make good grades. I'm an only child, that's my only problem. I fall in love with families. I spent my childhood at my Uncle Philip's house because he had six children. So much was going on over there. Nothing went on at home. The piano teacher came. Mother taught French in Decatur. Daddy ran the gin. We had dinner. We lit candles and put them on the table and talked about whether it would rain. We sat on the porch and talked to people who came over. We drove out to the fields and watched the cotton grow. I went to Lausanne School in Memphis, which is where I got to know the Standfields. Then I went to Vanderbilt. You get the picture. Everyone seeks that which they do not have. I seek excitement. But not to do it. Just to watch it going on. It was plenty of excitement to fly to New York with the Standfields to see an opera. Before they even decided to kidnap their mother.

Don't get me wrong. I agree in theory with what they had in mind. My mother's roommate from All Saints had her heart stop in the middle of a face-lift. I'd heard that story for years. Another friend of Momma's was blinded by a face-lift. Now she has a chauffeur and a dog and a cane.

★   ★   ★

"We don't have to sit by and let this happen." Cary was still making the case. "We don't have to sit around like a bunch of sheep while she lets some guy butcher her scalp. We could kidnap her. I've been thinking about it for days. We just cart her off and keep her until it's too late to do the surgery. You have to wait months for this guy. She said it was the last operation he was going to do before he went to Europe. He won't even be here to take care of her post-op. He sprang that on her yesterday. What if she's blinded like Sara's friend? Who do you think will have to take care of her the rest of their lives?"

"We could show her a video of the surgery." Kathleen spoke at last. "She's been brainwashed by her friends. We'll deprogram her."

"You'd kidnap her?" This from me.

"Yes, I think I would."

"Count me in," Arthur said. "When do we do it?"

"Monday afternoon. The surgery's Tuesday. She has an appointment at the beauty parlor Monday afternoon. We'll snatch her after that."

"And take her where?"

"I can get the Langs' house in Brooklyn. They're all in Italy. Donald offered it to us but Mother wanted to stay at the hotel so we'd be near Lincoln Center. We could take her there on some pretense and just not let her go."

"She'll kill us."

"She might be relieved. She was pretty mad when the doctor told her he wouldn't be here after the operation. He introduced her to some young guy who's going to take care of her. This short ugly guy. It's the old guy she's got the hots for. That's what this is about. I can tell by the way she talks about him."

"She doesn't want to do this. Look at how she's having to psych herself up. Having us all up here. Spending all this money."

"We have tickets to the opera on Monday night. Those tickets cost five hundred dollars. She'll die if we don't go."

"We can't worry about details. How can we get in the Langs' house?"

"It's a combination. He gave me all the numbers."

★   ★   ★

So the next thing I know it's Monday afternoon and I'm sitting in a rented Cadillac Coupe de Ville outside of Georgette Klinger's on Madison Avenue and Arthur is helping his mother into the car.

"We're celebrating," he was saying. "Sara won a scholarship. We have champagne. We're going out to Brooklyn to pick up Donald. He wants to celebrate with us."

"We have to be at the opera at eight. That's wonderful, Sara. I know your folks are proud. When did you find out?"

"Mother called and told me. They sent a letter. It's the Academic Excellence for Athletes Award. It's five thousand dollars." It was true about the scholarship. Only I had won it a month ago. So I didn't feel bad about lying to her. I almost never lie. There's no need to if you're an only child.

"I don't know how Arthur can keep up with you. You must have a room full of trophies."

"I don't keep them. Mother does. I just worry about the next tournament. Or I worry about my knee. I spend a lot of time worrying about my knee."

"All right then. Drive on, Kathleen. Let's go get Donald and celebrate." She smiled and patted me on the knee. Edwina's a wonderful woman. She's always been wonderful to me. I stared deep into her sweet funny face. I didn't see any lines. I just saw movement and laughter, Arthur's mother. I steeled my heart. Imagine letting anyone cut into that beloved skin.

"Is something wrong?" she asked. "Don't be afraid of success, Sara. I worry about young women fearing success. Arthur doesn't care if you excel. He brags about you to everyone, don't you, honey?" She put her other hand on his knee. She was sitting in the back seat between us. Kathleen was driving. Cary was riding shotgun. "Where are you going, Kathleen?" Edwina leaned up into the front seat. "You have to be careful where you drive in this city. Are you sure you know where you're going? Why did you rent a car?"

"I know where I'm going. I lived here for a year, remember?"

"Well, we can't be late to the opera. They won't let you in. *Das*

Rheingold. People are here from all over the world to see these operas. Now then, where is the champagne?"

"It's in the trunk. We wanted to wait until we got to Donald's. How was Georgette Klinger's?"

"How do I look?"

"You look great. You don't need a face-lift, Momma. You look perfectly all right like you are."

"Well, don't start that again. Tomorrow afternoon it will all be over."

"It won't be over." This from Arthur. "You'll be on Nembutal and Demerol and ibuprofen, maybe for months. You'll be on antibiotics until you've compromised your immune system. Your face will be bruised and puffy. You're risking your nervous system and muscular coordination. You're risking ending up with a tic."

"Jane Morris had it done and she looks marvelous."

"She was in pain for six months. Her daughter told me she was in pain for six months and couldn't sleep and now she's addicted to Xanax." This from me. I couldn't believe I said it.

"Well, I won't listen to this all the way to Brooklyn. I thought we were having a celebration for Sara. I'm too old to be afraid to take chances. I really want to stop talking about it. Sara, tell them to lay off their poor old mother." She smiled at me and pressed my hand. She kissed me on the cheek. I felt like a criminal and also Judas. We were violating her civil rights. I looked at the soft pretty skin along her hairline. I steeled my heart.

Thirty minutes later we were out in Brooklyn driving along a street with Italian restaurants on every corner. Cary was studying a city map. We found the neighborhood and pulled up before a tall brick duplex with a stone fence and a little courtyard. We parked and Arthur unlocked the gate in the fence and then the front door.

Donald Lang's parents are architects. From the minute we entered the courtyard we could tell we were someplace special. In the small courtyard were two Japanese magnolias and a statue of Venus leaning over to look at her hand. Very elegant and gracious, welcoming. The sidewalk was made of tiles with neat green grass growing in the cracks. Beside the door were pots of geraniums. The door was painted dark red with a brass plate for the combination lock. Inside, the house was stark and contemporary, more like a museum than a house. There were wide white sofas and black leather chairs. There was a television set behind a Chinese screen and Indian carpets on the floors. The kitchen opened into the living room. I opened the refrigerator. There were cheeses and wine and bottled water. "We are in Italy seeing palaces. Be welcome here," it said on a note propped against the wine bottle. I began to rethink my estimation of Donald Lang now that I had seen his home. No wonder he was so cautious. It was from living in a museum.

Cary and Arthur moved the screen from in front of the television set. "We have a surprise for you," Cary told her mother. "Sit on the sofa. We want to show you a video."

"You're full of surprises today. What's going on here, Cary? Is this about drugs? Because I'm not going to countenance anything like that."

"We want to show you a film," Arthur said. "We love you, Mother. Don't ask any more questions. Just watch this film for us."

"It's of you? You made a film for me?"

"Just watch it. Then you'll know."

"What time is it?"

"Four-thirty. I promise we won't miss the opera."

"How long is this film?"

"Twenty minutes. Come on, Momma. This is important to us." We surrounded her. She looked from face to face. Then she gave in. We settled down upon the sofas. Kathleen put the tape in the video player. I stood by the door.

"Lights," Kathleen said. I turned off the overhead lights. The film came on. A PBS special. The gory details of a face-lift. I waited until the surgeon made the first incision behind the ear. Then I slipped out the door and went into the kitchen and started eating cheese and crackers. I can't stand the sight of blood. I opened all the drawers and cabinets and inspected the silver and the china. Gorham and Spode and handmade pottery. She wouldn't prosecute her own kids, I decided. She wouldn't prosecute *me*.

When I went back into the living room the film was almost over. The patient was propped up in bed in the pressure bandages. Edwina was scrouched back into the sofa. "What time is it?" she was saying. "I appreciate all this but we really need to get back to the hotel."

"We aren't leaving yet." Cary walked over to the television set and turned it off. "What did you just see, Mother? What did that mean to you?"

"That you have decided to show me this gory film in the hopes that I will change my mind and not have the surgery done. That's obvious."

"Well?"

"Well, what?"

"Well, are you going through with this? After what you just have seen?"

"I am fifty-nine years old. I don't have long enough to live to go saving myself a little pain and discomfort. I want to have this done. I'm having it done."

"Jane Morris was in pain for six months. And she doesn't look that much better. She couldn't wear her glasses for ages. You want to be an invalid for half a year?" This from Cary.

"She doesn't look younger," Kathleen said. "She just looks like she had a face-lift."

"Her mouth looks funny," Arthur added. "You want your mouth to look like that?"

"I am not going to look funny. This man is the best plastic surgeon in the United States. Now let's get going. I appreciate your trying to do this. I'm not mad about it. But we're going to miss the opera. I want to be there before the curtain so we can see the crowd."

"Mother."

"What is it, Kathleen?"

"Your face could look like a mask. You can't do this. We just can't let you do it."

"You can't stop me." It became very quiet in the room. Edwina had known all along, I think. I moved back into the doorframe.

"You too, Sara? You're in on this?"

"Yes, ma'am. No, ma'am. I mean, I didn't think it up, but I think you shouldn't do it. You look fine. I mean, you look beautiful. You're one of the most beautiful women I know. If you do this, you won't be able to exercise for months. Think about it. You might straighten out some lines, but you'll lose your figure. God. I mean, no, I'm not in on it, but I don't want you to be mad at me. Okay, I'm in on it."

"Leave Sara out," Arthur said. "If you want to blame someone, blame me."

"All right." Edwina stood up and looked around. "I watched the film. Enough is enough. The opera starts at eight. Let's all just go back to the hotel and get dressed and forget all this."

"We're staying here." Cary stood up and faced her mother. "We aren't through talking. Do you know how delicate flesh and blood is, how intricate the connections are? The central nervous system, the dendrites, you want all that exposed to the air? The frontal lobes, the brain, Momma. The seeing, smelling, thinking, sensing, talking part. You're going to let somebody cut near that. You look fine. You don't need a goddamn face-lift."

"It's the money, isn't it? You don't want me to spend money on myself. That's it. It's always money with you, Cary."

"That's part of it. There isn't enough money for everything and this is going to cost a lot more than you know. Wait a minute. I want to show you something." Cary left the room to get her purse, which was on a table in the front hall. I looked at my watch. Six o'clock. Fourteen hours to go. How could we keep this up for fourteen hours?

"I want to use the phone." Edwina walked over to a table and picked up the phone but the phone was dead. We had removed the cords from the phones. She shook her head and pursed her lips together. For a moment I thought she might start yelling. Everyone at the Standfields' yells whenever they like, but usually not at each other, usually just at fate. They sort of yell up in the air.

Cary came back into the room carrying a sheaf of xeroxed papers. "Okay. Read this. This is a list of drugs taken by Jane Morris in a five-month period last year. Her daughter faxed it to us. They're getting ready to sue the doctor so they had to have the records. Look at this. Sit down a moment, Momma. Just read the list."

"We are going to miss the opera."

"No, we aren't. We have the car. I'll let you off in front of Lincoln Center." Cary pushed the sheaf of papers at her and she took them and sat down on the sofa and began to read. I walked over and read over her shoulder. It was a long list of antibiotics and painkillers and sleeping pills and tranquilizers. There was another list of special cosmetics and bandages and a wig. The total for both lists was five thousand, four hundred and thirty dollars.

"I knew it was the money," Edwina said, glowering at Cary.

"It's your health and mental stability," Cary shot back. "I don't want a crazy drugged mother."

Edwina dropped the papers in her lap. She looked around at her children. Then she began to cry. We all drew near. "You are so mean," she cried. "How can you be so mean to me? I love you so much. I'm trying so hard to find a way to live. Oh, God, I'm trying as hard as I can."

"Here, take this. It's a vitamin C." Arthur handed her a pill and a glass of water and she took it and put it in her mouth and swallowed. I couldn't believe she had done it. He handed the pill to her and she took it. Mothers and sons. Explore that if they lock you in a cell.

In five minutes she was nodding. In six she was asleep. "I don't believe you did that," I said. "You didn't do that while I watched."

"One Seconal compared to the list you just read?"

We put her to bed on the white sofa where she had fallen asleep. We straightened up the room and turned off the lights and went into the kitchen to sit around and feel guilty. "You and Arthur could go to the opera," Kathleen said. "Someone should go. She won't wake up. Cary and I can watch her."

"I don't think so," I said. "I don't think I could do it."

"I can." Arthur laughed. He was drinking milk and eating cookies. He's going to be a fat man. I will love him even more when he's

fat. If he gets fat, I'll get fat. We'll be fat together. If we aren't in jail.
"Come on, Sara. Let's go. If no one uses those tickets, she'll have a fit.
She'll be madder about wasting those tickets than anything else."

"She may never speak to us again." This from Cary. "Get ready
for that. She may not pay our tuition next year."

"Dad will pay it."

"I think we ought to call him. We ought to let him know about
this."

"Are you kidding?"

"Arthur, you and Sara go back to the hotel and see if there are any
messages and then go to the opera. We'll be fine here. She won't
wake up for hours."

We went outside. It was still light, just after seven. We got into the
Cadillac and drove into Manhattan and found a parking garage and
ran for Lincoln Center. We made it just before they closed the doors.

Das Reingold. It was superb. A metaphor for how the innocence
and beauty of the world were stolen and taken down into the earth to
be made into a ring of power. In the second scene, as the curtain rises,
the king and queen of the gods are asleep on the ground. It is dawn
on a mountain. They have nice clothes and food and weapons but no
home. They still have to sleep on the ground like animals. As the sun
rises and the mist clears away, a beautiful city appears in the distance.
Valhalla, a place for gods to live. Fricka, the queen of the gods, wakes
up. She shakes her husband. "Look at that," she says. "A city for us to
live in."

"I know," he says. "I paid two giants to build it for us."

"What did you pay them with?" she says, getting suspicious.

"I gave them your younger sister, Freia, Youth. One of them is
madly in love with her."

"My little sister, Youth? Oh, no, she is the treasure of the world."

"Well, we couldn't go on sleeping on the ground all our lives. We
had to have a city."

About that time the beautiful younger sister comes running onto
the stage with these ugly giants chasing her. She throws herself at her

sister's feet, begging for mercy, and in the end the king makes a deal with the giants that he'll go down into the earth and bring back the gold and give it to them in exchange for Freia. "Well, okay," the giants say. "You have until sundown to get it. Meanwhile, we will keep Freia as a hostage."

They take her away and as soon as she leaves the stage, the gods begin to age. Their faces wrinkle and they begin to stoop.

"Oh, my God," I whisper to Arthur. "This is too much metaphor. Let's go to the hotel and get the messages and then go back out to Brooklyn. Let's leave at intermission."

"There isn't any intermission. It's three hours nonstop. This is German opera."

"Be quiet," a man said in a foreign accent. The stage was dark. It was a set change. We grabbed our things and ran.

We went to the hotel and got the phone messages. We called the doctor's answering service and told them Mrs. Standfield had changed her mind and flown back home. We called the concierge and told him to hold the ballet tickets for Tuesday night at the desk. "At least she'll be able to see the ballet," I said. "That should cheer her up."

"Nothing's going to cheer her up. She's going to kill us."

"How long will she sleep?"

"Until five or six in the morning. It was a knockout dose."

"I couldn't believe she just took it, put it in her mouth and swallowed it."

"People trust doctors. They even trust first-year medical students."

"You slipped your mom a Mickey."

"I know. I did, didn't I?"

"What if she calls the cops?"

"She won't call the cops on us."

"What if she did?"

"Then there wouldn't be anyone left for her to love. That's what's wrong with her, Sara. That's why she wants to lie down on a table and get butchered. To have a different hope. God knows what she thinks it will do for her. Make her young again. Save her from the giants."

"She ought to have grandchildren by now. Only none of us wants to have them."

"It's the new world. People don't get what they think they ought to have. They have to think up new things to want."

"Elective surgery?"

"Maybe we should have let her do this." He sat on the bed and took my hand. Such a sweet, fine, chubby medical student. I did love him. That much was true.

"Maybe we should make love."

"Not right now. We need to get back out there and see what's going on."

She slept until dawn. "Think how tired she must have been," Kathleen kept saying. "She's just worn out with watching us grow up."

"We have to be more careful of her," Arthur kept saying. "We have to shield her from our pain."

"Bullshit," Cary said several times. "Children aren't responsible for their parents' lives. If she hadn't left Daddy, she wouldn't be alone. She left him when he was sick. I love her, but she's still a bitch."

"Maybe she wanted to get in on the modern world," I said once or twice. "Maybe she saw all these free young women and she wanted to be one."

"She was always free. A rich man's daughter and a rich man's wife."

"That's not freedom. That's chattel slavery."

"It's freedom to a starving peasant."

"It doesn't follow. It was slavery to her." And so on and so forth. We talked a lot that night. Since we didn't sleep.

"Some vacation," Arthur said. "What a pleasant rest." See, he's a real funny man and after this, I definitely will marry him.

Finally, it was dawn and she was waking up. We had put music on the CD player. We had made coffee. Kathleen had gone out to a deli and bought eggs and bread and butter and bacon and pancake mix and syrup. Arthur and I had slept a few hours, curled up in our clothes. Actually, it was the kind of night I'd always dreamed of. A family in crisis and me in the middle of it. Decisions to be made, sacrifices called for, furrowed brows, the quick darting glances moving among us. You drugged me, she was going to say. You are disinherited.

Forgive us, we will plead. We love you. We don't want your face cut off and sewn back on to make your mouth into a straight line.

"We're sorry," I said, as she opened her eyes. First one eye and then the other. "We love you. We did it for you."

"Where am I?" She sat up on one elbow. "What time is it?" She pulled herself into a sitting position, shook her head, looked at me, then shifted her gaze to Kathleen.

"We drugged you, Momma. You missed your appointment, by the way. There's no reason to get angry now. You aren't being rolled into surgery today." Kathleen leaned over and touched her mother on the arm. She kissed her forehead. Then she walked over to the television set and turned the plastic surgery tape back on. She had rigged it so that the opening scene was the surgeon poised above the patient with his knife. He cut into the flesh behind the ear, a long incision along the hairline and down below the ear. Blood seeped out. A nurse began to suction it.

Edwina sat up, stared at the set. She looked past me at Arthur. "Turn that off, please. Is there any coffee around here? My God, did I sleep on the sofa?"

"The coffee's ready," Kathleen said. "And I'm cooking pancakes and scrambled eggs and bacon. You can forgive us and eat with us or you can disinherit us. And don't get mad at Sara. She and Arthur are getting married. She's in this by mistake."

"I don't believe this," Edwina said. "Where's the phone, Kathleen? I have to call those people."

"We called them. We told them that you changed your mind."

Edwina shook her head. She lifted her arms to the ceiling. She fell back on the sofa and started laughing. "Oh, God," she said. "What have I wrought? This is unbelievable. I have to go to the bathroom." She stood up. "Is there a bathroom in this house?"

She left the room, barefooted, shaking her head from side to side.

"She isn't going to disinherit us," Cary said. "Let's get breakfast started."

"Next time it will be something worse." Kathleen walked into the kitchen and got out the bacon. "Next time it will be a man."

"Well, are you going to have her some grandchildren? Are you going to interrupt your medical school and deliver the heirs and heiresses?"

"Maybe Sara will?" They looked at me. I picked up a carton of eggs and began to break them into a bowl.

"Not anytime soon. I'm playing tennis."

When Edwina came back from the bathroom she had combed her hair and straightened up her clothes. It was amazing how well her hair had stood up, given the long sleep on the down sofa.

Arthur was setting the table. Edwina joined him and began to straighten the place mats and realign the silver. All the Standfields are perfectionists. Everything they do has to be just so. English genes. "I'm starving," Edwina said. "I suppose you know I'm going to lose a four-thousand-dollar down payment. There's no way he will give my money back."

"I'll get it back," Kathleen said. "Leave it to me. You want jelly or honey or both? The coffee's ready. You want it now or with breakfast?"

"Now would be lovely. What did Arthur give me?"

"A Seconal." Kathleen held out a cup of coffee to her mother. A beautiful cup and saucer with morning glories growing around the cup and handle. We had set the table with the prettiest china we could find. Food being cooked, sunlight coming in the window, life being led. Edwina took the cup of coffee and sat down in a chair at the table. "That's the first night's sleep I've had in weeks," she said. "I don't care what happens after a night like that. I didn't even dream."

"Then why were you doing it?" We all drew near. Moved around her.

"I don't know. I guess I thought it was my duty somehow."

"To not get old?" This from Cary.

"Well, not to be ugly. To go find love." Edwina hung her head, then started laughing again. "What did you tell them? Oh, my God, what did you say?"

"That you had changed your mind. That you were going home."

"We went to the opera," I offered. "It was the most beautiful thing I've ever seen. I brought you a program and a libretto. It's on again tonight. If we could get some tickets, I'll pay for them. I'd love to take you to the opera, Edwina. I bet we could get some if we tried."

"But there's the ballet," Cary said.

"There's a spectacular show at the Metropolitan Museum," Arthur added. "Ancient Greece. We could take you there."

"We'll do it all. Why not." Edwina reached out her hands and touched two of her children. "First let's eat. Someone say a blessing."

"Let me get the eggs," Kathleen decreed. "Sara, put the toast on the table."

A Wedding in Jackson

THEY WERE NOT getting married in a fever. Although they were young and full of hope and at least the bride seemed bright with passion. The boy was scared to death. His parents were there from Minnesota and his sisters stuffed into their ridiculous pink brides-maid's dresses. Well, there's no point in getting judgmental. The point is, I was there. I hadn't been to a family wedding in five years. I'd been too busy getting yet another anal-retentive Momma's boy to like me to have time for my family. From the age of fifty-four to fifty-eight I spent all my time and money getting this slightly younger man to squire me around and show the world I was still physically attractive. What a bore I must have been. Mooning around and getting dressed up to go to movies just so people would think I was getting laid. Not that what we were doing could be called getting laid. Still, it got the job done and I'm not complaining about him. It was my idea to begin with, then, suddenly, that spring I had let it go and I was free to go back to the bosom of my family.

My name is Rhoda, by the way. Rhoda Katherine Manning. You might have heard of me. I'm a famous scandal in some circles in the South. Our crazy cousin Rhoda, my respectable cousins call me, in Birmingham and Nashville and Memphis and New Orleans. Even some of the ones who are making it in New York City run me down.

Who cares, you might ask. Well, I cared enough to spend four years on this quasi-respectable man just to keep them at bay.

Then I was free again and the first thing I did was call my mother and tell her I would come to Jackson for the wedding of my great-niece, Annie Laurie. She's the first of her generation in our family to be married and I had made up my mind to be there. Was it my fault the plane couldn't take off from our goddamn fog-ridden mountain town?

I had gotten up at five-thirty in the morning to be out at the air-port for a flight at seven. I had spent two days packing a dress and hat and shoes and pearls and even bought new earrings. I had called my ex-daughter-in-law and begged her for an hour to bring her new boyfriend and my grandchildren and meet me there. I had acted with enthusiasm and good faith. No, it was not my fault that I was late.

If I were writing this as a play I would begin in my mother's house on Woodwind Lane in Jackson, Mississippi, where she is waiting for me to come and take her to the wedding. She won't ride in the car with my father and besides, he always rides with my brothers. The men against the world and so forth.

My plane was supposed to get in around noon, which would have given us plenty of time to make the wedding at four. Only the plane was not taking off. The plane was sitting on the runway with a light flashing in the cockpit saying the right engine needed oil. It didn't need oil. The switch to the light was broken and they didn't have one in Fayetteville, Arkansas. So, fifteen minutes went by and it was hot as Hades in the plane and I was wearing my allergy mask and reading Rilke. "All this was mission, but could you accomplish it? Weren't you always distracted by expectation, as if every moment announced a beloved?"

I'm a published author by the way, in case you want some cre-dentials. I'm an ex-alcoholic. My face is wrinkled but my legs are good and I'm in perfect health except for the allergies. Pollen, house dust, grasses, and seven kinds of mold. What else? I'm a lot of fun. People like to be with me. I'm likable and aware. Sometimes I'm smart. Lots of times I'm smart.

But back to the light in the cockpit. By the time they got it fixed the fog had rolled in and by the time it cleared I'd missed my connection in Memphis. The stewardess finally opened the door and told us to go back into the terminal and we did. I ran for it and reached the desk first and began to demand satisfaction.

There was none to be had. The best I could do by flying around half of Arkansas and Louisiana was to get to Jackson at two-forty. Give me back my money, I demanded. I'm driving. I had just spent seven hundred dollars putting Pirelli racing tires on my BMW and I was in the mood to drive. I collected my suitcase and ran for the car.

It was ten to eight. I have a friend who once made the trip from Fayetteville to Jackson in seven and a half hours and I thought I could do it. If I failed I would still make it to the reception. Seven and a half hours to drive, five minutes to dress, ten minutes to make it to the church. If I didn't stop to eat or drink I could make it. It was Holy Saturday, the day before Easter. I could make it if I tried.

I started up the curving mountain road leading from Fayetteville to Alma. I once killed a character in a novel on that road. Later, I brought him back to life in a short story.

Meanwhile, at Momma's house in Jackson, she is waiting for me. "I knew something was going on," she said, when I called to tell her where I was. She's an intuitive. Nothing gets past her. She is eighty-five years old and she has been there for every minute of her life. She is beloved in the world, worshiped really. She has never put down her pack for a moment or stopped to complain, except once when Daddy was going through his midlife crisis and "acting like a horse's ass." There are three profane things my mother has been heard to say. Hell's bells, tacky, and "he was acting like a horse's ass." She was a classics major. She believes in the Graces, in service and gentleness. I love her, that's the long and short of that, and I have given her plenty of heartbreak and disappointment. Also, I have acted out for her the life she never got to lead, have been selfish, spoiled, hot-tempered, all the things she married my father for. Is it my fault that's how the genes fell out? Is it my fault I have red hair?

So she is in Jackson waiting for me. Putting the bedspread I sent her from London on the bed in my room, making the pound cake, putting out the towels and the pink Vitabath, picking roses for the dresser. Here I am, up in the Ozark Mountains, dying of allergies and she is out in her backyard spraying poison on the roses without a sneeze. She could have given me her immune system in the gene exchange. I wouldn't have minded that.

The Pirelli tires were great. I drove up the mountain taking the curves at twice the speed on the posted signs and the car was sweet. The sun was bright, the mountains were beautiful, I had Mozart on the CD player, and I was going to make it. I stopped once to buy gasoline and a bottle of drinking water and kept on driving. At nine I drove into Alma and took the ramp to Highway 40, bound for Little Rock. Not a policeman on the road. Hardly any traffic. Holy Saturday. Everyone who was going anywhere was already there.

Wildflowers were growing in profusion along the highway. Blue cornflowers and the vibrant red triflora Lady Bird Johnson caused to be planted when she was First Lady. They bloom beside the highways all over the American South.

I drove eighty for a while, then eighty-five. The radar detector I paid five hundred dollars for in a fit of thinking the movies were going to make me rich scans five miles to the front and five miles to the back. Not a sound, not a beep.

Back at Momma's house she has decided what to do. Wait for me even if she's late to her great-grandchild's wedding. She wants to enter the church with her daughter on her arm. Her other choices are driving with Daddy or one of my brother Dudley's wives. The first one, the grandmother of the bride, the second one, who is still everyone's friend, or the fourth one, a twenty-eight-year-old student in graduate school. The third wife had not been able to come.

Maybe Mother is not waiting on me because she doesn't want to pick and choose among my brother's wives. Maybe she is waiting on me because she loves me. There's a thought. The squeaky wheel gets the grease and so forth. The squeaky middle child, that's me.

Whoever is in need. Isn't that the deepest truth of the maternal in-
stinct? Once a physician and I were sitting in a bar in New Orleans on
a rainy day in August discussing that. One of those hot muggy New
Orleans days that has finally turned into rain. We were in the
Napoleon House on Royal Street looking out into the rain and talking about women. This was years ago, before I believed in Germaine
Greer, when I only read her in a sort of dazzled haze. "There is an act
of volition in every pregnancy," he was saying. "And something else.
If I threw a baby down on the floor every woman in sight would rush
to pick it up. And some men too." I looked around me. It was true.
Even the woman wearing black and pretending to be gay. Even the
girl in the lace hat and patterned stockings, even the two charmers at
the bar.

"Then how will we ever control the world's population?" I asked.

"We won't. How about another drink?"

I passed the turnoff to Subaico, the Benedictine Academy where the
poet Francis Alter is buried. He was my first true writer friend. The
first blessed, gifted, cursed poet that I knew. Also, the most beautiful
human being I have ever seen. To be in his presence was to understand why men became the disciples of Christ. Existence changed
when he was around, became finer, clearer, more alive. He dedicated
his life to beauty, to art, poetry, freedom. Then he killed himself. He
showed me how to make my first book, chose the poems, put them
into order. He taught me how to find a cover, how to demand per-
fection. But that's another story. I didn't have time to take the turnoff
and visit his grave. Francis's bones are laid to rest. He has been in the
grave for fourteen years, has turned to dust. Dust also the roses we laid
upon his coffin, the tears the poets of Arkansas shed upon that hill on
that cloudy day that later turned to rain.

The highway from Russellville to Little Rock was deserted. Not a
beep on the radar detector as I cruised along at ninety miles an hour.
I was getting cocky now. If I got a ticket I could get it fixed. So I was
driving along like that, confident and cocky, and I made it to Little
Rock in three and a half hours. I cruised through the town and on

down to Pine Bluff, the ugliest town in the world. Then I was into the hardest part of the trip. The two-lane road from Pine Bluff to the Greenville, Mississippi, bridge.

The hardest and most sentimental. My most perfect lover was raised in a small town I was passing through. He had led his school-mates to state victories in three sports. I could have stopped on any corner and said, I used to be Raine's girlfriend, and men would have bowed to me.

Instead I kept on driving. I passed the state penitentiary at Cummins. I passed catfish ponds. I passed rice fields. I passed the place where I had been stopped once by a good-looking black patrolman who was immune to my scrawny white charms. Once I was going into a courthouse in New Orleans to pay a parking ticket and a black prisoner hanging out of a window in a neighboring jail had yelled down to me. "Where you going, you little ole dried-up white pussy?" I cherish that memory. It was such a beautiful piece of lan-guage, so funny and so bitter and so true. The sun had been so hot that day, beating down on the parking lot, and I had thought I looked so great in my new green dress.

At one o'clock I crossed the old suspension bridge that spans the Mississippi River at Greenville. I turned right onto Highway 454 and the vast fields of the Delta were all around me. The place that I call home. I passed the house built on top of an Indian mound. To my left were plowed fields, flat and verdant, waiting for seed. On my right were the dense woods of Leroy Percy Park, where I was taken for picnics as a child. I turned onto the River Road, Highway 1, famed in literature and legends. At the entrance to the park I turned left and headed east to Yazoo City. Nothing could stop me now. I was in the Delta and could drive a hundred miles an hour if I liked. No traffic, no policemen, roads as flat and straight as a line drawn with a T-square. Nothing to run into and nowhere to go but into a cotton field.

* * *

In Yazoo City I was stopped by a train crossing the main street of town. Forty minutes from my mother's house. One hour and ten minutes until the wedding and there I was, on the main street of Yazoo City with the streets full of Easter shoppers and a slow-moving train barring every street going east. I turned off the ignition and ran around to the back of the car and started getting out my things. I hung the suit up in the car. I got out high heels and hose. I put on a string of pearls and the earrings. I took the hat out of the hatbox and put it on my head.

"I'm late to a wedding," I called out. All around me the black and white citizens of Yazoo had stopped to watch.

"Hope you can make it," a man called back. "Good luck to you." The caboose came into sight behind the broken skyline of the town. Everyone waved and pointed. I turned on the motor, clutched the wheel, got ready to drive, my wide straw-colored hat at a rakish angle on my head.

At twenty minutes to four I pulled into my mother's driveway and honked the horn. She came out the door to the kitchen and shook her head. I loved her. She loved me. We had lived so long since I was formed inside her womb. She had held my head when I threw up. Had taught me to believe in fairies. Did I get out of the car and throw my arms around her and say, I love you, love you, love you, never die?

I did not. "Get that suit out of the backseat," I yelled. "I'll be dressed in five minutes."

She helped me carry the things into the house and stood leaning on the bedpost while I put them on.

"Where's the wedding?" I asked.

"Out in Madison County. Don't wear that silly hat, honey. This is only a little country wedding."

"I don't care. I want to wear it. I'm going to be me no matter where I go."

"Well, it looks ridiculous."

"I told my granddaughters to wear theirs. I have to match them."

"All right. Do as you please, as always."

"Let's go in your car. But I'm driving. I won't drive fast, I promise."

"The key's in the kitchen, on the rack." She led me out through the den. Every flat surface of the den is covered with photographs of her children and her sisters and her nieces and nephews and their children and husbands and wives and stepchildren and dogs and prizes and awards and sports events. Every person who comes into that room goes from wall to wall looking at photographs of themselves, checking to make sure they are well represented. One of the great moments of my life was one day when I walked into that den and noticed she had removed a photograph of Dudley standing over a dead lion and replaced it with one of me that had been in *Mississippi Magazine*.

We passed through this gallery and out into the hall and into the garage and got into her car and she opened the garage door with her genie.

We arrived at the church just as my youngest niece and her husband were going in the door. We followed them and found ourselves in a wide hall full of costumed people. The main sanctuary was in the midst of a dress rehearsal for the Passion Play.

There was a sign saying "Wedding" with an arrow pointing down a narrow hall and we followed it and made it to the ceremony just as the bride and groom were approaching the minister for the rites. I slid into a seat by my grandchildren and Momma sat with my brothers. The Baptist minister said a lot of things that burden the ear of an Episcopalian. Then the bridegroom kissed the bride and the recessional began. Everyone marched back down the aisle and the family rose and started kissing each other. I kissed my brother and his three wives and all their children and grandchildren. I kissed the people from Minnesota. I kissed my grandchildren, my ex-daughter-in-law, and her new boyfriend. He was a handsome man, as handsome as my son, who is the father of these children. She can pick them, I was thinking. She only wants the best. She doesn't care how long it takes. She waits for what she wants.

The boyfriend kept her close to him, his hand around her waist. He seemed kind, a kind man, the children seemed okay, at least the little girls did, they swirled around him, dancing with this idea of a daddy, even a borrowed one. I tried to get objective, really watch. In these days of reported child abuse everyone is suspect. The idea of a strange man in a house with their small precious bodies bothers me, even the kindest, most civilized-seeming man.

I pulled my grandson to me. He had gained weight, grown taller, was almost as tall as me. He looked at me as from a distance, resisted me somehow. That has never happened before between us.

"Let's go to the reception," Momma said. "They want us to get started."

"I'll take the children with me," I told my daughter-in-law. "Let Mother and me take them in the car." I pulled my grandson to my side. I held him there. I wanted to overpower him, surround him, make him safe, but maybe this time he wasn't going to let me tell him who to be.

Mother took the little girls by the hand. I followed with my arm around my grandson. As we moved down the hall we passed some of the costumed players. A sixty-year-old Mary Magdelene and a pair of Roman soldiers. "What's all that?" my grandson asked.

"A reenactment of the passion of Jesus," I answered. "A religious rite still practiced in many parts of the South."

"I don't believe any of that crap," he said. "It's just myth and superstition."

"Be quiet," Momma whispered, and swept us out the door. "This is someone's place of worship."

The reception was held at a lodge in the woods. An open building surrounded by pine trees and dogwoods in full bloom. There was a lake and a pier, which soon was filled with little girls in white dresses. Small boys fanned out along the lake's edge looking for snakes and frogs.

There were many delicate small trees just bursting into leaf. There were azalea bushes, pink and white and red with fresh May flowers. Inside were two huge cakes and a marvelous feast spread out upon a table. The bride and groom were shaking everyone's hands. "I want to talk to the bride," my six-year-old granddaughter whispered to me.

"It's just your cousin, Annie Laurie. You've talked to her lots of times."

"I want to talk to her. Take me over there." She took my hand and we went over and talked to the bride.

I have mellowed. I went around to each of my sisters-in-law and embraced them with real tenderness. I danced with my brother. I danced with my oldest grandson and taught him the two-step. I danced with my youngest granddaughter and one of her friends. I danced with every little girl at the party who looked like she needed someone to dance with. By then I had abandoned the hat. Mother had been right about the hat. Live and learn and mellow. Drive as fast as you can and try not to get a ticket.

At fifty-eight I have finally left my adolescence behind me. Lucky old fecund world. Whatever we lay down, there is always someone behind us to pick it up.

My grandson was sitting glumly in a chair. He had never had to put up with his mother having a boyfriend and he wasn't going to put up with it now. "What's wrong?" I asked him.

"Him. Edward. He kicked me going into the hotel."

"You must be mistaken. He wouldn't kick anyone. He's a sweet man."

"He kicked me. I don't like him."

"Oh, my. You want to ride around in the car for a while? Come on, get some cake and let's get out of here."

"I don't know."

"Please. I want to talk to you. I want to be alone with you. Get some cake and meet me at the door. Get me a piece of the chocolate one." He went off to get the cake and I found my mother and asked her for the car keys.

"What for?"

"I have to talk to Malcolm. He's having a fit."

"About the boyfriend?"

"Yes."

"It won't do, Rhoda. He's too young."

"No, he's not. You don't care how young Dudley's wives are. Ingersol's girlfriends. Why shouldn't she have some happiness? She's a wonderful mother. The best mother I've ever seen in my life. She's the light of my life. I want her to be happy."

"Don't talk so loud. This is Annie Laurie's wedding. Well, here they are." She found her keys in her pocketbook and gave them to me. "Don't be gone long. I don't want to stay forever. I don't want to drive home with your father." She looked in his direction. He has grown old this year, lost his power. All he cares for now is living, he wants to live forever, to go on breathing at any cost and she has begun to despise him for it. Her power, which was never physical, is still keen, and she still tries to use it.

I collected Malcolm and we walked out on the porch to go to the car. His mother and the boyfriend were sitting at a glass-topped table, laughing and drinking wine, talking to my nieces and their husbands. "We're going riding," I told her. "We want to be alone."

We went out to the parking lot and got into the car and my daughter-in-law followed us and got in the backseat.

"He's mad at Edward," I said. "He says Edward kicked him."

"They were just horsing around." She leaned up into the front seat and touched my hand. "He's the gentlest man on the earth. He wouldn't harm a child."

"You have to let your mother have a boyfriend," I began. "There's nothing wrong with that. She loves you. So do I. We love you more than anything in the world. We would never let anyone harm you in any way. We would kill or die for you. But you ought to let her have a boyfriend. She lets you have friends. Edward's a nice man. He's the nicest man I've met in years."

"No, he's not. He's mean to me." He scrunched down into the seat, looked at the floor. Heart of my heart, the dearest thing on earth to me. I touched his mother's hand. My son had destroyed every relationship I'd ever had after I divorced his father. That was with us in the car. And the pain my son had caused this woman. And the pain she had caused my son. And these children, our inheritance and legacy, our treasure.

"Okay," I said. "You need to have a meeting. You and your mother and Edward sit down and talk this over. Your mother says he was horsing around. Maybe you took it wrong."

"He did it to be mean."

"Okay. I'm going to send you some books about what to do when your mother has a boyfriend. Hell, maybe I'll send you Sophocles." My daughter-in-law laughed. For a moment the tension wavered. Like a thermocline, the water of laughter invaded the heat. Then the heat returned.

"If he's going to be around, I'll come and live with you," he said. "If you like me so much let me live with you."

Above us the beautiful light green leaves swayed in the breeze. Above them stretched the sky with its immensity and wonder. I looked into my ex-daughter-in-law's wide brown eyes. We had fought this child's father together. I had fought his father and grandfather and great-grandfather. We knew what we were up against. This will that grew stronger from generation to generation. That finally, in this child, had been mixed with her German, Dutch, and American Indian genes. Hybrid vigor. My Celtic craziness dissolved in more rational, cooler genes. Will and imagination and a sense of order remained of my genetic contribution. And the strongest of these was will.

There he sat, in the passenger seat of his great-grandmother's car, the end product of all this random *genius*, ready to defend his territory at any cost.

"I'm going to send you a book about a man named Oedipus," I said. "It will explain the psychological ramifications of this problem. Call me up when you've read it and we'll talk about it."

"I don't know what any of that means." He raised his head and looked at me. Gave me the full force of his gaze. He's an intuitive too. Nothing gets past him. There is no barrier between him and the world. Not a membrane to separate him from all that burgeoning wonder, all the glorious and inglorious knowledge of our being.

"I will love you till I die," I said. "I love you more than anyone. You are the dearest thing on earth to me."

"Let's go back to the party."

"We better," his mother added. "I have to see about the little girls."

The day wore on into evening. The little girls went off to spend the night with cousins. My ex-daughter-in-law and her boyfriend went off to party with my nieces.

I took my grandson to the mall. We bought some baseball shirts and a pair of striped shorts. We ate some junk food. We held hands and walked around and looked at things. He is five foot five inches tall now. As tall as I am. Soon it will be over, this part of it. The part when he was a child and I was his guardian angel. He will leave me and go off to the world. He will leave me here with memories of many days in many malls, of buying transformers and Lego sets and books and basketball shoes and posters of Jose Canseco. Baseball hats and tacos and pizza and frozen yogurt. Goofy golf and batting cages and long walks and bike rides and swimming pools. We have heard the chimes at bedtime, oh, the malls that we have seen.

"I love you," I kept telling him. "It's okay if your mother has a boyfriend. It will make her stronger. Anything that makes her stronger, makes you stronger. We are a family. We stick together."

"I wish you lived where I do. I wish you lived next door."

"I wish I did too. I hate to miss a day of seeing you."

After a while the mall began to close and we walked out into the parking lot and watched the black teenagers forming into groups. I held his hand and let him find the car for me.

We went over to my momma's house and slept in my old bed. We snuggled down into the sheets from London. I pulled his fine strong eleven-and-a-half-year-old body into my arms and held him there. "You are my angel," I said. "No one will ever take your place with me. Your mother and I love you more than you will ever know. No one will ever take her or me away from you."

"I don't think so," he said. I found his hand and held it. It is still the same size as mine. Delicate, with long thin fingers like his mother's. He is the catcher on his baseball team, the goalie at soccer. Always the dirtiest, hardest job in any sport. Because he can be depended upon.

"Go to sleep," I said. "Tomorrow's Easter. Grandmother dyed eggs for us to hide."

In the morning everyone reconvened in my mother's yard to hide Easter eggs and take photographs of each other. It was about evenly divided, between children who had been to Sunday School and the children of apostates.

The boyfriend moved among the children being charming. "My father is taller than you are," I heard the six-year-old girl tell him.

"No, he's not," I said. "Edward is taller than your father." He raised his eyebrows just an almost imperceptible amount and sighed, and seemed to thank me.

"Why did you introduce him to the children?" I asked my ex-daughter-in-law. "Why did you even let him meet them?"

"He asked to. I put it off as long as I could. Well, it's done now. Let's get this Easter egg hunt over and I'll take him home."

"This was a stupid idea. I shouldn't have talked you into coming. It was nuts. Coming up here into your ex-husband's family. Mother acting like the high priestess of a cult. The shrine of the double standard. My family in Jackson, Mississippi."

"It's okay. I know what I want. I won't let this stop me."

"Good. I'm glad to hear it." I hugged her to my side. This woman six inches taller than me who is the only daughter I have ever had, who has never let me down or disappointed me. This giver of grandchildren, whom I worship.

An hour later they drove away. The boyfriend driving. My ex-daughter-in-law riding shotgun with the six-year-old beside her. The older children on the backseat with their Walkmans plugged into their ears. "Thank goodness that is over," my mother said.

"What a mean thing to say," I said. "I'm pulling for her. I want her to be happy."

"He's too young," my mother said. "It's embarrassing."

Five days later I was in the kitchen of my house, leaning on a counter, hearing the fallout on the phone. "The boyfriend's gone," my ex-daughter-in-law is saying. "They scared him off."

"I'm sorry. It's my fault. I shouldn't have asked you to come."

"It had to happen. I'm a group of people. I'm four of us."

"Do you really believe that?"

"No."

"Is there something I can do?"

"I don't think so. I guess I have to ride it out."

"Fuck love. Fuck having lovers."

"Come on, Rhoda. It's not that bad. I had a good time for a while."

"Next time keep him to yourself. Don't even tell him you have kids. Don't tell me."

"I've had enough to last me for a while."

We hung up and I went out into my garden and started to water the hostas and the lilies. I pulled the garden hose around the hickory tree and started to turn it on. Then I changed my mind. To hell with nature. Let it take care of itself. I spotted a wasps' nest under the eaves by the garage. I went into the house and got a can of flying insect spray and sprayed it good. I doused it and then I sprayed some on a spider's web.

If I had been one of my grandfathers I would have gone out to the stables and saddled a horse and put a bit in its mouth and gone riding with my dogs at my heels. Instead, I went into the house and put on my running shoes and started out around the mountain. I don't have any German-Jewish or American Indian or Dutch genes. I'm a Celt. I pile up stones and keep a loaded pistol in my underwear drawer. My ancestors painted themselves blue and impaled each other on oak staves. I can't stand tyranny. From the world outside or the tyranny of the heart. How can I help anyone? I can't even help myself. I was GLAD HE HAD WON. GLAD NO ONE COULD TAKE HIS

MOTHER FROM HIM. GLAD HE KNEW HOW TO KEEP HER.

Even as I suffered for her I was glad no man would be in the house with those little girls, not any man, not the sweetest man in the world, in this chaotic world, vale of sorrows, vale of tears.

Too Much Rain, or,
The Assault
of the Mold Spores

⁒

THE SPRING Miss Crystal got her allergies was no joke. Creating jobs, Mr. Manny called it, and it did turn out to be quite an industry. By the time her nose quit running and she could talk again, there were fifteen different carpenters, four painters, two attic men, and half the teenagers in the neighborhood who knew the combinations to every door in the house. Two, two, four, two, three, is the front door combination in case there is anyone left in New Orleans who doesn't know it yet. There is nothing left in this house to steal anyway as Miss Crystal has turned out to be allergic to house dust as well as to mold spores and she is not taking any chances on any accumulating on any bric-a-brac. The allergy doctor showed Miss Crystal a blown-up photograph of a dust mite and that was the end of every book and statue and flower vase and piece of antique furniture in this house. We have gone completely modern for our interior with everything painted white and some new chairs by Mr. Mies van der Rohe who does not believe in chairs having arms on them. Also we have pulled up the carpets and put in black and white tiles that show every smudge and heel print and require a pair of floor cleaners coming in every Friday to vacuum and buff.

So much for the house. It was Miss Crystal's body that was the real battlefield. She even insisted that I go down and be tested even though I have never been allergic to anything in my life and wasn't showing any signs. Still, she pled and pled and finally I went on down and let them test me. They put sixty holes in your back and then you wait in this freezing cold room for twenty minutes and then they come back in to see if any of the holes have started itching or turning red. Then they put sixty more on your right arm with stronger chemicals in them and if that doesn't get a reaction they put sixty on your left arm. They were just debating whether to put a fourth set on my leg when I called a halt. Only one of all the holes had turned red and it was to a plant that grows up in Minnesota where I am not planning on going anytime soon and besides, I had to lead a youth group at four and it was growing late.

Another note. There was this nurse in white giving allergy shots to little children. The whole time I was waiting to be tested I had to watch that going on. She was standing in the hall with this tray full of dirty little bottles of different sorts of things people are allergic to. Ragweed, maple pollen, cedar dust, geraniums, and so forth. Each little child would come up and stick their arm out and she would dip a needle down into two or three of the jars, never watching what she was doing, just chatting with the parents and jabbing the needle in and out of the jar necks. Then she'd grab the child's arm and stick the needle in. I have never seen a nurse I trusted less. I wouldn't take those shots for anything in the world from that woman and I told Miss Crystal so. If you take them, I warned, demand another nurse.

The first thing the allergy doctor tried on Miss Crystal was having her stay in the house and putting her on some nose spray and a drug called Seldane that dries you up without putting you to sleep. I'd stick with Benadryl, I told her. You know you have strange reactions to prescription drugs. I have to take it, she replied. I have to put my faith in someone, so I have picked out Doctor Allensby.

So she began to take these Seldane tablets twice a day, once every twelve hours, and things picked up. Not only had her doctor recommended them but they were also recommended by a medical book we bought recently. Three days go by and all is going well. She is even able to go out in the yard to oversee the gardener.

The third afternoon she went down to the video store to get Crystal Anne a video and the girl in the store started talking to her about allergies and how everyone is getting them now and isn't it strange that it happened right when the pollution is getting worse and don't tell her it is only plants and trees making people in the United States get sick.

"I've got mine under control," Miss Crystal says. "I'm taking this new drug called Seldane. It's great. It makes you kind of hyper but I can stand it. It's better than not breathing."

"Oh, my God," the girl says. "My brother and I took that last year. It made us have terrible dreams. Very, very lifelike dreams."

"What did you say?" Miss Crystal says. "What did you just say?" It turns out she had been having terrible dreams for three nights but had not put the two things together. In the worst dream she and I are standing in a parking lot watching Mr. Manny drive the Lexus off the top of a cliff with the baby in the backseat. Mr. Manny is Miss Crystal's baby-faced and excessively brilliant husband. They have a mixed marriage which is doing better after many trials and tribulations. They met at a party in Pass Christian during the third day of the Six-Day War, when Miss Crystal was in her pro-Israeli syndrome and while Mr. Manny was obsessed with blonde Christian women, due to his having been sent to New England to school when he was thirteen years old. All of this came out in therapy. So they forged this troubled marriage out of these materials and they have this precious little girl, Crystal Anne, who is one of the two mainstays of my life. The other is my niece, Andria, who is at LSU leading the anti-establishment crusade. I have never been able to have a child of my own and for many years now I have seen that as a blessing in disguise. You get your heart tied up in children and you lose all sense of how to care for them and teach them to be strong. But back to Miss Crystal's dream.

The Lexus falls on its nose as we watch in terror and disbelief. Then a voice comes from the car. It is Mr. Manny's voice and he says everything is all right. He gets out of the car and then he reaches in the backseat and brings out the baby. They are both all right although they were not wearing seat belts. I think this dream is only a justification for Miss Crystal and Miss Lydia refusing to wear seat belts when they are together. Miss Lydia is Miss Crystal's best friend. She is a famous painter out in California who gets up to seventeen thousand dollars for every painting that she paints. Still, she and Miss Crystal are bad to act like adolescents when they get together. Many of their worst habits are on the wane now but they still like to ride around New Orleans with no seat belts. They say it is to prove there is no security, but I think it is more about not messing up their dresses when they are going out.

But back to the medical problems. You cannot win at this allergy game. Once your body goes autoimmune on you it is just one long trip to the doctor or the drugstore. Meanwhile, every tree and plant in New Orleans was bursting with blooms. Putting out pollen morning, noon, and night. "I am no longer part of the beauty of the world," Miss Crystal cried out at least once a day. "Now I have to hate the things I used to love so dearly."

"You never did pay much attention to flowers," I consoled her. "You'd rather be on the tennis court any day."

"I can't even play tennis with this going on," she answered. "I can see the pollen falling from the trees. The more I breathe, the more Seldane I have to take."

Here's what Mr. Manny decided we should do. All go to Florida and stay a few weeks and if Miss Crystal gets well, buy a house there for her to live in when the going gets rough in New Orleans.

It was Monday when we decided we should leave. By Tuesday afternoon we were out at the airport, only of course by then Mr. Manny had decided he couldn't leave his work. Now that he has quit his law firm and gotten into environmental work he is a worse workaholic than he was when he was only doing it to make money. He is fighting to save the wetlands and has almost completely stopped wearing ties.

So it was only Miss Crystal and Crystal Anne and myself who were boarding the plane. Crystal Anne and I sat together and Miss Crystal sat across the aisle reading a *Vogue* magazine and stopping every few minutes to blow her nose. "We will be there in two hours," I told her several times. "Buck up your courage. We have solved worse problems than this."

"You're right," Miss Crystal answered. "This is a very small problem. A problem we can fix."

"I was going to be the lilac fairy in the school play," Crystal Anne noted for the third time. "I'll never get to be the lilac fairy again."

"You are going to Florida instead," I told her. "Many little girls would give their eyeteeth for a week off from school to see the ocean."

We arrived in Saint Petersburg in the middle of the afternoon and a van from the hotel picked us up and carried us into town. It is a very spread-out city and quite clean and the hotel Mr. Manny had gotten for us was this very swanky hotel on the beach with an indoor pool and one outside near the ocean. Crystal Anne loves pools, although she also likes to swim in the ocean. Personally I do not like water that has chlorine in it. It reminds me too much of washday down in Boutte when my auntee would have water boiling with so much bleach in it the smell would fill the town.

We settled down in two rooms with a door that opened between them. There were balconies that looked out onto the beach and the Gulf of Mexico. Crystal Anne was enchanted by the balconies and kept going from one to the other putting her dolls on the chairs and making little nests for them overlooking the sea. She is eight years old now, just as sweet as an angel, which she has been ever since the day that she was born. Born sweet and stayed sweet. Also, she has a very fine brain and she knows how to use it. She is like Mr. Manny in that. She does not let outside influences change the way she sees things. If she has a flaw, it is that she is very rigid about her likes and dislikes. If she likes someone, she will stick up for them no matter what. If she takes a dislike to them, watch out. Well, she took a dislike to Mr. Hotchkiss, which Miss Lydia later said only proved once again that a little child should lead us.

But we had barely arrived and Mr. Hotchkiss had not showed up yet and so we took off our traveling clothes and went down to the pool to let Crystal Anne practice swimming.

The people around the pool were very friendly. There was a couple from Maine who had met each other at a support meeting they went to after their spouses died. His had died and hers had died so they got together and have lived happily ever after for two years. They each talked a lot about the people they used to be married to. It seemed that was most of their conversation, plus some jokes he was making about the fact that she was fifteen years younger than he was and other jokes about the fact that she smoked. She mostly talked about sailing the British Virgin Islands with her dead husband who was her age and what a good sailor he was and their narrow escapes.

I began to get the picture. Her on the sailboat with her young good-looking husband, the two of them tanned and sort of devil-may-care and smoking all the time. Him in a nice house with the mother of his children. Both of them happy and content and him never giving a thought to a younger woman until his wife died and forced him into it. He was very fat and jolly and glad to talk, and she was not pretty but she was vivacious and I began to take to her.

Another woman who said she was forty-eight was lying on a deck chair and she got into our conversation and began to tell all about her young husband and how her mother pretended not to know she was married to a man half her age and was supporting him. I really liked this woman a lot. Miss Martha Ann Hamblin from Saint Louis, Missouri. She was a snowbird, which means she goes to Florida to get away from snowstorms. Her husband was with her on the trip but he was off somewhere shopping for clothes. She was very vivacious too and had a pretty face. She kept laughing when she'd tell things about herself and she and Miss Crystal were establishing a rapport.

There weren't many other children at the pool. Just a fat girl about eight and another girl maybe twelve years old. Crystal Anne tried to make friends with the fat girl but the fat girl only wanted to play in her water wings and wouldn't dive or swim laps. I feel a great sympathy for fat children and always want to take over and change their diet although my niece Andria tells me that psychiatrists say many fat children are born to be that way and have a slow metabolism and should not be made fun of or have people always after them trying to change their diet.

We spent most of the afternoon by the pool or walking down to the ocean and back. Miss Crystal said she felt like a new woman from breathing the salt air. Crystal Anne was trying to get in one hundred laps before the sun went down. She was up to seventy-six when we made her give up and went up to our rooms to dress for dinner. The air down here in Florida is soft and fine and full of salt. So puffy and romantic. It is easy to see why all these people from up north come down here and decide to stay. Balmy is the word I'm searching for. Balmy is the only word for it.

There were two dining rooms in the hotel. The Palm Court, which is the finest one, and a more casual area called Sixteen Palms. We tossed a coin and the Palm Court won, so we dressed up in our best clothes and put the heated rollers on Crystal Anne's hair and dressed her in her new pink linen dress and down we went to have our first resort meal. There weren't too many people in the Palm Court when we got there, so we took a seat at the best table looking out toward the sea and began to talk about the salt air and why it always seems to mend anything that is wrong with you. We were laughing and carrying on and making fun of the menu when this very handsome man with black hair came in and took a seat at a small table facing us. He was very elegant, tall and thin and wearing a white linen suit like you see in movies set in Europe. He had on these little wire spectacles that made him look even more distinguished. While he was studying the menu the headwaiter came over and told him there was a telephone call for him and would he like a phone, but he said no, he wouldn't take it, he was eating dinner and would the headwaiter take a message.

Our dinner had been served but Miss Crystal had lost all interest in food. She started sitting up very straight in her chair and asking Crystal Anne things that I know couldn't really be of any interest to her. Also, she had taken off her glasses.

I have seen Miss Crystal get that way before, like she has seen a way out of a tunnel that she thought had no end. Like she had been asleep for days and all of a sudden woke up and started blinking.

She was not looking at him. Although by now he was occasionally raising his eyes above the little glasses and looking at her. That was about all that happened that night, except that he finished dinner before we did and passed by our table on his way to go stand on the patio and drink a brandy. "What a lovely child," he said, as he passed our table, this very cultured accent like he was from Boston or England or somewhere far away. Miss Crystal blushed and Crystal Anne bristled like he had said she was ugly. "I hate it when people do that," she said. "It's rude to act like children don't know you are talking about them."

The next morning, no sooner had we gone down to the beach and gotten settled on our striped beach chairs, when he came walking down to the water's edge. He had on a pair of blue jeans and a starched white shirt and some leather handmade sandals. In the morning light he looked even handsomer than he had the night before. He walked past us and stood a long time at the water's edge, letting us admire his back.

I should stop here and tell you something about Miss Crystal that you might miss if you only heard me tell the things she says and does. She is very lovely to look at. Not just the features of her face. She has a kind of glow about her, something coming from deep within that draws people to her. Everything she does has a kind of gracefulness and charm. I do not love her for nothing. It is because she has this glow of kindness, from the inside going out and it has always reached out to me. She does not think of me as a maid or a servant and I do not think of her as my employer. Not to mention that I have always been the highest-paid housekeeper in New Orleans and I have never had to ask for a raise. For a while there it looked as if Miss Crystal and Mr. Manny were in a race to see which one could pay more money to anyone who works for them. When Miss Crystal gave me the down payment for a house, Mr. Manny went right out and bought the gardener a pickup truck. Andria has paced up and down my living room a dozen times telling me this is a bad thing and we are all living in a fool's paradise but I do not care. Andria has set her sights on being a television anchorwoman and so it is necessary that she see everything in the most cynical light.

Back to Florida and the scene on the beach when Mr. William Hotchkiss from Atlanta, Georgia, showed up and went to stand at the water's edge looking out. We did not know at the time that it was Crystal Anne who was making him sad. It turned out he had a small daughter who had died several years before, carrying with her to the grave half his liver, which had failed to save her life. He had lain down beside her on a table at Mayo's Clinic and let them take out half his liver and stuff as much as they could fit into her tiny, sick body. After she died, his wife went completely crazy and started sleeping with everyone in sight and it ended in divorce. Now he was on a leave of absence from his job and was traveling around the country trying to find a place to think straight. He had come to Saint Petersburg because once, as a young man, he had sailed from there in an old patched-up sailboat with two other young men and made it to the Virgin Islands after having to build a de-salinater for water and making a rudder out of a dinghy seat. All of this came out later in conversation. For now, Miss Crystal was sitting up straight in her beach chair, Crystal Anne was getting nervous, and I was doing my usual thing, which is watch and reserve judgment until more information comes in. I have learned this counseling teenagers at my church.

"I'm not perfect," Miss Crystal says, meeting my eyes. "Life is short, Traceleen. Whatever winter offers, I will take."

"I see you're feeling better," is all I would say to that.

"I feel terrific, to tell the truth." She stood up and put her baby blue beach coat on over her suit. "I think I'll take a swim. The Gulf of Mexico, think about it, connecting to the Atlantic Ocean, the deep blue sea." She walked over in the direction of Mr. Hotchkiss, and I guess she must have said hello, or, Haven't we met somewhere before? or, Isn't it a nice day? because in a few minutes they were walking along the water's edge like they were old friends. She was telling him about her allergies, I suppose, because he was nodding his head.

* * *

I should stop and tell you something about this day. It was paradisical. Balmy and blue, soft, soft air, brilliant sun, low clouds on the horizon and everywhere the sound of the sea lapping on the sandy shores. My powers of observation fail me. Silk is the only word that fits this day.

Crystal Anne noticed her mother talking to Mr. Hotchkiss and she came out of the water and walked back over to me. About that time a man from the hotel came along and asked if we wouldn't like an umbrella and I said yes and he began to set up this very large green-and-white-striped umbrella above our heads. "Who is Momma talking to?" Crystal Anne asked. "Is she going to start flirting with men again?"

"Would you care to play tic-tac-toe?" I answered. "I brought a pad and pencils in case you'd like to play some games."

"Is that the man we saw last night at dinner?"

"I think so. Yes, I think it's the same man. He must be lonely. Down here at a hotel all by himself."

"If she starts flirting with men, I'm going home." Crystal Anne put on her hooded beach coat and pulled the hood up over her hair. "Why does she always have to do that?"

"Play me some games," I answered. "Leave your momma alone. Your momma is only talking to that man."

That night they started dancing. It was in the Palm Court again. There was a band playing South American dance music and Mr. Hotchkiss came to our table while we were waiting for the main course and asked Miss Crystal if she'd like to dance. They went out onto the dance floor and started dancing like they'd been dancing together all their lives. By now Miss Crystal had heard most of his story and her interest in him was furthered by sympathy.

She was wearing blue again, a long blue silk sheath with a little jacket. I had on my cerise cotton suit and Crystal Anne was wearing white with a pink sash, looking exactly like an angel.

That night she insisted on sleeping in my room with me. "I don't like Mr. Hotchkiss," she said, when we had turned off the lights and said our prayers. "I don't like the way he looks at me."

"He came down here because his little girl died and his wife went crazy on him. It won't hurt us to be nice to him."

"She's going to let him go to Disney World with us. Just because his little girl died doesn't mean he ought to dance with Momma all the time. If he goes to Disney World, I won't go." She rolled over with her face to the wall and put a pillow over her head and held it there.

"Go to sleep, honey. We're not in charge of everything that happens."

"We're on a planet," she said, rolling back over and throwing the pillow on the floor. "It's just a planet circling the sun. All around is darkest space."

"God is here," I put in.

"Maybe he is and maybe he's not. If he is, he's doing a terrible job."

In the end only Crystal Anne and I went to Disney World. Miss Crystal stayed at the hotel taking dancing lessons. Crystal Anne and I had a pretty good time. We had our photographs made and a five-minute video of us talking to Donald Duck. We rode about two dozen rides and ate lunch in Rapunzel's Tower and bought sweatshirts and sunglasses and got home about five in the afternoon completely exhausted. At least I was.

We went up to our rooms and Crystal Anne threw herself down on Miss Crystal's bed and started pouting. I was in the next room with the door open between the rooms.

"Did you have fun at Disney World?" Miss Crystal asked.

"No."

"Why not?"

"I wanted you to be there. People look at me funny when I'm with Traceleen."

"Why is that?"

"They think a maid is taking care of me."

"Do you think that?" I couldn't get up and close the door. I didn't know what to do. I coughed, but they did not seem to hear. I coughed again. "Come in here, Traceleen," Miss Crystal said. "This concerns you too."

"Black people should be at home taking care of their own families," Crystal Anne said. "That's what everybody thinks."

"I don't have any children but you," I answered. "This is my job, Crystal Anne. Also, my heart's desire. I love being in Florida with you. You know it's true."

"You're mad about Mr. Hotchkiss, aren't you?" Miss Crystal had decided to bite the bullet.

"I think it's going to be like it was in Maine with Allen. You and Daddy will get a divorce and I'll have to live in two houses like Augusta Redmon."

"I am only getting to know Mr. Hotchkiss so that when Lydia comes down here she will have someone to go out with. I'm trying to get Lydia to come and join us. I haven't told you yet because I wasn't sure she could come. Well, there it is, now you know and don't be disappointed if she doesn't come." Miss Crystal looked at me across Crystal Anne's head. It was the biggest lie I had ever heard her tell her child. The worst lie she had told since she quit drinking. It was a lie that was destined to draw me in. I took the bait. "See there, honey. It's not what you thought it was." Crystal Anne looked at me out of the bottom of her eyes. It is impossible to lie to her. Many children are that way. It is a gift they have.

"I'm going swimming," she said. "I want to get in some laps before dinner."

As soon as Crystal Anne left the room Crystal got on the phone and called Miss Lydia in California and began to plead with her to come and join us. "I'll buy the airplane ticket," she said. "I'll pay for everything. You better come and meet this man. He's a ten. You know you don't like any other kind."

So the upshot of it was Miss Lydia agreed to come the following day. It turned out she was in a lull between painting jobs anyway and thought she might drum up some portrait business among the snowbirds.

That night Miss Crystal went to work telling Mr. Hotchkiss all about how happily married she was and how careful everyone has to be around Crystal Anne because she is so sensitive and can read minds. Also, how fortunate everyone in Saint Petersburg was going to be when the best painter in the United States showed up for a visit and let ordinary people talk to her. I think Miss Crystal probably overdid it. Mr. Hotchkiss was so lonely and guilt-ridden over his liver not being strong enough to save his child that he was ripe for any kind of attention. We could have run in somebody with only half the personality of Miss Lydia and he would have been thrilled to meet her.

So Miss Lydia joined the party. She is a catalyst I guess you could call it. The ingredient that makes the pot boil over. She got off the airplane wearing this little black California outfit and carrying a rolled-up canvas under her arm. It was her latest painting, a portrait of a famous writer sitting beside a bowl of huge white roses. *Homage to Van Gogh*, it is called and we all agreed it was the best thing she had ever painted. Why she would roll it up and carry it across the United States on an airplane is beyond me but she says it is because of anxiety. She is continually worried that an earthquake will destroy one of her paintings before she has time to finish it or put it in a contest.

"I have just found out that much of what I have always thought of as anxiety is just plain fear," she started telling Mr. Hotchkiss as soon as they were introduced. (It is not the old-fashioned way to get a man interested in you but I try to keep an open mind about such things. In the old days we would look up at a man and say, Where did you get those big brown eyes? or something more along that line.) "All these years I assumed I was suffering the ordinary anxiety and depression common to artists when all along it was just plain old Midwestern fear."

"Imagine that," Mr. Hotchkiss said.

"I could have told you that," Miss Crystal puts in. "You've never been depressed, Lydia. Being afraid of earthquakes when you live on the San Andreas Fault is not neurotic. Why don't you move to New Orleans and live near me?"

"I might," she answered, and got this dark and serious look on her face and sat up straighter. "I'm rereading the *Chronicles of Dune*. I want to be a Bene Gesserit nun and have power over every aspect of my life. I am training myself to be constantly aware. And read body language." She looked directly at Mr. Hotchkiss, who was sitting like a perfect gentleman. He didn't move a muscle when she said that and I began to think maybe I had underrated him.

"Well," Miss Crystal said. "I think I'll join Crystal Anne in the pool. I want to get in a swim before dinner." Miss Crystal got up and went to join her daughter and Mr. Hotchkiss suggested that Lydia change her shoes and accompany him on a walk.

Lydia agreed and went off to her room leaving Mr. Hotchkiss and me alone. He looked off toward the sea, very gentle and companionable, and I reached in my bag for my knitting. I am knitting a pair of golf club covers for my niece Andria. It is tricky work and I forgot myself in it for a while. "I took up knitting once," Mr. Hotchkiss said. "When I was in the navy. I knitted seven scarves, each one longer than the last. The last one was seven feet long. It was my masterpiece."

"What sort of vessel were you on?" I asked.

"A nuclear sub. Imagine being young and unimaginative enough to do that." He laughed a gentle laugh and I thought for a moment he might cry. It is a strange thing about very handsome men as they grow older. Either they become great to match their beauty or a sort of fading begins. Their smiles lose all excitement. It's as if great beauty makes promises it cannot keep.

Miss Lydia reappeared, wearing shorts and a shirt and white socks and tennis shoes. She swept him up and took him off down the beach.

About that time who should come walking out of the hotel but Mr. Manny. He had finished up his work and decided to come down and surprise us. He came walking out of the hotel still wearing his suit and tie. Crystal Anne spotted him from the pool. She came tearing across the concrete and threw herself into his arms, getting him soaking wet.

Miss Crystal was slower in her welcome but I could see it was sincere. The things that have gone on between this pair that I have witnessed! Still, the love they have is always greater than their problems. They are smart enough for each other and can make each other laugh. "I look terrible" is the first thing Miss Crystal said. "My hair's wet. Why didn't you tell me you were coming? Come on, go up to my room while I get dressed."

"Crystal Anne and I will get a snack in the coffeeshop," I volunteered. Nothing makes me happier than the thought that Miss Crystal and Mr. Manny might spend an hour in bed. It looked like this might be the afternoon, so I grabbed up Crystal Anne and took her inside to eat bacon, lettuce, and tomato sandwiches and drink iced tea.

"Where did Lydia go with Mr. Hotchkiss?" she asked me. We were taking dainty little bites of our sandwiches, our backs straight, our napkins in our laps. Crystal Anne and I are not part of the messiness of life in the nineties.

"Lydia can take care of herself," I answered. "She has lived through two earthquakes all alone in a little house in a redwood forest. I wouldn't worry about her taking a walk with a man from Atlanta, Georgia."

"What does Mr. Hotchkiss do for a living?" She sat up even straighter and knit her eyebrows together in a perfect imitation of Miss Crystal's father.

"We haven't asked," I answered. "You know it is impolite to question people about their livelihoods. People will volunteer this information when they are ready."

"I don't like it when men don't go to work." She picked a piece of tomato out of her sandwich and laid it on her plate. "They should go to work in the daytime."

"Judge not that ye be not judged" is all I would say to that. We finished up our sandwiches and iced tea. Crystal Anne had added so much sugar to her tea that the bottom of the glass looked like a beach. She removed the ice, then took her red-and-white-striped straw and fashioned the sugar into a tiny sand castle. "Are you going to eat that sugar?" I asked.

"Yes," she said. She took her iced tea spoon and very carefully filled it with the castle and put it into her beautiful little pink mouth. I would rather have a meal with Crystal Anne than any king or queen on the earth. I have never had a meal with her that did not turn out to be memorable.

We wrapped up our bread crusts for the gulls and signed our bill and walked down to the beach to give the crusts away. There was no sign of Lydia and Mr. Hotchkiss. We walked along beside the water for a while, then we went up to our rooms to dress for dinner.

At seven that night Lydia and Mr. Hotchkiss had not been heard from. At seven-thirty we went to dinner without them. At nine Miss Crystal began to want to call the police.

At ten-fifteen the phone finally rang. It was Lydia calling from a bar in Tampa, begging them to come and save her. "He's drunk," she told Miss Crystal. "He said he'll kill himself if I leave him. He said he has no reason to live."

"I knew he was a kidnapper," Crystal Anne said, when Manny and Crystal had gone off to save Lydia. "You all go crazy if I speak to a stranger and Mother just takes up with a man she meets in a hotel and lets him take Lydia off like that."

"Your mother does the best she can," I answered. "You are too smart a little girl to start disliking your beloved mother just because she has flights of imagination."

An hour and a half later Manny and Crystal reappeared with Lydia. "I have spent my life trying to escape that bar," Lydia said. "Then I end up in it with this dull goddamn man from Atlanta. Will I ever learn?"

"Why did you go?" Crystal Anne had moved in closer. I couldn't believe we were letting her take part in this conversation.

"Because I felt sorry for him. And because he said he wanted me to paint his dead child. From a photograph, of course. He didn't bat an eyelash when I said twenty thousand dollars."

"Why don't you paint Crystal Anne instead?" Manny asked. "For, say, half that amount."

★ ★ ★

Which is how a spring that began with pollen, mold, and dust mites ended up in a glorious portrait of Crystal Anne wearing a green and white sprigged dimity garden dress and holding a hat in her hand. Beside her are squirrels and robins and bluejays and a turtle and her cat and many other of the creatures that she loves so dearly. Lydia stayed with us while she painted it and while she was doing the drawings Crystal Anne would add an animal every time she saw Lydia in a good mood. The painting is called *The Menagerie* and a copy of it was the cover of *New Orleans* magazine for August of last year. It has completely dominated the living room of our house and looks perfect with the stark floors and armless Mies van der Rohe chairs.

Actually, we would not have had to move all that furniture and paint all those walls if we had waited a few months. It turns out that Miss Crystal's allergies were really caused by all the antibiotics that she took when she had her teeth capped. What few allergies she has now can be controlled by nose spray and are only caused by the budding of the trees in spring and the going-to-seed of plants in the fall. Talking about things like that is work for a poet. If Mr. Alter hadn't killed himself he might be here to turn this experience into literature. In his absence I have tried to do the best I can. Here is my poem.

> *When the dew point rises*
> *When the buds appear*
> *"When Aprile with its sweete showeres"*
> *Fills the world with moisture*
> *This is the hour when the upper respiratory system*
> *Goes into high gear*
> *And we must accept*
> *We are not in charge here*

Paris

ᓂ

A YOUNG MAN is dead and maybe we could have stopped it.
That's what I wake up with every morning. Until a month ago I was
a completely happy person. Who knows, maybe I'll be happy again.

Reality expands exponentially. It meets itself coming and going. It
is a net, a web; touch one strand and the whole thing quivers. Get
caught and you cannot get away. Sticky stuff, reality. Spiders understand this metaphor. It had nothing to do with me. I say this over and
over again, like a mantra.

There was no reason why I shouldn't go to Paris. My young friend,
Tannin, was writing a book about me. He needed me to inspire him
and give him material. I don't think he knew he was writing about
me. He thought he was writing a book about three girls in Paris living in an apartment and talking all the time about their lovers. Only
all three sounded like me, my hysteria, how I make every utterance
an oath or a promise. I can't help it. I was poisoned in the womb. If
you don't buy first causes, don't read on.

I'm a journalist and a writer of novels. My name is Rhoda
Manning and I'm fifty-eight years old and you'd never believe that
either. People who believe in fairies don't age.

So on the fifth of May I climbed into the belly of the whale and crossed the Atlantic Ocean and arrived at Orly about seven in the morning. Tannin met me at the plane. His fifty-eight-year-old muse in a wrinkled white linen suit and two-inch spectator pumps getting bravely off a plane with her hair cut short for the mission. I used to have lovers his age. Now I only want the good part, the youthful energy, the sheer delight. Coming out to Orly at seven in the morning to squire me through customs. The ones I had for lovers might have done that. But none of them spoke flawless Parisian French.

There are many love affairs in the world, more ways to love, Horatio, than you dream of. I had been practicing all my life for this. Having brothers, raising sons, loving young men. And now, in my Senior Citizenship, Tannin had been delivered to me. To love, to understand, to nourish, to adore. He had written me a letter to say he liked a book I wrote. It was a book about a friend who died an early death. I will write about you, I had told the friend. I will not let you die. Do it, he had answered. If you write it from the heart, it will be good. I had and it was and I was as proud of it as anything I had ever written.

Also, it gave Tannin to me. The book had come to him from the Book-of-the-Month Club and he forgot to send it back. So he read it and then he wrote to me and told me he wanted to be a writer. I throw such letters away every day. This one was different. It had a lilt, a ring, it made me laugh. He asked my advice about writing schools and I told him to come up here. That Randolph was a genius and would not harm him. Randolph is the director of the writing program.

So Tannin came to Fayetteville and became my friend and the next thing I knew I was flying to Paris to "hang out with him" while he wrote his book.

He called me frantically two days before I left to say he had a visitor, a young man who had gone to Sewanee with him. "He's driving me crazy," he said. "He's in a terrible mood. He hates everything in Paris. I took him to hear Ravel at the Sorbonne. He hated Ravel. I hope he'll be gone by the time you get here, but he might not be. I'm really sorry. He just showed up. I invited him a year ago. I never dreamed he'd come."

"Maybe he's disoriented. That happened to me once, in Heidelberg. I just got completely disoriented. I had to go home."

"I don't know what's wrong with him. He quit his job a month ago. Maybe that's it. He was working for his dad in Nashville."

"Don't worry about it. Nothing will stop us from having fun in Paris. Did you get tickets to the ballet?"

"Yes. They're supposed to be good seats. They'd better be."

"My cousin plays in the orchestra. We'll meet her after the performance. I haven't seen her since she was in high school."

"Good. That's fine. We'll do anything you want to do. I'm so glad you're coming."

As soon as we collected my bags we went to my hotel and sat in the café drinking coffee and talking. We hadn't seen each other in four weeks but it seemed a year. Our sagas engage us. His are as real to me as mine. "So what's the friend's name?" I asked. "And is he better?"

"His name is William and he's worse. Now he has a cold. He's asleep in my room. He's going to the ballet with us tomorrow night."

"That's fine. I want to meet him. Don't worry, Tannin. Nothing is wrong. I'm elated to be here. Look at this weather. This is paradise. My plan is to stay awake all afternoon and take a sleeping pill and crash about six and sleep till dawn. How does that sound to you?"

"Fantastic. Should you be drinking coffee?"

"It won't matter. I have a Xanax. It will knock me out." We giggled. We laughed as if that were the funniest thing in the world, as if it were deeply, wildly, madly, hysterically funny.

We left the hotel and walked up the rue de Montalembert to the boulevard St.-Germain and followed it to the Seine. We stood on the bridge and watched people and talked about the swimming pool that had sunk in the river the night before.

"A floating swimming pool that's been here since the forties. Think what would have happened if it had been in the daytime. If people had been there. I wish I could have seen it sink."

"So do I. What a phenomenon. A huge floating swimming pool sinking into the Seine. *Mon dieu!*" We laughed again. It was incredibly, divinely, hilariously funny. No one ever gets that tickled when they are alone. Only two people can know something is that funny.

"In sight of Notre Dame Cathedral. This may be a sign. Listen, I told William I'd meet him for lunch. I never thought you'd want to stay awake. We don't have to go. I could go by there and tell him I'm not coming."

"I want to. Come on. I want to go. I really do. Why are you so worried about my meeting William?"

"Because it's your vacation. You shouldn't have to baby-sit my friends."

"I want to meet him." I took his arm and we walked along the river to the Jardin des Tuileries and across the gardens to the Café du Palais Royale, a bright café with pots of orange flowers and brilliant paintings on the walls. We found a table and sat down and began to read the menu. A young man came hurrying toward us through the tables. He had curly blond hair and blue eyes and looked enough like Tannin to be his twin. "William Watkins Weckter," Tannin said. "The fourth or fifth. My old roommate at Sewanee. He's dying to meet you."

"I read your books," he said. "I used to talk about them all the time."

"Oh, my. Sit down. Are you feeling better? Tannin said you had been sick."

"It's nothing. A summer cold. Well, I quit my job last month. I'm out on the street. That should give you a cold, don't you think?" He laughed and took a handkerchief out of his pocket and stood up and went outside and blew his nose. When he came back in he picked up the conversation and went right on. He didn't seem depressed to me. Just at loose ends, like half the young people I meet. No children, no responsibilities they can't leave. They are free, in the deepest and most terrible sense of the word. Cut loose, dismounted, disengaged. Not Tannin though, he's in love with the muse, the sight of his words upon the page. Artists are the same in any age, always lost and always found.

So here was William with a degree in history and a minor in biol-

ogy and nothing to do. He had worked for his father in an office supply store in Nashville for a while, now he was wandering around the
world. "I better see it while I can," he said. "When I go back to work
I won't have a vacation for a year."

"The age of commerce may be over," I said. "I've been thinking
of this. It's time for live theater, beautiful buildings, parks. There must
be things for young people to do that will engage them in their
brightest minds. It's this transition that is painful. Find out what you
want to do and do it. What do you want to do, William? Do you have
any idea?"

"Something worth keeping. Something I could talk about. When
I was young I liked to keep records. I wrote down what I did each
day." He looked off into the gardens outside the café. We finished
our coffee. William insisted on paying for our lunch. Nothing would
dissuade him. Then he left us, and Tannin and I walked back to my
hotel. There were young people dressed in costumes from the seven-
teenth century wandering around the Tuileries looking beautiful and
mysterious. They weren't selling anything. We couldn't figure out
why they were there.

"Gratuitous beauty," Tannin declared. "France. I am happiest
when I am here. It's my mother's fault. She did this to me."

"I'm fading," I answered. "Take me to my bed. I'll see you in the
morning."

Tannin delivered me to my hotel and I went upstairs and un-
packed and ordered some Evian and drank half a bottle of it with a
Xanax and went to sleep with the windows open. I was on the sev-
enth floor of the Hôtel Montalembert, where Buckminster Fuller
used to stay with his entourage. Outside my window I could see the
Eiffel Tower and the streets leading to the river and les Champs
Elysées. I slept. Like a lamb in a meadow I slept away the hours until
dawn.

I woke in Paris. I stretched out my muscles in the bed. Pulled the
beautiful pillows into my arms. Goose down, from some lovely flock
of geese somewhere in the land of France. This elegant old culture. I
lay in bed and looked around the room. It was black and white.

White walls, black painted furniture, a soft design on the chairs. Another bolder print on the bedcover. White linen drapes pulled back from dormer windows. I won't do a thing I don't want to do, I decided. I will not hurry. I curled back into a ball and daydreamed for a while, imagining the ballet we would see that evening. The Paris Opéra House with its ceiling painted by Chagall. Ballets by Balanchine and Robbins. I had not seen ballet in fourteen months. I was badly overdue for a ballet.

I rose from the bed and walked over to the window and stood leaning out the casement in my white silk nightgown. When I'm at home I sleep in flannel. See what this city does for me. I drank the rest of the Evian and dressed in a black pantsuit and went down to the café for petit déjeuner. A waiter brought me the *Herald Tribune* and I read Russell Baker's column and drank the best coffee in the world and ate a brioche and raspberries from the Dordogne. I was getting more civilized every minute. I was almost urbane. The city and the day stretched out before me. I thought of Tannin, not ten blocks away in his room overlooking the Luxembourg Gardens. I thought of William, with his upper-respiratory infection and his pretty face. I thought of my young cousin playing her violin at the Paris Opéra. I thought of Chagall and the light coming in the glass windows onto my table and the perfect weather and how lucky I was to live in such a world.

I went upstairs and changed into street shoes and left the hotel and walked for an hour, exploring side streets, stopping at a salon to make an appointment for my hair, windowshopping.

When I got back to the hotel there were messages. Tannin was coming to take me to lunch. My cousin was home and would I call her. It made me giddy, to be in a city this beautiful, in cool weather, with young people to talk to, and nothing, not a single thing going wrong, and no longer in boyfriend jail. I was not in love with anyone and I did not want to be. BOND NO MORE, it said on notes I had scattered around my house. I had written it and I meant it. I was free to let the whole world be my lover.

Free at last from the obsessive weight of love affairs. Free from waiting around a hotel room for a husband or a lover to decide what I could or could not do. Free from men turning on television sets.

I combed my hair, put on my two-inch heels, went down to the lobby and Tannin was there, smiling and embracing me, as excited as I was. We left the hotel and walked until we found a sidewalk café that we liked and sat in the shade of a plane tree giggling and talking and telling stories and watching everything. There is nothing on earth like friendship. It is God's love, God's ambrosia, the one thing we never have to pay for or regret.

"That man is looking at you." Tannin laughed. "Men have been checking you out all morning."

"It's the damnedest thing. I mean, *mon dieux*, the minute you stop being available, men start wanting you. They can smell it a mile away. It has nothing to do with age or beauty."

"It's true. If we think we can't have it, it becomes interesting to us."

"You can't manufacture it. You have to really be out of the game. I am. You can't imagine how much I do not want to have another affair of any kind."

"Look at that, Rhoda. Over in the corner." I glanced at the couple kissing in the corner. A middle-aged man and a woman in a low-cut blouse. They looked like some inferior breed of human, the expression on their faces was completely infantile.

"Do you think they just did it or are they just about to go somewhere and do it?"

"Probably both." A waiter approached the couple and set a huge glass of ice cream with whipped cream and cherries and chocolate sauce down in front of the woman. The man picked up a spoon and began to feed her. Tannin touched my arm. We shook with laughter. We almost fell off our chairs. We could not contain ourselves. We paid the bill and walked off down the street and found a building to lean against and laughed until we cried.

I slept in the late afternoon and dressed and met Tannin and William in the lobby and we set out for the opera house. "I've never seen a ballet," William said. "Is it okay to admit that?"

"I was older than you before I saw one that was good," I answered. "This is the World Series you're going to see. Except for Maurice Béjart and the Ballet of the Twentieth Century. That's the best to me, the nonpareil."

Later, after the first ballet, which was the Balanchine, he said, "Don't the ones in the chorus mind? They never get to be the star?"

"Prima ballerinas," I told him. "Listen, these are great athletes. They don't mind someone being the prima ballerina any more than a football team minds having a great running back. They have a wonderful life. They live to dance, to be up there on that stage, with that music, doing this for us. Dancers never grow old. I wish I could have been one."

"Well," I grudgingly admitted, later, in the lobby, at intermission, with a glass of wine. "They ruin their feet. They tear up their toes. What they're doing is unnatural, but that's why it's so hard and why the excitement of it never dies."

We went back to our seats, which were in a box to the left of the stage. Above our heads, the divine ceiling by Chagall. The curtains opened. Two dancers came on stage. Behind them were the flats which had also been painted by Chagall. *Entree et pas-de-deux*. Magic. *Danse des garçons* with tables covered by umbrellas. More magic. Then the *danse des filles*, with small umbrellas everywhere. It was the dance of the day we had just spent in Paris, with the burden of weight dissolved in color. The human spirit turned loose to fly, transcend itself. This ballet alone would have been worth the trip across the ocean.

I had arranged for us to meet my cousin after the performance. May Chatevin Debardeleben. Her name was almost whispered in my family. She's in Paris, they would say. She plays the violin for the Paris ballet.

She was just as I remembered her, a blithe young girl with long dusty blond hair and violet eyes. Even as a child she had carried herself with dignity and grace. It had not surprised me when I heard she had flown the coop, escaped the massive tentacles of our family.

We found her in the orchestra pit, holding her violin against her black taffeta dress. I introduced everyone, embraced her, and begged her to come to dinner with us. "All right," she said. "Let me put this violin away. I won't bother to change to street clothes, if you don't mind." She was so absolutely southern, the same young girl from Abbeville, Louisiana, where her mother played the organ at the Episcopal Church.

While she put the violin in the case I squeezed Tannin's hand. I was so proud of my lovely young cousin. All this time William had not spoken. Now, when May Chatevin snapped the clasps on the case, he reached out a hand and took it from her. "I played a violin when I was a kid," he said. "But I had to stop."

"Oh, why was that?" She was wearing large hornrimmed glasses. She reached up and took them off as she waited for his answer.

"Because it interfered with baseball practice. Then I broke a finger and it was in a cast for a year."

"That's terrible." She moved near him. "That's the worst thing I ever heard."

"I used to love the way it fit into the case."

"You could start again. It's not too late."

"You think so?"

"Sure. There are wonderful teachers here. Do you speak French?"

"I won't be here long."

"Let's start walking," Tannin said. "You can't solve this on an empty stomach."

We had dinner at a brasserie along the Seine. The lights from the barges going along the river climbed the trunks of the trees, then filled the crowns, then climbed back down. Afterward, an afterglow. A heavy metaphor for love, if anyone needed one in Paris.

May Chatevin and William were in love before we even got to the brasserie. They had paired up as soon as we left the opera house. They walked behind us, their heads bent toward one another. I had forgotten how fast it happens, had forgotten young men's bodies, the cold shaking power of desire, had been glad to forget it, as I now had other things to do, being in the universe on this clearer, older plane.

"My guardian angel must have finally made it across the ocean,"

William was saying across the table. "Everyone who goes to Sewanee gets a guardian angel. When we go onto the campus we check him at the gates. When we leave we pick him up again. We don't need him at Sewanee, you see, as it's the closest place to heaven." William laughed out loud. He was laughing at everything. And his cold had disappeared. It was the truth, what I told his parents later. He was the happiest young man I'd ever seen. In contrast to Tannin, who is as hysterical as I am. Searching, searching, dreaming, playing out the string. Philip Larkin has a metaphor for this. People sitting on the cliffs waiting for a white-sailed armada of hopes to come in. They arrive, Larkin says, but they never anchor. "Only one ship is seeking us," the poem ends. "A black-sailed unfamiliar, towing at its back a huge and breathless silence. In its wake, no waters breed or break."

The four of us became inseparable. We went to the Sorbonne to hear a string quartet play Brahms. We walked in the Tuileries and had lunch at Les Deux Magots. We strolled the boulevard St-Germain and went to Sulka to look at the ties. We walked along the Seine and saw the small blue asters in the flower shops and I told the story of V. K. Ratcliff's trip to New York City to the wedding of Eula Varner Snopes to the Jewish Communist and how V. K. bought a tie the color of asters and how the Russian woman kissed him on the mouth as she tied it around his neck.

We talked of writing and painting and music. We harvested the beauty of the city and fed it to each other. One day we rented a car and drove to Dieppe to see the coast. On the way home the skies were full of clouds and over a field of young corn we watched three parachuters playing with the wind. We talked of books we had read and artists we admired. We went to the Rodin museum and stood in line for fifty minutes. "Rilke came here every afternoon," Tannin said. "He adored Rodin. '*Rodin, c'est lui qui a inspiré le poete,*' Ran Rilke."

"I want to buy the tickets," I said. "Tell me what to say?"

"*Quatre. S'il vous plaît.*"

"*Quatre. S'il vous plaît,*" I told the lady in the cage and counted out the money as if I were six years old.

The *billets* were beautiful, reproductions of the statue called *Le Bourgeois de Calais*, 1895. Musée Rodin, 77 rue de Vareene, Paris.

We had an audience with the brilliant translator, Barbara Bray, and took her to a concert with us at a cathedral. May Chatevin and I had our hair done at Julien et Claude, Haute Coiffure, St-Germain-des-Près. We stood outside the Louvre and watched the tourists going in. We bought a disposable camera and took photographs of each other by the statues of the continents. We went to Chanel and saw Catherine Deneuve shopping for costumes for a movie. We pretended not to know who she was and looked the other way.

Often, in the afternoons, May Chatevin and William would disappear until suppertime. Tannin had sworn off women until his book was finished. And I had found out a wonderful thing. You do not have to be getting laid to be ecstatic in this city which worships love.

Often while they were gone we went somewhere and wrote in our notebooks. He needed a château for a love scene in his book and we found one in the country and went there several times to draw it in our minds.

"William's sister is calling him twice a day," Tannin told me. "His family's furious. They want him to come home."

"His sister?"

"She's visiting Rome with her husband. She wants him to come there and go home with them."

"What does he tell them?"

"He tells them no. He says he's in love with a girl from the States."

"What's going on?" I asked my cousin, when I had her alone one afternoon.

"I'm in love with him. I want him to stay here with me."

"How could he work? An American can't get work in Paris."

"It's a problem." She looked right at me. That old fierceness, selfishness, call it what you will. In the last two generations our family has a divorce rate about twice the national average. The reason is that look. This arrogance we breed or foster, here it was again, in Paris, in this twenty-nine-year-old girl with her perfect ear and talented hands. "I'm writing a symphony. The Saint Louis Symphony is going to perform it when it's done. I can't leave now. This city is my muse. I have to stay another year or two."

"Then what will happen?"

"I don't know. I want him to stay. He can live with me. He knows that. He can get a visa."

"What would he do for money?"

"I don't know. Maybe we have to live today and not think about it." I had been wrong. She had stopped being southern. She stood beside the window in my room, looking out onto the roofs of Paris. She was where she had meant to go, she was where she meant to be.

I changed my plane reservation. I decided to stay another week. One morning Tannin met me in the hotel café for breakfast.

"He's leaving at noon," Tannin said. "He's run out of money and his sister won't leave him alone. He's going to Rome and fly home with them in his brother-in-law's plane. His family has lots of money, but they won't give it to him."

"They shouldn't. That's good. That's right."

"He's in love with your cousin. That's our fault, Rhoda. We did that, you and I. He's really broken up about leaving. Do you think she loves him?"

"She loves her work. She's writing a symphony. She wrote one last year that was played by the New Orleans Symphony Orchestra. She has an agreement to write one for Saint Louis. She's going to be a star. Yes, I think she loves him. She wants to keep him here for a pet."

"He came home early last night. I guess they had a fight."

"It's not our fault, Tannin. That's nuts to think that."

We left the café. We walked to the Champs Elysees and window-shopped. We went to the Luxembourg Gardens and rode the carousel. We bought beignets with powdered sugar and sat upon a bench and ate them with our fingers.

"I'd better call May Chatevin when I get home," I said. "She has to play tonight. Maybe we can meet her later and get some supper."

"It's not our fault, Rhoda, remember that."

"I know. It isn't. By God, it has nothing to do with us. We didn't do it."

Neither was it our fault that the Italian Mafia chose that day to load up a car with plastic explosives and drive it into the train station in Firenze just as William got off the train. For what? To turn around and come back to Paris? To buy a package of cigarettes? To call May Chatevin?

I don't buy group guilt. Or any of that politically correct bullshit. Most of the people in the world are doing the best they can with whatever knowledge they have managed to attain or been fed by whatever myths they were raised under. So, somewhere in the darkness of the underside of existence in the ancient land of Italy, someone, or two or three benighted souls, stuffed a Fiat full of explosives smuggled in from God knows where and with or without a driver ran it into the side of the old section of the Firenze train station where maybe William had just disembarked long enough to buy a sandwich or a drink or a newspaper. He was trying to learn Italian, he had said, one night when we were sitting beside the Seine using all our pidgin languages. Tannin is the only one of us who has mastered anything other than English, although May Chatevin's French is charming and she gets by.

Tannin and May Chatevin and I were together that night. We left my hotel about six and walked to the Jardin des Plantes to see the menagerie. It was cool that evening and May Chatevin was wearing pale yellow silk pants and a green silk jacket. Her hair was pulled back into a chignon. I thought she looked like her mother that night, as she was sad and trying to hide the sadness. "I couldn't leave now," she said a dozen times. "I couldn't just leave all this and go back home. I think he understood that. Did he say anything to you, Tannin? What did he say?"

"That he is in love with you, of course. He doesn't know what he's going to do. Maybe go to work for his brother-in-law. Make some money and come back for you."

"You could go and visit him," I put in. "Surely you don't have to work incessantly."

"Until I finish the symphony I can't take a day away from it. I've wasted two weeks as it is, but not entirely. I've been working in the mornings." We were walking along the rue Claude Bernard, trying to find our way to the boulevard de Vaugirard, where there was a Brazilian restaurant Tannin knew about.

After dinner we decided to see the late showing of *Much Ado About Nothing* in English with French subtitles. It was over about eleven-fifteen and the two young people left me at my hotel and Tannin walked May Chatevin home. He is struggling with his novel and takes every opportunity to put off going home to write it, which he does in the middle of the night no matter how much I lecture him on the efficacy of the morning hours.

I went up to my room and turned on the television set for the first time since I'd been in Paris. I turned on CNN and settled back into the pillows with a glass of Evian. It was the first event on the news. The train station in flames, people running with their hands up in the air, firemen spraying the flames with chemicals, demolished automobiles parked outside the station.

I watched the full report. Then I called Tannin. He returned to my hotel and came up to my room and we began to call crazily around three countries trying to find something out.

"Let's go down there," I said. "Rent a car."

"We have to stay here. He might have my address with him if he was hurt. He might call."

"What about May Chatevin?"

"Wait until morning. If she knew she would have called. What could she do this time of night?"

"It wouldn't be him. He wouldn't die. He's not the type."

"Anyone can die, Rhoda. Anytime. Anywhere."

"Thinking he was a failure?"

"He didn't think that. He just couldn't decide what to do."

"We're overreacting. I shouldn't have called you. You should be at home doing your work."

"Do you think he was in it?"

"I don't know."

"Neither do I."

Tannin slept on the sofa in my room. We woke up early and dressed and went to May Chatevin's apartment. She had read it in the paper. "If he wasn't hurt, he would have called us," she kept saying. "He said he'd call when he got there."

"We can't be sure."

"Then why hasn't he called?"

"What's his sister's name?

"I don't know."

"Should we call his parents in the States?"

"No. Oh, God, no. What if he's all right?"

In the end Tannin and May Chatevin had a car delivered and started driving. I stayed by the phone. They stopped and called every two hours. In between the second and third call the American embassy called to say his name was on the list of the dead.

THE LIST OF THE DEAD. In June, in a peaceful Europe, the summer he was twenty-five. Random, inexplicable.

I told her when she called at three that afternoon. They went on to Firenze to see if they could claim the body. I asked the embassy to get me his parents' phone number. I sat in zazen on the floor of my room and waited for the courage to make the call. I could have looked out the window and seen the Eiffel Tower if I wanted to.

I got his father on the phone. I told him his son had been completely happy when he left for Rome. I told him his son had been the happiest man I had ever known. I asked if I could meet the daughter in Firenze. If I could do anything at all for them. I gave them my phone number in the United States. I said they could come to visit me and I would tell them about every minute of the weeks gone by. "He was the happiest young man I've ever known," I told them. "What fine parents you must have been. What a delightful son you had." Had. Here in the maya of space and time. On the planet Earth, in nineteen hundred and ninety-three A.D., in the only world there is.

★ ★ ★

Two days later Tannin and May Chatevin got back to Paris. They had met the sister. Tannin had helped identify the body. May Chatevin had lost ten pounds. I put her to bed in her apartment with one of my three remaining Xanax tablets. I sat in her living room while she slept and tried to read *Le Monde*. Tannin had gone home to rest.

"Get up tomorrow morning and write," I told him. "Now will you believe? Now will you go on and write your hero's death?"

"No," he answered. "I'm going to skip over to the part that takes place in the United States. After the child is born."

"Requiem. Yes, go on."

"We got a dog the last year we were at Sewanee. This brown dog we found at the pound. We had to hide it from the landlord."

"What happened to it?"

"He took it to Nashville and gave it to his mother. I guess she's still got it. He used to let it ride in the car with him everywhere he went. That dog loved to ride in automobiles. He'd put his paws up on the window and stick his head out. Everyone knew our dog. We called it Vain for a girlfriend he once had."

"I told his father he was the happiest man I had ever known."

"He might have been. Now he is. Now he doesn't care." We had been whispering. Now we embraced. He left me there. I opened French *Vogue* and began to read an article about how to dye the hair on my legs. We don't really need hair on our bodies anymore. But nature keeps it there in case things change.

The Raintree Street
Bar and Washerteria

ℭ

THERE WERE FOUR POETS at the bar and the son of a poet
tending bar and the Piano Prince of New Orleans playing ragtime in
the next room. It was a good day at the Raintree Street Bar and
Washerteria. It was a Wednesday afternoon and it was ninety-nine
degrees in the shade and (because of that) there was no one in the bar
but people other people could trust. All the rich ladies and Tulane
students had found air-conditioned places to hang out in and people
who needed the Raintree to keep their lives in order could lounge
around the bar sipping beer and listening to the Piano Prince play
"Such a Night" and "Junko Partner" and "I Walk on Gilded
Splinters" while in the back room the washing machines and dryers
did their accustomed work. It was June in New Orleans, Louisiana,
and it was exactly as hot as it was supposed to be.

"Fuck a bunch of rich women chasing my ass all over town," the
Most Famous Poet in New Orleans was saying to the Jazz Poet.
"Fuck them calling me on the telephone. I can't even take a shit
without the goddamn phone ringing off the hook. 'Finley, is that
you? You don't sound like yourself, honey. Is something wrong?' Is
something wrong, you goddamn bitch, you bet it's wrong. Leave me
alone. Oh, please, for God's sake, leave me alone." The Most Famous
Poet laid his head down on the bar and the Jazz Poet raised an eye-
brow in the direction of the bartender.

"Come on, Finley," the bartender said. "Come lie down on the sofa in the office. You got to save yourself for the night. Jay-Jay's coming to sit in with the band and Johnnie Vidocavitch will be here. You don't want to use it up in the daytime, do you? Come lay down."

"Lie," the Most Famous Poet said. "Chickens lay." His head was almost to the edge of the bar, his right hand shoved his beer farther and farther down the bar. The phone beside the cash register was ringing. "Don't answer it," he continued. "I'm not here. Say Finley isn't here. Finley is in Galway where he wants to be. Finley gone bye-bye. For God's sake, Charles Joseph, help me." Now he was all the way down and the Jazz Poet moved behind him and propped him up and held him to the bar.

"Who doesn't he want to talk to?" the Jazz Poet asked. "Who's he hiding from now?" The Jazz Poet had only wandered in to wash a load of clothes. He hadn't meant to get so deep into poetry on a Wednesday afternoon in June.

"The society lady painter. The one that does the cartoons of her friends."

"Oh, shit," the Jazz Poet said. "I remember her."

"She came in here last night all gussied up in black. She'd been to that Andy Warhol thing at the museum. Her mother was with her. Her mother's as bad as she is. Her mother was chasing ass all over the bar. They parked right out front and left the motor running. She's been stalking Finley for days. I guess he laid her. He shouldn't lay them if he doesn't want them coming after him."

"Christ," the Jazz Poet said. "Jesus Christ."

It was June of 1979. A hard time for poets in New Orleans. Every society woman in town who wasn't into tennis was into poetry. They were trying to be poets, but they didn't know how. Some of the ones who were into tennis were also into poetry. They were into poetry but they didn't know how to do it yet. They didn't know how to write the poems or what poets to talk about or how to get anyone to publish the poems they wrote in case they wrote them. There wasn't a big poetry hook-up yet. Of course, over at Tulane a real poet was teaching a poetry class but it met at inconvenient hours for society women just getting into poetry and besides you had to already know how to do poetry to get into it.

Society women are hard to keep out of something once they decide they want to be in, however, and they had discovered the Raintree Street Bar and Washerteria. One of them had even brought her maid over one day pretending their washing machine at home was broken. There she was, sitting at the bar drinking beer and pretending to be a poet and going back every now and then to make sure the maid wasn't bored.

The society women were being terribly frustrated by the world of poetry in nineteen hundred and seventy-nine and if there is one thing a society woman won't put up with it is being frustrated or bored.

"Finley started a poetry magazine with her," the bartender was explaining. "She got drunk one night and gave him a check for five thousand dollars to revive *The Quachita Review*. Now she's making him do it."

"They asked me for some stuff," the Jazz Poet answered. "They said they'd pay five dollars a line. I gave them a poem. First American Non-exclusive Serial Rights only, of course. Well, it looks like he's out, Charles Joseph. You want to leave him here on the bar?"

"Move his beer. No point in having to clean that up."

Sandy George Wade made his way down Raintree Street from the streetcar stop on Carrollton Avenue, walking as fast as ninety-nine degrees in the shade would allow him to walk, admiring the windows of the little old-fashioned shops, pawn shops, and shoe repair shops and an antique store and a bakery. He had the address of the Raintree in his pocket. A poet named Francis Alter who came to teach at his reform school had given it to him a few months before. "Go by there," the poet had said. "There are good people there. People who will help you."

"Can I say I'm a friend of yours?"

"Sure. There are people there who know me. They know my work."

"Are you famous?"

"They'll know my work. Poets know other poets by their work. Go there if you get lonely in New Orleans. Keep this address. You might need it someday." The poet had folded up the piece of paper with the address of the Raintree on it and watched while Sandy put it in his pocket.

Sandy arrived at the door of the Raintree and looked inside and saw the Jazz Poet holding up the Most Famous Poet at the bar and heard the Piano Prince playing "High Blood Pressure." *I get highhhh blood pressure when I hear your name.* It looked like a good place to stop. It looked like a place where a man could begin to straighten something out. The Jazz Poet was wearing a clean white T-shirt and a panama hat. He looked like a poet should look and Sandy walked on down the bar and took a seat beside him and ordered a beer.

"Did any of you ever know Francis Alter?" he asked. "He told me I could find friends here if I used his name."

"Francis," the Jazz Poet said. "You know Francis?"

"I knew him down in Texas. I was in his class."

"He's the best. The absolute nonpareil. The very best. Look, we've got to get this guy to the office. You want to help?"

"Sure. I'll be glad to help. Who is he?"

"He's a great poet. The best in New Orleans."

Sandy and the Jazz Poet eased Finley off the stool and moved him to-ward the office, with the bartender leading the way. "Don't answer it," Finley kept calling out. "Tell her I'm not here."

"He's not here," the bartender said. "That's for sure."

"Finley in spirit land," the Jazz Poet added. "Hey, I could make a poem of that. Finley gone to spirit land where no rich lady bother him. Not make him read her dreadful poems. Not make him listen to her whine. No ladies call him on the phone. No magazines send him rejection slips. No blues in spirit land. Goddamn, Charles Joseph. Listen to this. Ain't No Blues in Spirit Land. What a riff."

"That's good," the bartender agreed. "That's really good, Dickie. Especially the last line."

"Where are we going?" Sandy asked. He was now the sole support of Finley. The other two were leaning against the walls talking. The four of them were wedged into a small hall between the bar and the washerteria. The air was thick with the exhaust from the dryers. The smell of panties cooking, Sandy decided. Little flowered panties getting cooked.

"Turn in that door," the bartender said. He took back his part of the burden, hooked his shoulder under Finley's arm, and began to drag him to the door. "Right in there, that's the office." Sandy pushed open the door and they entered a small neat room with a large sofa in one corner.

"Right there," the bartender directed. "Ease him down. That's it. He'll be okay as soon as he gets some sleep."

"What's wrong with him?" Sandy said. "Who doesn't he want to call him?"

"He's in deep trouble," the bartender answered. "They put an article about him in the paper and now all the society women are after his ass. It happens. I told him not to let them interview him. My old man's a poet. I slept in a bed once with W. H. Auden. I know about this stuff."

"You slept with Auden?" the Jazz Poet said. "You never told me that."

"He was passed out in my bed, in Starkville, when he came to read, the last year before he died. He slept in his clothes. God, he was a lovely man."

"I envy you so much," the Jazz Poet said. "I would give anything to have had your childhood."

"It was nice," the bartender agreed. "I wouldn't trade it."

"Who's Auden?" Sandy asked. "Is he some friend of yours?"

"Let's go back to the bar," the Jazz Poet answered. "I want to hear about Francis. All my life I wanted to meet that man." He put his arm around Sandy's shoulder, and, with the bartender leading the way, they went back down the hall and out into the lofty beer- and cigarette-laden air of the Raintree bar. The sky had darkened. It was going to rain. The Piano Prince had just returned to the piano after taking a break to get a fix in the men's room. He smiled upon the world. He lifted his genius-laden fingers and dropped them down on the piano and began to play his famous rendition of "Oh, Those Lonely, Lonely Nights."

"This poetry seems like a good deal," Sandy began. "I like the feel of it. I'd like to get in on some of it."

"It's about death, baby," the Jazz Poet answered. "But it's to keep the skull at bay. I wrote a poem about waiting in the welfare line that got me so much pussy I had to change my phone number. I just wrote down what everybody said while we waited to get our checks. That line used to stretch all the way down Camp Street from the old Times-Picayune Building past Lafayette Square to the Blood Bank. I met some characters in that line who were unforgettable and I made the longest poem in the world out of it and used to put it on down at this theater we had on Valencia Street. I had to beat them off with a stick when I'd do my welfare line poem. I'll do it for you someday."

"It's great," the bartender put in. "It's a great poem."

"But enough about me," the Jazz Poet added. He pushed his panama hat back from his brow and wiped his face with a pale orange and white bandanna, then tied the bandanna around his neck. He could see their reflection in the bar mirror. Charles Joseph's back in his ironed white shirt and the good-looking new kid and his own hat and bandanna and strong hawkish profile. "Tell me about Francis," he went on. "I'd give anything to know him. He's the best there is, the absolute best."

"I thought you said that guy was."

"He's the best there is down here. Francis is the best in the United States. He's a god."

"I'm going to go see him," Sandy said. "He said I could go up there to Arkansas and help him run some lines."

"I'll go with you. God, I'd love to go up there. Do you think he'd mind if I came along?"

Oh, those lonely, lonely nights. Oh, those lonely, lonely nights. In the adjoining room the Piano Prince was playing his heart out. He was in heaven, back in the arms of his honey juice and as soon as he finished here he'd be back in his bed with his monkey in his arms. *Monkey, monkey, monkey,* the Piano Prince sang to himself and laid down his heart into his hands. *Oh, those lonely, lonely nights. Oh, those lonely, lonely nights.*

"That guy is really good," Sandy said. "That guy is something else."

"Yeah, that's the Piano Prince. He's an addict. He plays to get his fix. He's the best. He's so popular now he doesn't come here often anymore. Oh, shit, look out there." He pointed out the window to where a big green Mercedes Benz was pulling up beside the curb. "That's the Lady Jane coming after Finley. Oh, yes, it's her and who the hell is that she's got with her?" A short busy-looking woman in a white tennis dress got out of the car and came in the door with a determined look on her face. Right behind her, in her wake as it were, was a taller, thinner woman with long red hair. They moved like an armada into the bar and took up a determined position near the cash register. "Is Finley here?" the woman asked the bartender. "Tell me the truth, Charles Joseph. Have you seen him?"

"He was here a while ago," the bartender answered, "but now he's out."

"Well, I have to find him. Where did he go?"

"What do you need Finley for?" the Jazz Poet put in. "It's nice to see you, Janey. Who's this with you?"

"Allison Carter, the painter. You know her work. I had that show for her, remember? Allison, this is Dickey Madison. Hayes Madison, Junior. His daddy's the district attorney. He's our Jazz Poet. You ought to hear him sometime. Have you seen Finley, Hayes? We really need to find him. It's about *The Ouachita.*

"He was in here a while ago. What's the problem?"

"We have to see the printer. The printer won't fix the typos. It's a mess. We took it to that place on Marengo and they promised they'd have it by last week and now it isn't finished and they won't fix the typos. Your poem looks great."

"She has a poetry magazine," the Jazz Poet explained to Sandy. "She revived an old one called *The Ouachita*. He knows Francis Alter, Jane. He's going up there to visit him."

"You know Francis Alter?" The woman turned her attention to Sandy. "Where did you know him?"

"He taught at a school I went to. He told me I could come and see him anytime I wanted to."

"What school?"

"Down in Texas. You wouldn't of heard of it. It's really small."

"Oh, okay. Well, if you see him tell him we'd really like to publish some of his stuff. What did you say your name was?"

"Sandy. Sandy Wade."

"This is Allison Carter, Sandy. She's a painter. She's great. She's going to do our cover. So, do you think Finley's coming back?"

"He might be back tonight," the bartender said. "He said he wanted to come hear the band. Johnnie Vidocavitch is going to sit in, and . . ."

"Tell him to call me," Jane said. "Tell him I'm looking for him. Look, could we have a Diet Coke? I really need something to drink." The bartender got two not particularly clean glasses down from a shelf and put some less clean ice in them with his not very clean hands and filled them from a hose that led God knows where, to some subterranean Diet Coke well. Lady Jane shuddered and reached in her purse and took out five dollars and laid it on the counter. She held the dirty germ-filled Diet Coke at a distance from her tennis dress.

"So," she said. "You know Francis Alter? That's amazing. I've been trying to meet him for years. I'd give anything to be in his class."

"Are you a poet too?" Sandy asked.

"Well, sort of. I mean, I haven't published anything yet but I'm learning. I've been so busy getting this magazine published I don't have time to write. Well, come on, Allison. Let's get out of here. Jesus, it's so hot in here. It's so hot everywhere. You really need some air conditioning in this place." She put the untouched drink down on the counter and left the change beside it and took her friend's arm and left the way that she had come, in a hurry, and went out and into the car, which she had left running with the air conditioner on.

"Who was that?" Sandy asked.
"That's why Finley can't answer the telephone."

At nine o'clock that night they were all back at the bar. The band was filing in, beginning to warm up. The regular drummer was at the bar, drinking water and talking to the new bass player. Sandy had been home and showered and changed and put on his best white Mexican wedding shirt and his earring. The Jazz Poet had gone home and collected his lady, the ex-lesbian minimalist poet, Kathleen Danelle. Finley had sobered up and washed his face and hands and put on his painted Mirò tie. The Piano Prince had had another fix. The sun was all the way down behind the levee and now it was only ninety-two degrees in New Orleans, Louisiana, and the big fan that blew the air around the Raintree Street Bar and Washerteria could make some headway in its work to make the poets and other patrons more comfortable in their progress through the month of June, nineteen hundred and seventy-nine. The pinnacle year of poets in New Orleans. The year the ladies loved the poets. The year the poets got all the pussy and the preachers got none. Those were the days, the people from the Raintree would say later. Those were the years.

This night, the sixth of June, nineteen hundred and seventy-nine, was the beginning of the end for the poets of New Orleans, but they didn't know it yet. So far only six people in New Orleans knew that Francis Alter was dead. A married lady named Crystal Weiss knew it and her husband, Manny, and their two children and their two best friends. They had known it since seven o'clock. They had all been out to eat to celebrate the remission of a terrible leukemia inside a child of their two best friends. A gala celebration at a famous steak house. They had feasted on steak and fried potatoes and buttered mushrooms and salad smothered in Roquefort dressing and several bottles of fine red wine. A nineteen fifty-nine Mouton Rothschild from Manny Weiss's legendary cellar. The Weisses had even let the children have a glass of wine. Drink up, they said to their children. Cancer is on the run. Man has triumphed once again.

After they had finished all the food and wine, they had gone to the Weisses' house to sit around the pool and celebrate some more. Then the phone rang. A chill of premonition went around the people at the pool. Something's wrong, everybody said. Something's happened.

Manny answered the phone. Francis is dead, the caller said. Francis shot himself.

It was unbelievable. Francis had just been in New Orleans visiting all of them, charming them to death with his beauty and poetry, charming their children, charming the sick boy, charming their parents and the people they invited to meet him, charming the maids and yardmen, charming the birds down from the trees. Then he had gone home to his meager poet's cottage and lain down upon a bed and shot himself through the heart. He had gone into a bedroom and lain down upon a bed and blown his heart to smithereens. He had decided to put an end to all his poetry and pain and the hard work it is to be alive. Besides, he believed that if he killed himself everyone would be sorry and not be able to forget him. He was right about that.

As soon as the phone call came all the people around the Weisses' pool felt guilty for being alive. The Weisses' best friends soon went home. The Weisses' children were sent to their bedrooms to watch their television sets. The Weisses started getting very drunk. Then Crystal Weiss decided it was time to drive down to the Raintree and tell the poets. "The poets should know," she told her husband. "You stay here with the kids. I'm going to tell the poets."

"You shouldn't drive," he said, halfheartedly.

"It doesn't matter. I'm not drunk."

"Okay," he said and let her go. As soon as she left for the Raintree he went downstairs to his darkroom and began to print a roll of film he had taken when Francis was visiting them. It was a film of a Martin Luther King parade they had gone to with the poets. It began with a series of photographs of Francis eating breakfast in their dining room, smiling and charming everyone in sight. Manny cut off a negative of Francis sitting at the breakfast table and began to make a print. It was pitch-black dark in the darkroom and the face of the dead poet floated up in the developer, eyes first, then nose, then chin. "My God," Manny cried out loud and fled from the room. "This is nuts. What am I doing mixed up with these crazy people?" He left the print in the developer and ran up the stairs and into his little four-year-old girl's room. He covered her with a blanket and took off her shoes and turned off her television set and kissed her on the head. Then he went into his fourteen-year-old stepson's room and sat down beside him on the bed. "What are you watching?" he asked.

"Nothing," the boy said. "Is Francis really dead? Francis is dead? He said he was going to take me fishing. He said we were going camping on the White River. He said he was coming back."

Crystal Weiss drove drunkenly in the direction of the Raintree. No one at the Raintree knew yet that Francis had killed himself. No one knew anything except that the night was young and Johnny Vidocavitch was coming to sit in with the band and they had plans for one another. Finley's plan was to get the married lady to leave him alone. Hopefully, to give him five thousand more dollars for the magazine and still leave him alone. The Jazz Poet had two plans, one, to get Finley and the rich lady to do a special issue of the magazine featuring only his poetry and, two, to get Sandy to take him up to Arkansas to meet Francis Alter.

The bartender, Charles Joseph, had a plan to write a novel about the whole bunch of them, using their real names and then taking them out later so they couldn't sue him. Maybe also change the name of the street and get his dad to edit it since his dad was a sober man who worked hard and taught school as well as being a poet. His dad was extremely worried about Charles Joseph wasting his youth tending bar. He'd be glad to edit a novel Charles Joseph wrote so he'd have a chance to get rich and make something of himself. If I could get a million dollars for a book I'd be in high cotton, Charles Joseph was thinking. I'd go off to the islands and never come back. I'd drink all day and play cards and get all that island pussy. What a lovely deal. Charles Joseph rubbed his rag across the bar, fixed drinks, opened beers, rang up charges on the cash register, whistling to himself, lost in island dreams, singing along with the music on the juke box. *Iko, Iko, . . . Iko, Iko, Ole. Laissez les bons temps roule. Oh, those lonely, lonely nights. Oh, those lonely, lonely nights.*

About nine-thirty the rich lady, Jane Monroe, and her girlfriend, Allison, and her mother, Big Jane, who was even richer than her daughter, came breezing in the door. They stopped at the cash register to talk to Charles Joseph. "I don't know whether to get a table on the dance floor or the other room," Jane asked. "What do you think?"

"The dance floor," Charles Joseph said. "Johnny Vidocavitch is sitting in. It might be the last time he ever plays here."

"This is so exciting," Big Jane said. "This reminds me of the south of France."

"Get a table, Momma," Jane said. "I've got to talk to Finley." She had spied him at the end of the bar talking to Sandy.

"What do you guys want to drink?" Charles Joseph asked.

"A martini," Big Jane answered. "Make it a double." She smiled a curved smile through her third face-lift, wrinkled what was left of the skin around her eyes. "I love martinis. And load it up with olives."

"Coming up." Charles Joseph smiled back, thinking about her tons of money, thinking about the story he had heard about her dancing naked on the bar at Lu and Charlie's. "Now that would be something to see," he said out loud.

"What?" Big Jane asked. "I don't understand."

"I heard you were a great dancer," he said. "I heard you could dance like everything."

"We'll try it later," she answered. The smile had straightened back out. She moved in. "Come try me out." She took the martini he offered her. "You look like your daddy," she added. "I knew him when he was young."

"Go to the table, Momma," Lady Jane said. "I'm going to talk to

Finley. Come on, Allison." She pulled her guest down to the end of
the bar where Sandy was telling stories of the great poet.

"He's the most beautiful man I ever knew," Sandy was saying. "He
makes everything seem important. He read us poems, Yeats, Rilke,
Rimbaud."

"Oh, my God," Jane said. "I'd give anything to hear him read. He
won't give readings. Tulane offered him two thousand dollars and he
wouldn't come. And here he is, down in Texas, reading to a bunch
of kids. Oh, God, that's just like poetry."

"He made poetry seem the most wonderful thing in the world.
I'm going up there to see him. I'm going to help him run some lines."

"I'm going too," the Jazz Poet put in. "He's going to call and ask
if I can come. I worship Francis Alter. I worship at his shrine."

"He steals from black people," Finley muttered. "He steals everything he writes from them."

"Oh, sure," Jane said. It was her chance to pay him back for all the
times he had never called her up. "Oh, sure, you're not jealous or
anything, are you, Finley? You're so great, of course. Why would
you be?"

"What are you doing here, Jane?" he answered. "What do you
want with me?"

Crystal Weiss came into the Raintree and stood beside the cash register for a moment watching the dancers in the adjoining room. Big
Jane was jitterbugging with a martini glass in her hand. The wife of
the owner of a steamship line was dancing with a tall skinny poet who
taught at UNO. A fat poet was seated at a table with glasses all around
him looking wise and cynical. He was the Fat Cynical Poet. Many
people were afraid of him. Johnny Vidocavitch had shown up and
was playing the drums like all hell had broken loose. The Piano
Prince was playing standing up. I hate to tell them, Crystal thought. I
don't know if I want to be the one to spread this. Of course she was
dying to be the one to tell, dying to be known as the first one who
knew, dying to be remembered as the great poet's friend. She

arranged her face into a mask of sadness and mystery and despair and walked down the bar to where Finley was sitting between Jane Monroe and Sandy. "Can I talk to you?" she said. "I have to tell you something private." Jane Monroe flinched, Sandy admired the blonde intruder's long white dress and long white hair. Finley got up off the stool and walked with Crystal to the hall.

"What's up?" he asked. "What's happened?"

"Francis is dead. He shot himself. It's true. It's really true. I talked to James and to Sam. They saw it. People were in the house. He did it with people in the house."

"Oh, God, oh, my God."

"I know. Oh, Finley. He's gone. Gone forever." She let Finley take her into his arms and then she began to cry. Then the terrible news spread around the bar and into the adjoining room and the Fat Cynical Poet stood up and shook his head back and forth and the bartender opened himself a beer and the band began to play "The Saint James Infirmary Blues" as slowly as they could play and all the dancers stopped and stood around and looked each other over. A death had come among them. A poet had died by his own hand, had given the lie to all the gaiety and pussy and beer and poetry and jazz.

"Such a night," the Piano Prince began to play. *Sweet confusion under the moonlight.*

Among the Mourners

ℭ

THE SPRING that I was thirteen years old a poet we knew died and we had to have the funeral. It was the most embarrassing thing that ever happened to me in my life. In the first place he killed himself and the police couldn't even get his briefcase open to find the suicide note, and in the second place it almost broke up my parents' marriage. Not that my mother minded my father offering to have the funeral. Somebody had to do it, I guess, and our house is always full of people anyway. She just goes back to her room and reads magazines until they go away. My dad is head of the English Department and there are always poets around telling Dad their problems. I'm used to them and so is she. But this was different. All those police cars pulling up in front of the house and my little sister running around in her pajamas in the front yard and everybody over there smoking cigarettes like it was going out of style. This was several years ago when a lot of people still smoked inside the house.

How would you feel if you had just gotten the first boyfriend you ever had and every time his parents drove by your house there were cars parked all over the yard and police cars in the driveway? I was mortified. His name is Giorgio and his mother is from Peru and his father is Jewish and they don't have things like that at their house. They are very religious. Giorgio goes to the Catholic church with his mom and goes to the temple with his dad. They teach in the Foreign Language Department and they don't always have to have crazy people around like you do if your father is head of the English Department.

Giorgio speaks about fifteen languages and he is so good-looking you wouldn't believe it. He's pretty short but I'm glad he is. I couldn't stand it if he was playing football and I had to get out there and cheer for him getting his nose broken or his teeth cracked. I'm on the Pep Squad. I didn't want to go out but my mother made me. She's always trying to make me have a normal life. Only how can I? With all my dad's crazy friends coming over all the time and my crazy little sister running around naked and failing the first grade. I think they got her mixed up in the nursery. I don't believe she's kin to me.

Anyway, this poet that used to come over all the time and talk to Dad shot himself because his girlfriend had talked his wife into divorcing him and the next thing I knew there were about a hundred cars parked all over the yard on the day after Giorgio finally told me he liked me. My cousin bet him ten dollars he wouldn't tell me, and he called me up that night and told me. I don't think he got the ten dollars but he didn't care. He was so glad to have me for a girlfriend. He's in Gifted and Talented and so am I. I've been liking him for ages but I didn't know it until he called me up. That was about six o'clock one afternoon. That night the poet shot himself and the people started showing up.

"Aurora," my dad says, when he called me into his office to tell me what was going on. "Mr. Alter has killed himself and the widow is going to stay here until we can figure out a way to bury him."

"Why'd he do that?" I asked.

"We don't know. We'll need your room if Mr. Seats comes in from Saint Louis. You remember Mr. Seats? He used to teach here."

"He can't have my room. I'm making a project for Swim Team. It's the decorations for the banquet next week." I backed off toward the door. If you get into my dad's office he can talk you into things. It's like there's not enough oxygen in there when he really gets something on his mind. "Take Annie's room. It's filthy anyway. She's such a pig."

"Aurora."

"Yes, sir."

"A man has killed himself. We have a civilized duty to mourn when someone dies. If Mr. Seats comes we will need your room."

"I didn't kill him. Why should I give up my room?"

"Aurora, I am deeply disappointed in you. It makes me very sad to hear you talk that way. Mr. Alter was a guest in this house. He was a friend of mine and your mother's. We are going to pay him the respect that's due."

"If someone kills themself they don't get my respect."

"Alice Armene! Come in here!" So he starts screaming for my mother. He always blames her when he gets mad at me. As if she can stop it. Sometimes I think I'm the one who was switched in the hospital. Here's what they do that drives me crazy. They preach all the time about reason. *Dharma*, my dad calls it. He is so big on dharma. Then the first time something happens they start acting like these big Christians or something and having all these rituals.

By ten o'clock the next morning the house was full. Mr. Seats caught the first plane he could get and came on down and put his suitcase in my room. I will say this, he didn't touch anything. He just put his suitcase down and went into the living room and started watching television with Mother. He used to be a poet but he had just got this job sending in dialogue for *Days of Our Lives* so he had to watch all the soap operas all day even while he was mourning. He was the best friend of Mr. Alter and had just seen him a few weeks ago. Also, he was suffering a broken heart because the person he loved in Saint Louis wouldn't get a divorce and marry him. He was telling Mother all about it the first day he was there and she's sitting on the sofa with him patting him on the hand. That's what almost broke up my parents' marriage, not to mention almost got the television taken out of our house for good.

So here they are, all sitting around the house drinking beer and iced tea and eating all the food everyone kept bringing over and waiting for the police to finish their investigation so they could bury the body. Giorgio's mother said she thought they should stop making a big deal out of someone young and in good health who would kill themself. "It ees an unholy act," she kept saying in this beautiful accent she has. They only live three blocks from us so I started staying over there all the time. I couldn't stand it at my house with all those people coming in and out the doors and Momma sitting in the living room with Mr. Seats holding his hand.

My dad is insanely jealous of my mother. He won't let anyone near her. He fell in love with her at first sight. She was second runner-up for Miss Tennessee and he met her when his roommate at the University of Kentucky had him up to visit one Thanksgiving vacation. She was good friends with his roommate's sister and she came walking into a room and he was instantly in love with her. Then he swept her off her feet and married her and brought her to Fayetteville, Arkansas, to live. As soon as they got here they had me on a freezing cold January night. I'm an Aquarius, born in my own time, only my parents don't like for me to talk about astrology. They say it's lower-middle-class superstition and not worthy of me. They are afraid I'll get into a coven or something when I grow up if I start believing in astrology.

They had Annie seven years later, although they didn't mean to. My mom is a sculptor although she hasn't had time to do it since Annie was born. Annie wouldn't even go to kindergarten half the time. Then she failed the first grade. All she wants to do is ride her stupid bike or run around with hardly any clothes on or just hang on Dad like some kind of monkey. She adores him.

So what does she do while this funeral is going on but run around in these little pink nylon pajamas that are about ten years old and too short for her and go from person to person being cute and getting people to talk about her to Dad. She's a slut if I ever saw one. She'll do anything for attention. That's why she failed the first grade. Just to get attention.

"It makes me sick," I told Giorgio. We were sitting on the front wall looking at the house. You've never seen so many people going in and out of a house in your life. Mom's going to have to throw the carpets away. There won't be any way to clean them. "He thinks it is his job," Giorgio says. He's sitting right next to me and I can smell the Peruvian perfume his mother puts on everything he wears. Just to think I waited all these years to have a boyfriend and the minute I get one they start having this six-day funeral at my house.

"A wake," my dad told me. "This is the wake."

"When are they going to bury him?" I ask. I don't say another word about Mr. Seats living in my room. He has barely opened his suitcase the whole time he's been here. He thinks Mr. Alter has been appearing to him. Like a ghost. But does my father start screaming and say don't start getting into that lower-middle-class superstition? No, of course not. He just gets this really serious look on his face and lets Mr. Seats talk all he wants about seeing Mr. Alter's ghost behind the rocking chair in the living room and also in the front yard near the maple tree. I bet Mr. Seats told that story about fifty times in one day. Every time I would walk through the room, trying to get something to eat or take a bath or finish my decorations for the Swimming Team banquet, there he would be, telling about the ghost behind the rocking chair.

"Are you coming to my banquet?" I asked my mother finally. She and Mr. Seats were in the living room watching *The Young and the Restless*. Mr. Snider was with them. He's my father's student assistant. Dad told him not to let them watch the television alone. I heard Mr. Snider laughing and telling that to the widow like he was trying to cheer her up. Anyway, I believed it because every time they were in there with the TV on, Mr. Snider was there too.

"They should not have eenvolved you in thees death," Giorgio's mother said to me. "Thees murder."

"I can't even take a bath," I told her. "It's a good thing I'm on the Swim Team. I might get impetigo or something. I was late to practice yesterday because my mother couldn't back out of the driveway. They had this man there from the radio station. They've been playing a special program of all the dead guy's favorite music on the student radio station. He was there getting everyone to tell him what to play."

"Thees ees so morbid, you poor baby girl." Giorgio's mother asked me to eat dinner with them that night so I called and they said I could and Giorgio and I went into his room and listened to music and played Scrabble. Just the two of us. No one bothered us or came in. Well, he's an only child, and his father is a workaholic so there wasn't anyone there but us and his mother and I could tell she wanted us to be in love. She was real excited because I'm in Gifted and Talented too.

"I want Giorgio to have friends who share hees interests so he won't get involved with thees football people." You should hear her say involved. She gives it about fourteen syllables. She grew up speaking French and Spanish and English and I could just live over there listening to her talk.

I guess you think we were in there kissing and making out but you are wrong. I would never take advantage of that woman. I wouldn't violate Mrs. Levine's trust for fifteen-carat diamonds in my ears. I wouldn't hurt that woman for all the money in the world. I love her with all my heart. Even if Giorgio did quit liking me I would never do one thing to make Mrs. Levine unhappy. If it hadn't been for her I would never have made it through that week.

Finally, on the Friday after he killed himself on Saturday, the police released the body and they all went up to the cemetery and buried him. He didn't have any parents. He was an orphan from the word go, which is what made it so tragic. The only one who had ever loved him was his wife and he betrayed her with another woman and then he couldn't face the consequences of what he had done.

"Thees happens every day in my country," Mrs. Levine told me. "We do not theeenk these things are tragedies. Tragedy ees for the poor widow or the child who loses his mother or when there is a war. Thees young man will have eternity to regret hees act. It would be better if the living walked off and forgot hees selfish life."

"Can Aurora spend the night tonight?" Giorgio asked. "She can sleep in the guest room. She hasn't had any sleep in days, Momma. She has to sleep with her little sister."

"I'm an insomniac anyway," I added. "But that's okay. I can take it another night."

"Of course not. Of course you can stay here with us. I will call your mother and see if thees is all right with her, then?"

So listen, my parents are so wrapped up in this funeral they said yes. They let me spend the night at a boy's house. I couldn't believe it. I was afraid to go home and get my pajamas and toothbrush. I was afraid my mom would change her mind if she saw me. Sometimes she can read my mind like a Gypsy.

I sneaked in the side door and grabbed some clothes and stuffed them in a bag and almost made it back out into the yard when Dad caught me. "Where are you going?" he says. By now they have buried Mr. Alter and are back at our house sitting around discussing the funeral. I'm in the back hall about four feet from the kitchen and Dad's blocking the way to the door.

"I'm going to church with the Levines," I said.

"You're doing what?" My father has spent his life listening to students. There is no fooling him. I raised my head and looked him in the eye. "I think they're going to the synagogue," I said. "Or maybe to St. Joseph's. I'm freaking out from this funeral, Dad. The Levines asked me to stay with them. Mom said I could."

"Mr. Harris?" It was this graduate student named Bellefontaine who's a big favorite of my dad's. He had a faded red corduroy shirt in his hand. "This was one of Francis's shirts. We thought you might like it for a souvenir. We cleaned out his closets like you said. We brought this to you. I don't know. Maybe you don't want it." He stood blocking the door to the kitchen with the dead poet's shirt in his hand. My dad reached out and took it. I went under their arms and made my escape. "I have to go," I said. "They're waiting for me in the car." I was out of the door. I had just told two lies in a row to a man who never forgets anything and is never fooled. I lit out across the patio and took the short cut to the Levines' house across the backyards of my piano teacher and some people from Indiana that no one ever sees.

Giorgio and his mother were waiting for me. They were making paella for dinner. Mr. Levine was going to be late. We weren't going to have to wait for him.

Everything went along just fine until Mr. Levine came home and he and Mrs. Levine went to bed, leaving Giorgio and me alone. "You want to go for a walk?" he asked. "They won't mind. They don't care what I do."

"It's ten-thirty at night. Sure. I'd love it. We can walk up to the store." I was about five feet away from him. He smelled like that perfume. He reached out and took my hand and we just walked on out the door. "We can go to the park," he said. "Sometimes I go there at night. It's not too far."

"I can walk a hundred miles. Who cares how far it is." So we started off down Washington Avenue. It was in between semesters at the college and the town was quiet. We walked down to Highway 71 and crossed at the IGA. There wasn't anyone around but old Donnie Hights, who is a lunatic that walks the streets all the time saying hello to people. He gives me the creeps but Dad says he is proof there is still freedom in the United States and to count my blessings and be polite.

Anyway, he was standing on the corner by the Shell station so I held on tighter to Giorgio's hand and we crossed 71 and started up toward Washington Elementary School.

"That's where I learned to read," I commented. "Right there in that corner room. Mrs. Nordan taught me. She's the sweetest lady in the world. I adore her."

"I adore you," Giorgio says. He said that. Right there by the corner of the school on Maple Street. He got real near me and sort of breathed into my hair.

That's all that happened then. We walked up Maple and cut over at Doctor Wileman's house and went on down to the park. At the wooden bridge we stopped and sat down and started kissing. We just started kissing without saying a thing. I bet there wasn't a person left in the park. If it hadn't been for the lights in the houses on the hill there wouldn't have been any light except for the moon and stars. "This is just like the old shepherds in the Bible," I said at last. "Or else the Druids. It makes me think of death to be alone in the night. Does it you?"

But all Giorgio did was put his hand on my breast and keep it there. I would have made him move it but I wanted to know what it felt like. It felt good. I can tell you that much. If I hadn't had to think about what it would be like when my dad got me in his office and started screaming at me I might have just let him keep it there all night.

"We better get back," I said. I was kissing him as hard as I could in between talking but I still have my braces on and it hurts to kiss very hard with them. Besides, last week I got a free certificate to TCBY for not breaking any pieces off of them for a month and I was trying to get another one. "You better stop doing that," I added, and pushed his hand off of my breast.

He didn't fight me. He just ran it down my shorts and stuck his finger up inside my underpants. Just stuck it right up around the edge of my underpants. I don't know what would have happened but a car full of teenagers pulled up on Wilson Street and got out and started running for the swing sets which are only forty feet from the bridge where we were lying. Something crashed in the creek. It was probably just a beer can but it sounded like a hydrogen bomb.

I stood up and dusted myself off. I already had about five hundred chigger bites but luckily I wouldn't know that until morning.

That's all there is worth telling about that night. We walked back to the house. Giorgio was acting like he was mad at me. He was pouting if you want to know the truth. He was acting like he was about five years old. He's spoiled rotten, to tell the truth.

Besides, in another year he'll be too short for me. We're already the same height and my mom is five foot seven and my dad's six five. It wasn't going to last.

So I don't care if he told my best friend he doesn't like me anymore.

Mr. Seats has twin boys my age who live up in Minnesota. When he comes down next winter to be the Poet in Residence he's going to bring them with him. He thinks they will both fall in love with me. "They always fall in love together," he told me, while he was packing up his stuff to leave my room. "You can have them both, Aurora."

So what do you think? Do you think Giorgio quit liking me because I let him put his hand on my breast? Or because I didn't let him put it in my pants? Or because there were police cars outside my house for seven days?

My dad would say that's like trying to figure out why Mr. Alter killed himself. He believes in the theory of random acts. He thinks lightning strikes. He thinks we should just live every day and do the best we can.

Also, this is the last funeral we'll have to have. Before they left Dad called all the people into the living room and told them this was the last time he was going to a suicide's funeral. If anyone else killed themself they were on their own for getting buried. "This has had a negative effect on my children," he said. He knew I was listening in the hall. "I am worried that I allowed them to witness it. Aside from that, I love you all and I wish you well." I noticed as soon as Dad made his announcement that Mr. Seats went into my room and took a shower and put on a shirt and tie and starting acting like a grownup. My dad has the power to do things like that to people but he usually saves it up and only uses it at the end.

My parents are very cool people to tell the truth. They aren't even going to make Annie go to summer school. They're just going to let her run around all summer in her bathing suit and try again next year. This is very advanced behavior for academics and everyone was congratulating them on it when they were getting in their cars and leaving. You're right about Annie, people were saying. Let her be a child. Don't push her, and so forth.

Of course, why should they worry? They've got me. And I have them again. More than I need. The television has a sign on it that says,

GOODBYE, SEQUENTIAL THOUGHT, and a schedule of times when Annie and I are allowed to watch it. Although I think the sign is really just to remind my mother that Mr. Seats has whored himself by agreeing to write the dialogue for a soap opera.

Now that I know what it is they do when they go into their room at night I am looking at them with different eyes. I feel sorry for them, to tell the truth. If I had to do that stuff every night I might not be able to stay in Gifted and Talented or even be on the Swim Team. Here's the way I look when I start thinking about it. Very soft around the mouth and chin, like Bambi, sort of big-eyed and stupid, bowing my head to chew a little piece of grass.

Very helpless and half-asleep, while all around me for all I know the forest might be catching fire.

The Stucco House

TEDDY was asleep in his second-floor bedroom. It was a square, high-ceilinged room with cobalt blue walls and a bright yellow rug. The closet doors were painted red. The private bath had striped wallpaper and a ceiling fan from which hung mobiles from the Museum of Modern Art. In the shuttered window hung a mobile of small silver airplanes. A poet had given it to Teddy when he came to visit. Then the poet had gone home and killed himself. Teddy was not supposed to know about that, but of course he did. Teddy could read really well. Teddy could read like a house afire. The reason he could read so well was that when his mother had married Eric and moved to New Orleans from across the lake in Mandeville, he had been behind and had had to be tutored. He was tutored every afternoon for a whole summer, and when second grade started, he could read really well. He was still the youngest child in the second grade at Newman School, but at least he could read.

He was sleeping with four stuffed toys lined up between him and the wall and four more on the other side. They were there to keep his big brothers from beating him up. They were there to keep ghosts from getting him. They were there to keep vampires out. This night they were working. If Teddy dreamed at all that night, the dreams were like Technicolor clouds. On the floor beside the bed were Coke bottles and potato-chip containers and a half-eaten pizza from the evening before. Teddy's mother had gone off at suppertime and not come back, so Eric had let him do anything he liked before he went to bed. He had played around in Eric's darkroom for a while. Then he had let the springer spaniels in the house, and then he had ordered a pizza and Eric had paid for it. Eric was reading a book about a man who climbed a mountain in the snow. He couldn't put it down. He didn't care what Teddy did as long as he was quiet.

Eric was really nice to Teddy. Teddy was always glad when he and Eric were alone in the house. If his big brothers were gone and his mother was off with her friends, the stucco house was nice. This month was the best month of all. Both his brothers were away at Camp Carolina. They wouldn't be back until August.

Teddy slept happily in his bed, his stuffed animals all around him, his brothers gone, his dreams as soft as dawn.

Outside his house the heat of July pressed down upon New Orleans. It pressed people's souls together until they grated like chalk on brick. It pressed people's brains against their skulls. Only sugar and whiskey made people feel better. Sugar and coffee and whiskey. Beignets and café au lait and taffy and Cokes and snowballs made with shaved ice and sugar and colored flavors. Gin and wine and vodka, whiskey and beer. It was too hot, too humid. The blood wouldn't move without sugar.

Teddy had been asleep since eleven-thirty the night before. Eric came into his room just before dawn and woke him up. "I need you to help me," he said. "We have to find your mother." Teddy got sleepily out of bed, and Eric helped him put on his shorts and shirt and sandals. Then Eric led him down the hall and out the front door and down the concrete steps, and opened the car door and helped him into the car. "I want a Coke," Teddy said. "I'm thirsty."

"Okay," Eric answered. "I'll get you one." Eric went back into the house and reappeared carrying a frosty bottle of Coke with the top off. The Coke was so cool it was smoking in the soft humid air.

Light was showing from the direction of the lake. In New Orleans in summer the sun rises from the lake and sets behind the river. It was rising now. Faint pink shadows were beginning to penetrate the mist.

Eric drove down to Nashville Avenue to Chestnut Street and turned and went two blocks and came to a stop before a duplex shrouded by tall green shrubs. "Come on," he said. "I think she's here." He led Teddy by the hand around the side of the house to a set of wooden stairs leading to an apartment. Halfway up the stairs Teddy's mother was lying on a landing. She had on a pair of pantyhose and that was all. Over her naked body someone had thrown a seersucker jacket. It was completely still on the stairs, in the yard.

"Come on," Eric said. "Help me wake her up. She fell down and we have to get her home. Come on, Teddy, help me as much as you can."

"Why doesn't she have any clothes on? What happened to her clothes?"

"I don't know. She called and told me to come and get her. That's all I know." Eric was half carrying and half dragging Teddy's mother down the stairs. Teddy watched while Eric managed to get her down the stairs and across the yard. "Open the car door," he said. "Hold it open."

Together they got his mother into the car. Then Teddy got in the backseat and they drove to the stucco house and got her out and dragged her around to the side door and took her into the downstairs hall and into Malcolm's room and laid her down on Malcolm's waterbed. "You watch her," Eric said. "I'm going to call the doctor."

Teddy sat down on the floor beside the waterbed and began to look at Malcolm's books. *Playing to Win, The Hobbit, The Big Green Book*. Teddy took down *The Big Green Book* and started reading it. It was about a little boy whose parents died and he had to go and live with his aunt and uncle. They weren't very nice to him, but he liked it there. One day he went up to the attic and found a big green book of magic spells. He learned all the spells. Then he could change himself into animals. He could make himself invisible. He could do anything he wanted to do.

Teddy leaned back against the edge of the waterbed. His mother had not moved. Her legs were lying side by side. Her mouth was open. Her breasts fell away to either side of her chest. Her pearl necklace was falling on one breast. Teddy got up and looked down at her. She isn't dead, he decided. She's just sick or something. I guess she fell down those stairs. She shouldn't have been outside at night with no clothes on. She'd kill me if I did that.

He went around to the other side of the waterbed and climbed up on it. Malcolm never let him get on the waterbed. He never even let Teddy come into the room. Well, he was in here now. He opened *The Big Green Book* and found his place and went on reading. Outside in the hall he could hear Eric talking to people on the phone. Eric was nice. He was so good to them. He had already taken Teddy snorkeling and skiing, and next year he was going to take him to New York to see the dinosaurs in the museum. He was a swell guy. He was the best person his mother had ever married. Living with Eric was great. It was better than anyplace Teddy had ever been. Better than living with his real daddy, who wasn't any fun, and lots better than being at his grandfather's house. His grandfather yelled at them and made them make their beds and ride the stupid horses and hitch up the pony cart, and if they didn't do what he said, he hit them with a belt. Teddy hated being there, even if he did have ten cousins near him in Mandeville and they came over all the time. They liked to be there even if their grandfather did make them mind. There was a fort in the woods and secret paths for riding the ponies, and the help cooked for them morning, noon, and night.

Teddy laid *The Big Green Book* down on his lap and reached over and patted his mother's shoulder. "You'll be okay," he said out loud. "Maybe you're just hung over."

Eric came in and sat beside him on the waterbed. "The doctor's coming. He'll see about her. You know, Doctor Paine, who comes to dinner. She'll be all right. She just fell down."

"Maybe she's hung over." Teddy leaned over his mother and touched her face. She moaned. "See, she isn't dead."

"Teddy, maybe you better go up to your room and play until the doctor leaves. Geneva will be here in a minute. Get her to make you some pancakes or something."

"Then what will we do?"

"Like what?"

"I mean all day. You want to go to the lake or something?"

"I don't know, Ted. We'll have to wait and see." Eric took his mother's hand and held it. He looked so worried. He looked terrible. She was always driving him crazy, but he never got mad at her. He just thought up some more things to do.

"I'll go see if Geneva's here. Can I have a Coke?"

"May I have a Coke." Eric smiled and reached over and patted his arm. "Say it."

"May I have a Coke, please?"

"Yes, you may." They smiled. Teddy got up and left the room.

The worst thing of all happened the next day. Eric decided to send him across the lake for a few days. To his grandmother and grandfather's house. "They boss me around all the time," Teddy said. "I won't be in the way. I'll be good. All I'm going to do is stay here and read books and work on my stamp collection." He looked pleadingly up at his stepfather. Usually reading a book could get him anything he wanted with Eric, but today it wasn't working.

"We have to keep your mother quiet. She'll worry about you if you're here. It won't be for long. Just a day or so. Until Monday. I'll come get you Monday afternoon."

"How will I get over there?"

"I'll get Big George to take you." Big George was the gardener. He had a blue pickup truck. Teddy had ridden with him before. Getting to go with Big George was a plus, even if his grandfather might hit him with a belt if he didn't make his bed.

"Can I see Momma now?"

"May."

"May I see Momma now?"

"Yeah. Go on in, but she's pretty dopey. They gave her some pills."

His mother was in her own bed now, lying flat down without any pillows. She was barely awake. "Teddy," she said. "Oh, baby, oh, my precious baby. Eric tried to kill me. He pushed me down the stairs."

"No, he didn't." Teddy withdrew from her side. She was going to start acting crazy. He didn't put up with that. "He didn't do anything to you. I went with him. Why didn't you have any clothes on?"

"Because I was asleep when he came and made me leave. He pushed me and I fell down the stairs."

"You probably had a hangover. I'm going to Mandeville. Well, I'll see you later." He started backing away from the bed. Backing toward the door. He was good at backing. Sometimes he backed home from school as soon as he was out of sight of the other kids.

"Teddy, come here to me. You have to do something for me. Tell Granddaddy and Uncle Ingersol that Eric is trying to kill me. Tell them, will you, my darling? Tell them for me." She was getting sleepy again. Her voice was sounding funny. She reached out a hand to him and he went back to the bed and held out his arm and she stroked it. "Be sure and tell them. Tell them to call the president." She stopped touching him. Her eyes were closed. Her mouth fell open. She still looked pretty. Even when she was drunk, she looked really pretty. Now that she was asleep, he moved nearer and looked at her. She looked okay. She sure wasn't bleeding. She had a cover on the bed that was decorated all over with little Austrian flowers. They were sewn on like little real flowers. You could hardly tell they were made of thread. He looked at one for a minute. Then he picked up her purse and took a twenty-dollar bill out of her billfold and put it in his pocket. He needed to buy some film. She didn't care. She gave him anything he asked for.

"What are you doing?" It was Eric at the door. "You better be getting ready, Teddy. Big George will be here in a minute."

"I got some money out of her purse. I need to get some film to take with me."

"What camera are you going to take? I've got some film for the Olympus in the darkroom. You want a roll of black-and-white? Go get the camera and I'll fill it for you."

"She said you tried to kill her." Teddy took Eric's hand and they started down the hall to the darkroom. "Why does she say stuff like that, Eric? I wish she wouldn't say stuff like that when she gets mad."

"It's a fantasy, Teddy. She never had anyone do anything bad to her in her life, and when she wants some excitement, she just makes it up. It's okay. I'm sorry she fell down the stairs. I was trying to help her. You know that, don't you?"

"Yes. Listen, can I buy Big George some lunch before we cross the Causeway? I took twenty dollars. Will that be enough to get us lunch?"

"Sure. That would be great, Teddy. I bet he'd like that. He likes you so much. Everybody likes you. You're such a swell little boy. Come on, let's arm that camera. Where is it?"

Teddy ran back to his room and got the camera. He was a scrawny, towheaded little boy who would grow up to be a magnificent man. But for now he was seven and a half years old and liked to take photographs of people in the park and of dogs. He liked to read books and pretend he lived in Narnia. He liked to get down on his knees at the Episcopal church and ask God not to let his momma divorce Eric. If God didn't answer, then he would pretend he was his grandfather and threaten God. Okay, you son-of-a-bitch, he would say, his little head down on his chest, kneeling like a saint at the prayer rail. If she divorces Eric, I won't leave anyway. I'll stay here with him and we can be bachelors. She can just go anywhere she likes. I'm not leaving. I'm going right on living here by the park in my room. I'm not going back to Mandeville and ride those damned old horses.

Big George came in the front door and stood, filling up the hall. He was six feet five inches tall and wide and strong. His family had worked for Eric's family for fifty years. He had six sons and one daughter who was a singer. He liked Eric, and he liked the scrawny little kid that Eric's wife had brought along with the big mean other ones. "Hey, Teddy," Big George said, "where's your bag?"

"You want to go to lunch?" Teddy said. "I got twenty dollars. We can stop at the Camellia Grill before we cross the bridge. You want to do that?"

"Sure thing. Twenty dollars. What you do to get twenty dollars, Teddy?"

"Nothing. I was going to buy some film, but Eric gave me some so I don't have to. Come on, let's go." He hauled his small leather suitcase across the parquet floor and Big George leaned down and took it from him. Eric came into the hall and talked to Big George a minute, and they both looked real serious and Big George shook his head, and then Eric kissed Teddy on the cheek and Big George and Teddy went on out and got into the truck and drove off.

Eric stood watching them until the truck turned onto Saint Charles Avenue. Then he went back into the house and into his wife's work-room and looked around at the half-finished watercolors, which were her latest obsession, and the mess and the clothes on the floor and the unemptied wastebaskets, and he sat down at her desk and opened the daybook she left out for him, to see if there were any new men since the last time she made a scene.

June 29, Willis will be here from Colorado. Show him the new po-ems. HERE IS WHAT WE MUST ADMIT. Here is what we know. What happened then is what happens now. Over and over again. How to break the pattern. Perhaps all I can do is avoid or understand the pat-tern. The pattern holds for all we do. I discovered in a dream that I am not in love with R. Only with what he can do for my career. How sad that is. The importance of dreams is that they may contain feelings we are not aware of. FEELINGS WE ARE NOT AWARE OF. The idea of counterphobia fascinates me. That you could climb moun-tains because you are afraid of heights. Seek out dangers because the danger holds such fear for you. What if I seek out men because I want to fight with them. Hate and fear them and want to have a fight. To replay my life with my brothers. Love to fight. My mascu-line persona.

Well, I'll see Willis tonight and show him the watercolors too, maybe. I'll never be a painter. Who am I fooling? All I am is a mother and a wife. That's that. Two unruly teenagers and a little morbid kid who likes Eric better than he likes me. I think it's stunting his growth to stay in that darkroom all the time. . . .

Eric sighed and closed the daybook. He picked up a watercolor of a spray of lilies. She was good. She was talented. He hadn't been wrong about that. He laid it carefully down on the portfolio and went into her bedroom and watched her sleep. He could think of nothing to do. He could not be either in or out; he could not make either good or bad decisions. He was locked into this terrible marriage and into its terrible rage and fear and sadness. No one was mean to me, he decided. Why am I here? Why am I living here? For Teddy, he decided, seeing the little boy's skinny arms splashing photographs in and out of trays, grooming the dogs, swimming in the river, paddling a canoe. I love that little boy, Eric decided. He's just like I was at that age. I have to keep the marriage together if I can. I can't stand for him to be taken from me.

Eric began to cry, deep within his heart at first, then right there in the sunlight, at twelve o'clock on a Saturday morning, into his own hands, his own deep, salty, endless, heartfelt tears.

Big George had stopped at the Camellia Grill, and he and Teddy were seated on stools at the counter eating sliced-turkey sandwiches and drinking chocolate freezes. "So, what's wrong with your momma?" Big George asked.

"She fell down some stairs. We had to go and get her and bring her home. She got drunk, I guess."

"Don't worry about it. Grown folks do stuff like that. You got to overlook it."

"I just don't want to go to Mandeville. Granddaddy will make me ride the damned old horses. I hate horses."

"Horses are nice."

"I hate them. I have better things to do. He thinks I want to show them, but I don't. Malcolm and Jimmy like to do it. I wish they were home from camp. Then he'd have them."

"Don't worry about it. Eat your sandwich." Big George bit into his. The boy imitated him, opened his mouth as wide as Big

George's, heartily ate his food, smilingly let the world go by. It took an hour to get to Mandeville. He wasn't there yet. He looked up above the cash register to where the Camellia Grill sweatshirts were prominently displayed—white, with a huge pink camellia in the center. He might get one for Big George for a Christmas present or he might not wait that long. He had sixty-five dollars in the bank account Eric made for him. He could take some of it out and buy the sweatshirt now. "I like that sweatshirt," he said out loud. "I think it looks real good, don't you?"

"Looks hot," Big George said, "but I guess you'd like it in the winter."

Teddy slept all the way across the Causeway, soothed by the motion of the truck and Big George beside him, driving and humming some song he was making up as he drove. Eric's a fool for that woman, George was thinking. Well, he's never had a woman before, just his momma and his sisters. Guess he's got to put up with it 'cause he likes the little boy so much. He's the sweetest little kid I ever did see. I like him too. Paying for my lunch with a twenty-dollar bill. Did anybody ever see the like? He won't be scrawny long. Not with them big mean brothers he's got. The daddy was a big man too, I heard them say. No, he won't stay little. They never do, do they?

Teddy slept and snored. His allergies had started acting up, but he didn't pay any attention to them. If he was caught blowing his nose, he'd be taken to the doctor, so he only blew it when he was in the bathroom. The rest of the time he ignored it. Now he snored away on the seat beside Big George, and the big blue truck moved along at a steady sixty miles an hour, cruising along across the lake.

At his grandparents' house in Mandeville his grandmother and grandfather were getting ready for Teddy. His grandmother was making a caramel cake and pimento cheese and carrot sticks and Jell-O. His grandfather was in the barn dusting off the saddles and straightening the tackle. Maybe Teddy would want to ride down along the bayou with him. Maybe they'd just go fishing. Sweet little old boy. They had thought Rhoda was finished having children and then she gave them one last little boy. Well, he was a tender little chicken, but he'd toughen. He'd make a man. Couldn't help it. Had a man for a father even if he was a chickenshit. He'd turn into a man even if he did live in New Orleans and spend his life riding on the streetcar.

Teddy's grandfather finished up in the barn and walked back to the house to get a glass of tea and sit out on the porch and wait for the boy. "I might set him up an archery target in the pasture," he told his wife. "Where'd you put the bows the big boys used to use?"

"They're in the storage bin. Don't go getting that stuff out, Dudley. He doesn't need to be out in the pasture in this heat."

"You feed him. I'll find him things to do."

"Leave him alone. You don't have to make them learn things every minute. It's summer. Let him be a child."

"What's wrong with her? Why's she sick again?"

"She fell down. I don't want to talk about it. Get some tea and sit down and cool off, Dudley. Don't go getting out archery things until you ask him if he wants to. I mean that. You leave that child alone. You just plague him following him around. He doesn't even like to come over here anymore. You drive people crazy, Dudley. You really do." She poured tea into a glass and handed it to him. They looked each other in the eye. They had been married thirty-eight years. Everything in the world had happened to them and kept on happening. They didn't care. They liked it that way.

Teddy's uncle Ingersol was five years younger than Teddy's mother. He was a lighthearted man, tall and rangy and spoiled. Teddy's grandmother had spoiled him because he looked like her side of the family. Her daddy had died one year and Ingersol had been born the next. Reincarnation. Ingersol looked like a Texan and dressed like an English lord. He was a cross between a Texan and an English lord. His full name was Alfred Theodore Ingersol Manning. Teddy was named for him but his real father had forbidden his mother to call him Ingersol. "I want him to be a man," his father had said, "not a bunch of spoiled-rotten socialites like your brothers."

"My brothers are not socialites," Teddy's mother had answered, "just because they like to dance and have some fun occasionally, which is more than I can say for you." Teddy always believed he had heard that conversation. He had heard his mother tell it so many times that he thought he could remember it. In this naming story he saw himself sitting on the stairs watching them as they argued over him. "He's my son," his mother was saying. "I'm the one who risked my life having him. I'll call him anything I damn well please."

Teddy's vision of grown people was very astute. He envisioned them as large, very high-strung children who never sat still or finished what they started. Let me finish this first, they were always saying. I'll be done in a minute. Except for Eric. Many times Eric just smiled when he came in and put down whatever he was doing and took Teddy to get a snowball or to walk the springer spaniels or just sit and play cards or Global Pursuit or talk about things. Eric was the best grown person Teddy had ever known, although he also liked his uncle Ingersol and was always glad when he showed up.

All his mother's brothers were full of surprises when they showed up, but only Uncle Ingersol liked to go out to the amusement park and ride the Big Zephyr.

Ingersol showed up this day almost as soon as Big George and Teddy arrived in the truck. Big George was still sitting on the porch drinking iced tea and talking to Teddy's grandfather about fishing when Ingersol came driving up in his Porsche and got out and joined them. "I heard you were coming over, namesake. How you been? What's been going on?"

"Momma fell down some stairs and me and Eric had to bring her home."

"Eric and I."

"I forgot."

"How'd she do that?"

"She said Eric tried to kill her. She always says things like that when she's hung over. She said to tell you Eric tried to kill her." There, he had done it. He had done what she told him to do. "If she divorces Eric, I'm going to live with him. I'm staying right there. Eric said I could."

His grandfather pulled his lips in. It looked like his grandfather was hardly breathing. Big George looked down at the ground. Ingersol sat in his porch chair and began to rub his chin with his hand. "You better go see about her, son," his grandfather said. "Go on over there. I'll go with you."

"No, I'll go alone. Where is she now, Teddy?"

"She's in bed. The doctor came to see her. He gave her some pills. She's asleep."

"Okay. Big George, you know about this?"

"Just said to bring the boy over here to his granddaddy. That's all they told me. Eric wouldn't hurt a flea. I've known him since he was born. He'll cry if his dog dies."

"Go on, son. Call when you get there." His grandfather had unpursed his mouth. His uncle Ingersol bent down and patted Teddy's head. Then he got back into his Porsche and drove away.

"I'm going to stay with Eric," Teddy said. "I don't care what she does. He said I could stay with him forever."

Ingersol drove across the Causeway toward New Orleans thinking about his sister. She could mess up anything. Anytime they got her settled down, she started messing up again. Well, she was theirs and they had to take care of her. I wish he *had* thrown her down the stairs, Ingersol decided. It's about time somebody did something with her.

Teddy's mother was crying. She was lying in her bed and crying bitterly because her head hurt and her poems had not been accepted by *White Buffalo* and she would never be anything but a wife and a mother. And all she was mother to was three wild children who barely passed at school and weren't motivated and didn't even love her. She had failed on every front.

She got out of bed and went into the bathroom and looked at how horrible she looked. She combed her hair and put on makeup and changed into a different negligee and went to look for Eric. He was in the den reading a book. "I'm sorry," she said. "I got drunk and fell asleep. I didn't mean to. It just happened. *White Buffalo* turned my poems down again. The bastards. Why do I let that egomaniac judge my work? Tell me that."

"Are you feeling better?"

"I feel fine. I think I'll get dressed. You want to go out to dinner?"

"In a while. You ought to read this book. It's awfully good." He held it out. *The Snow Leopard*, by Peter Matthiessen.

"Has the mail come?"

"It's on the table. There are some cards from the boys. Malcolm won a swimming match."

"I wasn't sleeping with him, Eric. I went over there to meet a poet from Lafayette. It got out of hand."

Eric closed the book and laid it on the table by the chair. "I'm immobilized," he said at last. "All this is beyond me. I took Teddy with me to bring you home. For an alibi if you said I pushed you down the stairs. I can't think about anything else. I took that seven-year-old boy to see his mother passed out on the stairs in her pantyhose. I don't care what you did, Rhoda. It doesn't matter to me. All I care about is what I did. What I was driven to. I feel like I'm in quicksand. This is pulling me in. Then I sent him to Mandeville to your parents. He didn't want to go. You don't know how scared he is—of us, of you, of everything. I think I'll go get him now." Eric got up and walked out of the room. He got his car keys off the dining-room table and walked out into the lovely hot afternoon and left her there. He got into his car and drove off to get his stepson. I'll take him somewhere, he decided. Maybe I'll take him to Disney World.

Teddy was sitting on an unused tractor watching his grandfather cut the grass along the edge of the pond. His grandfather was astride a small red tractor pulling a bush hog back and forth across a dirt embankment on the low side. His grandfather nearly always ran the bush hog into the water. Then the men had to come haul it out and his grandfather would joke about it and be in a good mood for hours trying to make up for being stupid. Teddy put his feet up on the steering wheel and watched intently as his grandfather ran the bush hog nearer and nearer to the water's edge. If he got it in the water, they wouldn't have time to ride the horses before supper. That's what Teddy was counting on. Just a little closer, just a little bit more. One time his grandfather had turned the tractor over in the water and had to swim out. It would be nice if that could happen again, but getting it stuck in the mud would do. The day was turning out all right. His uncle Ingersol had gone over to New Orleans to get drunk with his mother, and his cousins would be coming later, and maybe they wouldn't get a divorce, and if they did, it might not be too bad. He and Eric could go to Disney World like they'd been wanting to without his mother saying it was tacky.

His grandfather took the tractor back across the dam on a seventy-degree angle. It was about to happen. At any minute the tractor would be upside down in the water and the day would be saved.

That was how things happened, Teddy decided. That was how God ran his game. He sat up there and thought of mean things to do and then changed his mind. You had to wait. You had to go on and do what they told you, and pretty soon life got better.

Teddy turned toward the road that led to the highway. The Kentucky Gate swung open, and Eric's car came driving through. He came to get me, Teddy thought, and his heart swung open too. Swung as wide as the gate. He got down off the tractor and went running to meet the car. Eric got out of the car and walked to meet him. Crazy little boy, he was thinking. Little friend of mine.

The Blue House

NORA JANE'S GRANDMOTHER lived in a blue frame house
on the corner of Laurel and Webster streets. It was there that Nora
Jane was happy. There was a swing on the porch and a morning glory
vine growing on a trellis. In April azaleas bloomed all around the
edges of the porch, white and pink and red azaleas, blue morning glories, the fragrant white Confederate jasmine, red salvia and geraniums
and the mysterious elephant ears, their green veins so like the ones on
Nora Jane's grandmother's hands. Nora Jane hated the veins because
they meant her grandmother was old and would die. Would die like
her father had died, vanish, not be there anymore, and then she
would be alone with only her mother to live with seven days a week.

"Let me set the table for you," she said to her grandmother, waking beside her in the bed. "Let me cook you breakfast. I want you to
eat an egg."

"Oh, honey lamb," her grandmother replied, and reached over
and found her glasses and put them on, the better to see the beautiful
little girl, the better to be happy with the child beside her. "We will
cook it together. Then we'll see about the mirlitons. You can take
them to Langenstein's today. They said they would buy all that you
had."

"Then I'd better hurry." Nora Jane got out of bed. If she was going to take the mirlitons to Langenstein's she wanted to do it early so she wouldn't run into any of her friends from Sacred Heart. She was the only girl at Sacred Heart so poor she had to sell vegetables to Langenstein's. Still, they had not always been poor. Her grandfather had been a judge. Her father had gone to West Point. Her grandmother had sung grand opera all up and down the coast and auditioned for the Met. She kissed her grandmother on the cheek and swung her long legs out of the bed and began to search for her clothes. "You cook breakfast then," she said. "I'll go pick the mirlitons before it gets too hot."

She put on her shorts and shirt and found her sandals and wandered out into the backyard to pick the mirlitons from the mirliton vines.

A neighbor was in the yard next door. Mr. Edison Angelo. He leaned over the fence. "How's everything going, Nora Jane?" he asked. "How's your grandmother?"

"She's feeling fine," Nora Jane said. "She's fine now. She's out of bed. She can do anything she likes."

Nora Jane bent over the mirliton vines. They were beautiful, sticky and fragrant, climbing their trellis of chicken wire. The rich burgundy red fruit hung on its fragile stems, fell off into Nora Jane's hands at the slightest touch. She gathered a basketful, placing them carefully on top of each other so as not to bruise them. Mirlitons are a delicacy in New Orleans. The dark red rind is half an inch thick, to protect the pulp and seeds from the swarming insects of the tropics, for mirlitons are a tropical fruit, brought to New Orleans two hundred years ago by sailors from the Caribbean. Some winters in New Orleans are too cold for mirlitons and the fruit is small and scanty. This had been a warm winter, however, and the mirliton vines were thick with fruit. Nora Jane bent over her work. Her head of curly dark black hair caught the morning sun, the sun caressed her. She was a beautiful child who looked so much like her dead father that it broke her mother's heart and made her drink. It made her grandmother glad. Nora Jane's father had been her oldest son. She thought God had given Nora Jane to her to make up for losing him. Nora Jane's grand-mother was a deeply religious woman who had been given to ecstatic states when she was young. It never occurred to her to rail at God or blame him for things. She thought of God as a fallback posi-tion in times of trouble. She thought of God as solace, patience, wis-dom, forgiveness, compensation.

Nora Jane's mother had a darker meaner view. She thought God and other people were to blame for everything that went wrong. She thought they had gotten together to kill her beautiful black-haired husband and she was paying them back by staying inside and drinking herself to death. Still, it wasn't her fault she was weak. Her mother had been weak before her and her mother before that. It was their habit to be weak.

Nora Jane's grandmother came from a line of women who had a habit of being strong. One of them had come to New Orleans from France as a casket girl, had sailed across the Atlantic Ocean when she was only sixteen years old, carrying all her possessions in a little casket and when she arrived had refused to marry the man to whom she was assigned. She had married a Welshman instead, a man who had been on the boat as a steward. Each generation of women was told this story in Nora Jane's grandmother's family and so they believed they were strong women with strong genes and acted accordingly. When she was about four years old Nora Jane had looked at the strong story and the weak story and decided to be strong. It was the year her fa-ther died and her grandmother sat in the swing on her porch and watched the morning glory vines open and close and the sun rise and fall and believed that God did not hate her even if he had allowed her son to die in a stupid war. Many of the men who fought with him had written her letters and she read them out loud to Nora Jane. One young man, whose name was Fraser, came and stayed for five weeks and painted the outside of the house a fresher, brighter blue and put a new floor in the kitchen of the house. Every day he sat on the porch with Nora Jane's grandmother as the sun went down and talked about the place where he lived. A place called Nebraska. When all the painting was done and the furniture put back in the kitchen, he kissed

Nora Jane and her grandmother good-bye and went off to see his own family. After he was gone Nora Jane and her grandmother would talk about him. "Where's Fraser gone?" Nora Jane would ask.

"He has gone to Nebraska," her grandmother would answer. "He went to try to find his wife."

"Where's his wife?"

"He doesn't know. She got tired of waiting for him."

"She's sad, like Momma, isn't she?"

"I think so, some people get sad."

"But not us, do we?"

"Let's walk over to the park," her grandmother said, and got up from the swing. "Those Emperor geese are dying to see you. They're waiting for you to bring them some bread."

"Then do I have to go home?"

"Sometime you do. Your mother doesn't like it if you stay here all the time."

"I'll go tomorrow. In two days I'll go back over there."

"We'll see. Put on your shoes. Those geese are waiting for you by the bridge."

Of course sooner or later she would have to go back to her mother's house and watch her mother cry. Although the older she got the less she had to put up with it. Her mother's house was seven blocks from her grandmother's house. Her mother's house was in the three hundred block of Webster Street and her grandmother's house was in the five hundred block of Henry Clay. By the time she was six years old Nora Jane was allowed to walk from her grandmother's house to her mother's house anytime she wanted to as long as the sun was up. She knew every house and yard and porch and tree between the three hundred block of Webster Street and the five hundred block of Henry Clay. She knew which fences made the best sound when she ran a stick along the railings. She knew which dogs were mean. She knew which people got up early and which ones were sleepyheads. She knew who took the *Times-Picayune* and who did not. When the golden rain trees bloomed and when the magnolia blossoms opened.

Hello, Nora Jane, everyone would say. How you keeping? How's everything with you?

Nora Jane carried the basket of mirlitons up the wooden steps to the kitchen. Ever since she was a small child she had sat on those steps to dream. She dreamed of elves and fairies, of ballet dresses and ballet shoes, of silk and velvet and operas and plays. There were photographs of her grandmother in operas in a book in the house. Photographs of long ago before her grandmother's face got old. In one photograph her grandmother was wearing a crown.

Nora Jane paused on the stairs, resting the basket of mirlitons on the rail. A fat yellow jacket buzzed past the door, a golden Monarch beat against a window, a blue jay flew down and sat upon a yard chair. Nora Jane walked on up the stairs and into the kitchen. It was seven o'clock in the morning. Already the sun was high. It was time to go to Langenstein's. "I'm going right now," she called to her grandmother. "I'll eat breakfast when I get back."

"Have a piece of toast then. Take it with you."

"I'm fine. I want to get these over there while they're fresh." She kissed her grandmother on the cheek and walked out through the rooms. It was a shotgun house with one room right behind the other. Her grandmother let her leave. She knew why Nora Jane wanted to get to Langenstein's so early and she approved of it. It was the same reason she swept her porch at dawn. Ladies didn't do housework. Ladies didn't sell vegetables to the grocery store.

Nora Jane proceeded down the street, down Webster to Magazine and over to Calhoun, past Prytania, Camp, Coliseum, Perrier and Pitt to Garfield, past the Jewish cemetery and into the parking lot of Langenstein's, which is the richest grocery store in New Orleans, perhaps the richest grocery store in the world. A few ladies were already parking their cars and going in to wheel small old-fashioned carts through the narrow aisles. Past shelves of exotic imported foods and delicatessen items, past chicory coffee and avocados and artichokes and stuffed crabs and seafood gumbo and imported crackers and candy, past wine vinegar and

Roquefort cheese and crème glacée and crawfish bisque and crawfish étouffée and potage tortue and lobster and shrimp ratatouille.

An old lady was being helped from her car by her chauffeur, a young woman in a tennis dress bounced by with a can of coffee in her hand, a fat white cat walked beneath a crepe myrtle tree, a mockingbird swooped down to pester it. Nora Jane ignored all that. She hurried across the parking lot and into the office and found Chef Roland at his desk. He was a man who loved the world. He loved food and God and music and all seven of his children and the idea of Food and God and Music and Children. He cooked all day and listened to his employees' troubles and then went home and listened to his wife's troubles and drank wine and talked on the telephone to his brother who was a Benedictine monk in Pennsylvania and wrote long impassioned letters to his brother who was a Jesuit in Cincinnati. Dear Alphonse, the letters would begin. Put down your apostasy and your rage. Please write to Maurice. Maurice longs to hear from you.

It concerned a religious schism that had split Chef Roland's family. For seven years his younger brothers had battled over the matter of birth control. Look at little Nora Jane, Chef Roland told himself now. No family, only one old grandmother and a mother better left unsaid. No brothers or sisters or aunts. A family which has died out. This one little blossom on the vine.

He got up from his desk and wrapped the little girl in his arms and kissed her on the top of her head. "Ah, these mirlitons," he said. "What a casserole I will make of these. Is this all? Only one basketful? You will bring me more?"

"I'll bring some more over later. If mother gets up. We wanted to bring you some early in case you needed them."

"How old are you now, Nora Jane?"

"I'm fourteen. I'll be fifteen pretty soon. This summer. You like them? You think they're beautiful?"

"Magnificent. Always your grandmother's vegetables are magnificent. I want the asparagus this year. All that she can spare." He was writing out a receipt for her to cash at the checkout stand. He knew why she was in a hurry. The Whittingtons were proud. The grandmother had sung with the opera. His father had heard her sing. He handed the receipt to her. She folded it and stuck it in the pocket of her shorts. Such a lovely child, he thought, a lovely child.

"You will come and work for me this summer?" he asked. "I will teach you to cook for me. You think it over, huh?"

"If I can," she said. "I might help the sisters with the camp at Sacred Heart. How much can you pay?"

"Four fifteen an hour and you will learn to cook. That's worth something, even for a pretty girl like you, huh?"

"I know how already. Grandmother taught me. We made a Charlotte Rousse for her birthday." Nora Jane giggled. "And we made an angel cake but it fell, because the stove is old. We need a new stove but we don't want to waste our money on it."

"I will call your grandmother and speak to her. She will tell you to come and work for me. Better than little children all day. I'll teach you a trade."

"Okay," Nora Jane said politely. "I'll think it over. I have to go now," she added. "Is there someone up front to cash this?"

"Yes, they're open. Run along then. But let me know."

"I will." She left the office and went into the store, down between the aisles of imported foods to the checkout stand. She collected three dollars and seventeen cents and put it in her pocket, then she started home, up the street of crushed-up oyster shells, past a line of azalea bushes that grew out onto the sidewalk. A black and white cat moved lazily along beside her, then disappeared into the open door of the Prytania Street Liquor Store. I better go by Momma's and get some clothes, Nora Jane decided. If I go now she won't start calling Grandmother's all day and driving us crazy.

Chef Roland stared down at his desk. Poor little girl, he was thinking. Of course she doesn't want to come work in the deli, but it's all I have to offer her. Poor baby, poor little thing.

The phone was ringing. Chef Roland pushed a button and answered it. It was his brother Maurice calling from Pennsylvania.

"So you're back from Rome," Chef Roland began. "Well, did

you tell them what I told you to tell them? Did you, Maurice? Did you or not? Answer my question."

"I want to come visit you when I get through here," Maurice said. "Can I come down for a few days? I want to talk with you, Roland, bury the hatchet, smoke peace pipe."

"What did you tell them, Maurice? Did you tell him what I said or not?"

"What's wrong, Roland, how are you in such a bad mood so early in the day? Is Betty all right? Are the children okay?"

"I just had a visit from the daughter of Leland Whittington, your old schoolmate that died fighting for the pope in Nam, Maurice. It broke my heart so early in the morning. Poor little fatherless thing. Poor little girl."

"No one with Leland's heart and will could be an object of pity. God, he was a beautiful man."

"Leland is dead, Maurice, and I want to know if you told the pope what I told you to tell him. It's the modern world. We have to move with it or be responsible for all this sadness. It's our fault, it's on our shoulders. The edict was preposterous."

"I'll be there in a few days or a week. Is that all right?"

"Of course it's all right. I'll tell everyone you're coming."

"I have to go now. We have prayers."

"Pray for sanity," Chef Roland said. "Pray to have some goddamn common sense."

Nora Jane crossed Prytania and walked down Camp to Magazine, then turned and went down Webster Street into the Irish Channel. The sun was higher now, people were coming out onto their porches, opening their Saturday newspapers, people jogged by in jogging suits, rode by on bicycles headed for the park. Maybe she won't be up yet, Nora Jane thought. And I can just grab some clothes and leave a note. She's getting worse. She really is. She's worse than she was at Mardi Gras or on their anniversary. Well, forget that. It doesn't matter. It isn't my fault. Remember Sister Katherine said never to think it's my fault. It's not my fault. It's not my fault.

Nora Jane passed her godmother Leanie's house, hurried by so she wouldn't get stopped and have to talk. She hurried on down the street and turned into the yard of her mother's white frame house. It wasn't a bad house. Only Francine never cleaned it up right and it smelled like furniture polish and cigarettes. It smells like a bar, Nora Jane decided. That's what it smells like.

"Nora Jane, is that you?" Her mother was up, walking around in a bathrobe, her hair tied back with a string. "Oh, honey, I just called your grandmother and no one answered. I was so lonely. I had bad dreams all night. Oh, I'm so glad you're home. Look, could you go down to the corner and get me a package of cigarettes?"

"I just came by to get some clothes. I have to go to school today. They have a special day."

"No one told me about it."

"I'm in a hurry. Didn't Grandmother tell you? Why didn't she answer the phone? Well, I guess she was in the yard." Nora Jane swept past her mother and went into her room and began to fill the basket with clothes, socks and underwear and cotton shirts and a dress for Sunday. She threw the things into the empty basket. Her mother stood in the door watching her.

"You won't go get me some cigarettes?"

"I don't have time. I have to hurry."

"I want you back here tonight. I can't stay here at night by myself."

"I'll come back if I can." Nora Jane threw one last pair of underpants into the jumble of clothes and turned to face her mother. "I have to go now. I haven't had any breakfast. I went to sell the mirlitons at Langenstein's. I'm going. I'm starving."

"You could eat here. I'll fix things for you."

"Like what? Some rotten oranges, like last time. I'm not eating out of that kitchen until you get someone to kill the roaches. I told you that. And I'm not sleeping here. I don't want to listen to you cry." Nora Jane passed her mother in the bedroom doorway. Her mother reached for her, almost had her in her arms. "Let go of me," Nora Jane said. "Don't hold me. I have to go." She pushed her mother away and walked back through the house and out onto the porch and down the steps. Her mother followed her.

Nora Jane stopped to inspect her broken bike. "I thought you were going to get my bike fixed," she said.

"I couldn't do it, honey. There wasn't any money."

"Okay, well, I'm off." She switched the basket to the other arm, opened the gate and struck off in the direction of the park. She had decided to walk back through the park to see what was going on. There was always something happening in Audubon Park on Saturday morning. Besides, there was a grove of birch trees Nora Jane liked to walk through for luck. Her grandmother had told her it was a copy of a sacred grove of trees in Greece where the philosophers had lived.

Nora Jane entered the park at Prytania and walked through the lucky grove of trees and over to the flower clock. A race was forming. Forty or fifty people in their running clothes were milling around the fountain and the clock. A young man was doing T'ai Chi beside the fountain. Kids rode by on bikes. Suddenly, Nora Jane was embarrassed to be there carrying a basketful of clothes. She hurried out of the park and back toward her grandmother's house. I'm so hungry, she told herself. I shouldn't have waited so long to eat.

She felt bad now. She was hungry and it made her cold. She hurried back down Henry Clay and turned into her grandmother's yard. A radio was playing, much too loudly. It was WTUL, Leontyne Price singing *Tosca.* "Vissi d'arte" from *Tosca.* That was wrong. Her grandmother never played music loudly enough to be heard in the yard. Of course, sometimes she might sing along with an aria and then her voice might reach the street, but never for long, never long enough to bother other people.

This radio was too loud. It made no sense. Nora Jane dropped the basket on the porch and went on in. There was no one in the living room. In the dining room where the radio sat upon a shelf, a dust cloth was lying on the floor. That was also wrong. Her grandmother did not leave dust cloths lying on the floor. "Grandmother," Nora Jane called. Then she looked into the bedroom. Her grandmother was lying on the floor, crumpled up on the rug beside the bed. The beautiful voice of Leontyne Price continued with the aria. Nora Jane moved like water into the bedroom and knelt down upon the floor. She covered her grandmother's body with her own and began to weep.

A neighbor found them. She had heard the music and begun to worry. April is the cruellest month, the neighbor said to herself, for she was an English teacher. Breeding lilacs out of the dead land.

"Oh, honey," the neighbor said, holding the weeping child. "I'm so sorry. So very sorry."

"I can't live with my mother," Nora Jane said. "I can't do it. Where will I live?"

"Maybe you can," the neighbor said. "We all have to do things we don't want to do." She tried to lift the child, to make her stand up.

Nora Jane lay back down upon her grandmother's body. The sirens were making their way down Henry Clay. The noise of the sirens filled the air.

Later that afternoon they came to take the body away. Two men in a station wagon wrapped the grandmother's body in a sheet of canvas and carried her out of the living room and down the stairs and put her into the back of a wood-paneled Oldsmobile station wagon and drove off down Henry Clay as if they were going to a ball game. So that's it, Nora Jane thought, pulling a morning glory pod off the vine and tearing it to pieces with her fingers. That's all there is to it, just like I knew it would be. She's gone and this will be gone too.

She tore some more buds off the vine and squeezed them in her hand and wouldn't let anyone talk to her and went out into the backyard and stood by the mirliton arbor wondering what part of the opera was playing when her grandmother died. I could go in there and find the record and put it on but they probably wouldn't let me, she thought. She climbed the stile that led over her grandmother's back fence into Mr. Edison Angelo's yard and went out that way and over to the Loyola University library and checked out the phonograph record and went into a booth to play it for herself. It was a very old and scratchy record from the collection of Mr. Irvine Isaacs, Junior. Leontyne Price with the Rome Opera House Orchestra under the direction of Oliviero Fabritiis, the same recording Nora Jane had learned to sing the opera from. She sat in the booth and sang the opera with Miss Price and cried as she sang. Nora Jane had inherited her grandmother's voice. People acted so funny when they heard her voice that Nora Jane had decided long ago to keep it to herself. It was a promise she managed to keep most of her life. For almost all of her life she only sang to people she loved or people she wanted to solace or amuse. For nearly all the years of her life she managed to keep her voice to herself.

II

Of course, now everything had to change. After the funeral, after the grievers and the mourners were gone, after the sisters left and her mother was still sober, had been sober for four days, had sworn to Sister Katherine to stop drinking if she wanted Nora Jane to stay. Had settled for a bottle of pills instead, had agreed to put away the bottle if she could have the pills and was in her bedroom now, like a zombie against her pillows with the radio on low, playing jazz. After all of that Nora Jane looked around the house to see what she could do. I could clean it up, she decided. I could call that damn Francine and make her get over here. Nora Jane searched in her mother's address book, found the number and got Francine on the phone.

"I'm sorry about your grandmother," Francine began. "The Lord gives and the Lord taketh away."

"Forget that, Francine. I need you to come and help me clean this place up. I can't live in this mess. Bring your husband's truck. We're going to throw some things away."

"Right now?"

"Right now. I will pay you three dollars an hour if you bring the truck. Can you come? I'll get somebody else if you won't." Nora Jane sniffed, waited, began to get mad. If there was anybody who made her madder than her mother, it was Francine. "I don't care if you do or not. Say if you will."

"I'll be there. Soon as I can get on a uniform."

"Bring the truck."

"If I can get hold of Norris."

By the time Francine got there Nora Jane had emptied the kitchen cabinets of rotten potatoes and empty bottles and half damp grocery sacks. She had filled the grocery sacks with broken cups and half-used boxes of cereal. She had reamed out the kitchen of her mother's house. And called the Orkin man. "I have money to pay you with," she told him. "If you come right now and spray us with everything you've got."

By the time her mother woke up the dining room rug was on the truck and a broken chair and stacks of magazines. The living room rug was rolled up on the porch to go to the cleaners and Francine was mopping the wooden floors with Spic and Span. "What's going on?" her mother asked, coming out into the living room, still wearing the dress she had worn to the funeral. "What's going on? My God, Francine, what are you doing?"

"We're cleaning up this house," Nora Jane said. "Go back to sleep. I won't live in a pigpen. The Orkin people are coming in a minute."

"Where's the rug?"

"We're throwing the dining-room rug away. I won't live in a house with a rug like that. And this one's going to the cleaners. Francine's going to take it on the truck."

Nora Jane's mother sat down in a chair. Her little navy blue and white print dress hung in waves around her legs, her collar was awry. The Valium was in charge. She was powerless in the face of Nora Jane's rage. Powerless in the face of anything. She pulled her legs up onto the chair. "Am I in the way?" she asked. "Do you mind if I sit here?"

★   ★   ★

Later, in the late afternoon, after Nora Jane had paid Francine her wages and the kitchen and dining room and Nora Jane's bedroom had been cleaned to her satisfaction and the Orkin man had come and sprayed so much Diazinon and Maxforce and Orthene around the house that even with the windows open it was hard to breathe, Nora Jane and her mother dressed in cotton dresses and walked down the street to eat oyster loaves for supper at Narcisse Marsoudet. "It looks wonderful," her mother said. "I can't believe you did all that in one day. I can't believe she's gone. Now you are the only one, Nora Jane. The last of the Whittingtons."

"Don't talk about it," Nora Jane said. "I don't want to think about it anymore."

"I'm not going to drink, my darling honey. I'm going tomorrow to the meetings that they have. I won't ever drink again, you can depend on that."

"I want to get an air conditioner," Nora Jane said. "Mr. Biggs said there would be enough money when they sold her house. They said I could have enough for anything I'd need. And a new refrigerator. I can't stand to have that old thing anymore." They passed Perlis' Department Store and turned down Magazine to the café.

"I won't drink anymore, honey. You can depend on that." Her mother caught sight of herself in the store window. How pale she seemed, how slight beside her striding daughter. It seemed impossible, the day, the world, the store window and its terrible reflection. The huge old liveoak tree beside them and its roots. Her terrible mean teenage daughter, the death of Lydia and the sisters saying terrible things to her, the gaping hole in the earth and Lydia lowered into it, only six, seven, eight hours before, her dining room rug from Persia thrown away and nothing to take its place, poison everywhere.

"You might not," Nora Jane said, continuing to look straight ahead. "I'll believe it when I see it."

No sooner were they in the restaurant than it began. A white-coated waiter with a towel over his arm came to take their orders. "I'd like a Seven-Up," Nora Jane said. "And a glass of water."

"A glass of white wine," her mother added. "A Chablis. But anything will do. Your house wine will be fine."

"Just a glass. One little glass." She looked at Nora Jane. "One little glass with dinner."

"No, you don't," Nora Jane said. "Don't do this to me."

"Would you like a little while?" the waiter asked. He stepped back. He'd been through this plenty of times before and he wasn't in the mood to go through it again. My God, between a mother and a child. This girl doing it to her mother. What little beasts they were. The waiter knew he would never do that to himself. Load himself down with parasites, little beasts and bitches like this frowning child. Jesus, the waiter thought. I can't believe people do that to themselves.

"Just bring our drinks," the mother said. "We'll order later."

"I won't order," Nora Jane said. "I won't stay here and watch you get drunk. I'm leaving."

"It's only one drink. Only a glass of wine."

"No. I won't stay." Nora Jane got up, pushed her chair back into the table. The waiter backed up further. Nora Jane picked up a handful of crackers from the table and put them in her pocket. She was furious and she was starving. She had been so busy cleaning up the house she had forgotten to eat. She took a second handful of crackers and turned to leave.

"Don't you do this," her mother said, and rose to her feet. "If you do this you will be sorry. I won't put up with this." The waiter came back with a tray, took the glass of wine and set it before her. Put the Seven-Up at Nora Jane's empty place. Nora Jane picked it up, drank it greedily, put the glass back down.

"Sit down," her mother said. "I order you to sit back down." Nora Jane turned and walked out of the restaurant.

"Have your wine?" the waiter said. "I don't know where they come from, these modern kids. I mean, who do they think they are, anyway? Drink your wine and I'll get a menu. You go on and enjoy your dinner and don't worry about her."

He had noticed the nice diamonds on Mrs. Whittington's hands, the nice legs, the scared gentle face. Probably a lonely divorcée. He might end up with a really big tip if he played his cards right. He leaned over the mother and straightened her silverware. "I'll get you more crackers," he said. "Don't worry about the kid. They all act like that nowadays."

Six blocks away Chef Roland was making crawfish étouffée. His brother Maurice was coming that afternoon. Maurice who had given his life to God. "He knows nothing of the real world," Chef Roland said. His wife Betty was listening, leaning against the sink drinking coffee and watching her husband cook. She loved to watch him cook, loved to be in bed with him on top of her, she loved him. Anything he believed she tried to believe, anything he said she agreed with. They had a happy marriage. No one believed it, but it was true. Roland and Betty Dupre had a happy marriage and had always had. At night they got into the bed and touched each other from head to toe and cuddled up like bears. In the daytime they worried about their children and cooked and ate. It was a good life, a happy life and neither of them were ever sick.

"Martin's gone to his baseball game," Betty said. "I hope they win."

"They'll win, or they will not. Life is hard, Betty, don't let them forget that."

"If you say so."

"Maurice doesn't know it. How could he. He never pays taxes. He doesn't have to watch the world going to pot around him, he doesn't see the wholesale prices I'm paying for fish this week. What does Maurice know? He doesn't know the real world. He's lost touch with reality."

"When does he get here?"

"His plane gets in at seven-forty. We'll take the twins and go."

"What about Martin?"

"Leave the food on the stove. He'll get home."

"Can I taste it?"

"Sure you can. Come over here." She put the coffeecup down and went to stand beside him at the stove. He held out a spoon, blew on it to cool it down. Waited. She raised her lips to the spoon, tasted, almost swooned. It was perfect. Anything Roland did was perfect. He was a perfect man, the best chef in all New Orleans and he still found time to cook a meal for his family. "Oh, oh," Betty said. "Oh, oh, oh."

Chef Roland pushed the pot to the back of the stove, turned off the burner, and took his wife in his arms, ran his hands up and down her back, caressed her. He was still caressing her when the twins came in, two boys as alike as blossoms on a stem, Matthew and Mark, they were eleven years old, awkward and gangly and tall for their age, very funny, very skinny, very crazy and brave. They rode trick bicycles around the neighborhood, put the seats of the bikes on stilts, built ramps and ran the bicycles off of them. They were always getting cuts, breaking bones, having to be hurried to the emergency room. Roland and Betty adored them, thought they were wonderful.

"It's time to go to the airport," the twins said, coming in and beginning to eat homemade cake, cutting slices and eating it with their fingers as their parents embraced. "We better go or we'll be late. Martin's not going is he? He's at a game."

"Come along then." Chef Roland released his wife and removed his apron. He doted a moment upon his identical gangly sons. Largess, the great bounty of the earth which had supplied him with a life of adventure and good work and a gentle wife and three daughters and four sons. "Get a fork," he said. "What will people think if they see you eating with your fingers?"

"There's no one here," the twins said, and laughed their secret identical laugh.

"You're right." Chef Roland gathered his family and began to march out through the rooms of his huge Victorian house, past the dining room with its beautiful unbleached domestic drapes his wife had made to save him money, down the hall past the polished stairs, into the parlor and out of the double doors with the broken lock.

Nora Jane was coming up the sidewalk, tears running down her face and her fists clenched in rage. "Can I stay with you?" she asked. "Momma's drinking wine. She's at the restaurant drinking wine so I left. I'm never going back."

The family curled around her. Chef Roland took her into his

arms, the twins patted her. She was their baby-sitter when their sister was away at school.

"Don't cry," they all said. "You can stay. Come on, we're going to the airport to get Father Maurice. You want to go with us to the airport? There's room. There's lots of room."

"Don't cry," Chef Roland said. "Come get in the car. We're going out to Moissant to get my brother."

Maurice was no more in the car than the argument began. Nora Jane was sitting in the back of the station wagon with the twins. Betty and Chef Roland and Maurice were in the front.

"Well, your buddies have certainly done it down in South America," Chef Roland began. "I guess you're proud of that?"

"In what way?"

"You know goddamn well what way. In the birth control way. No solving it now. Let 'em starve. Right, Maurice?"

"You think you can solve the problems of South America by killing babies."

"Killing babies! Jesus, Maurice, you sound like a born-again Baptist. Killing babies, I'm hearing killing babies. Jesus, Betty, did you hear that?"

"I didn't see you killing any of yours," Maurice said.

"Yeah, but I stopped having them."

"I stopped having them," Betty put in.

"We stopped having them. I didn't kill my wife. I didn't have a bunch of kids I couldn't feed or house. They're all born addicted now in Peru. Half of them are born addicted to cocaine. You call that Christianity, Maurice? You think that's what He wanted you to do?"

"Oh, Roland, don't do this to me. I've looked forward to this so much. I can't tell you how I've missed all of you."

"You don't miss shit, Maurice. You guys sit up there and lay down edicts. You went to Rome last month, didn't you? Weren't you the personal envoy of the bishop? And what did you do? Did you speak up or did you get drunk and kiss ass?"

"Watch out," Betty said. "You almost hit that car."

"It's his brother?" Nora Jane asked the nearest twin.

"Yeah." The twins giggled. "Isn't it wonderful?"

"Right here in New Orleans," Chef Roland went on. "We got kids being born to thirteen-, fourteen-year-old girls. We got poor little girls with no homes having babies. You want me to kill you, Maurice? I'm thinking of killing people if it doesn't stop. The Church has to join the modern world. The Church has to help, not this anti–birth control crap. I've had it. I don't go anymore. We don't go, do we, Betty? We don't send the kids."

"I'm so sorry," Maurice said. "I can't tell you how that saddens me."

"Are you going to spend the night?" Matthew asked Nora Jane. "Are you going to live with us now? You can have our room. We'll let her stay in our room, won't we, Mark?"

"Her grandmother just died," Chef Roland explained to his brother. "She's got a bad situation at home."

"It isn't bad," Nora Jane spoke up. "My mother drinks because my dad died. It's not too bad. I just don't like it when she drinks. She quit for six weeks."

"I'll go over there tonight," Chef Roland said. "We'll get it straightened out. Meanwhile, you stay with us. There's plenty of room. You can have a room with Margaret Anne. You don't have to stay with them." He swerved to avoid a city bus, turned onto Webster Street and resumed his argument. "Life is short, Maurice, the life of the planet may be short. We can't let people suffer. People suffer because of your bullshit. You're too smart to keep on buying all that crap. I'm ashamed of you. You had a good mind before the Jesuits got hold of you."

"Oh, Roland, we need to have a long talk. I can't believe I find you so full of venom. Sadness and venom. What do you have to be sad about? We will go for a walk together. It has been so long since I've seen the park."

"I go to the park all the time," Nora Jane said. "I never miss a

Saturday. There's a grove of trees that is sacred to Apollo. My grandmother knew the man who planted them."

"She's Lydia Whittington's granddaughter," Chef Roland explained. "Remember that time Momma took us to hear her sing?"

"I heard your grandmother sing Madame Butterfly," Maurice said. "A long time ago when New Orleans was a center of the arts."

"We have a boomerang," Matthew said to Nora Jane. "We can go throw it in the park tomorrow. You want to throw our boomerang?"

"I don't know," Nora Jane said. Her sadness had lessened in the presence of Chef Roland and his family. Her sadness was turning back into rage. She remembered the real world. She was Lydia Whittington's granddaughter. She had a reputation to maintain. "I better go on home and see about Momma," she added.

"You stay with us," Chef Roland said. He turned the station wagon into the driveway and parked by the old garage. The twins got out and took off running into the house, planning on getting in a few minutes of worthless trashy television before someone turned it off. Betty went to look for her son Martin, who was on the baseball team but didn't get to play very much. She was always thinking about him when a game was going on, praying that he got to play, wondering if anyone had called him Four Eyes or hated him for striking out.

"I think I'll go on home," Nora Jane said, getting out. "Thanks for letting me go to the airport with you. It was nice to meet you, Father Maurice. I hope I'll see you again while you're here."

"Let me go talk to her," Chef Roland said. "Your mother likes me. I can talk to her."

"She'll be okay. She'll be asleep by the time I get home. I'm okay. I'll call you if I need any help. Thanks again for letting me go with you. I had a nice time." Nora Jane was moving away.

"Let me walk you home," Father Maurice said. "Let me go home with you."

"No, it's okay. I shouldn't have come over here. It's all right. It really is. I'll be okay." She had gained the sidewalk now. The man looked after her, not knowing what to do, not knowing where the lines were drawn in the problem of Nora Jane.

"I'm okay," she called back. "I really am." She waved again and hurried off down Webster Street. I am okay, she decided. It's all inside of me, heaven and hell and everything. I don't have to pay any attention to her. All I have to do is go to school and wait to get out of here. I'll get out sooner or later. That's for sure. At least I don't have a bunch of brothers and sisters to argue with. Their house is as bad as Momma's is.

She stopped on the corner and looked down the long green tunnel of Henry Clay. Past the houses where the rich satisfied people lived. "I'll get rich someday," she said out loud. "Whatever you want you get. Well, it's true." I'll be leaving here before too long. I'll have a job and a boyfriend and the things I need. Remember what I read in that poem. "Oh, world, world, I cannot get thee close enough." Remember that and forget the rest.

Love at the Center

$\mathcal{P}$

AN INTERESTING story was developing down at the Washington Regional Medical Center for Exercise. The boy who runs the machines was falling in love with a black-haired nurse. Black-eyed and black-haired, olive-skinned, muscular, vivacious. She is in here every afternoon putting in forty-five minutes on the StairMaster, then working out on the weight machines. Most of the habitués are older people, recovering from heart surgery and strokes, overweight housewives, retired college professors, or the doctors from the hospital themselves, always running on tight schedules and looking at their watches and being beeped.

So it was a light and vibrant thing to have this flirtation going on. I'm one of the housewives, but I wasn't always this way. I used to be a reporter for the *Times-Picayune* in New Orleans. And a lesbian. Then I gave it up for a stockbroker and moved up here with him. It's okay. Sometimes I miss the city and my women friends. Then I drive down there and stay a few days and maybe get high and lie around someone's French Quarter apartment flirting with young women and feeling evil. Bobby doesn't care. He's not that sure of his sexual orientation either. You can bank on that. That's his favorite expression. You can bank on that.

Well, I'm fifty-four and my trips to the South happen less often.

I'm into health. One hundred and forty pounds, five feet six. It looks better than it sounds. I have this muscular physique. I never appreciated it until I started working out with weights. You wouldn't believe how I muscle up.

Well, back to the love affair that was about to happen. It hadn't happened yet. Nothing had happened except that every time the nurse came in the door this beautiful young man would brighten up. Shine, beam, shimmer. It was spring in the Ozark Mountains and, except for the pollen in the air, it was paradise. Daffodils and black-eyed Susans, dogwood, violets, apple trees in bloom, all the dogs barking, mourning doves walking the yards in pairs, rainy afternoons and brilliant sunsets. Who wouldn't fall in love if they needed to?

Andy Buchanan was the boy's name and he wasn't a boy. He must have been at least twenty-five. The black-haired nurse was named Athena, if you can believe that. Athena Magni. On the day things heated up I was on a treadmill at the back of the room. There are three treadmills in a row facing a large window that looks out on the street and two more in the back of the room. Usually I get one by the window and watch people coming in and wave at children who stop and look into the center as if they had never seen old people exercising before. But this day the treadmills by the window were taken and I was on one of the ones at the back.

The retired head of the English Department was on the one beside me. We were discussing John Fowles when I saw Athena come in and sign in on the sign-in sheet. Andy came out of the office and stood beside her, very close in the narrow space between the sign-in desk and the office door. His face was lit from within. She laughed and tossed her coal-black hair and then she went into the dressing room to change into her leotards. Andy stood smiling after her. I turned and met the English teacher's eyes and we started giggling. He is sixty-seven years old and he only has one leg. We got to laughing so hard his good leg almost slipped off the moving belt. He had to grab the handrails to keep from falling.

"Hero and Leander?"

"Romeo and Juliet. With a name like that she's Greek or Italian. If he's Baptist and she's a Roman Catholic, we've got problems."

"Come live with me and be my love."

"But at my back I always hear time's winged chariot drawing near, et cetera. What role do you want?"

"The chorus, or the soldiers on the watchtower." He moved the good leg to a new position and slowed the treadmill down. His name is Doctor Wheeler and he always exercises in his coat and tie, which completely cheers me up even on the bleakest day.

A few minutes later Athena came out and climbed on a StairMaster. As soon as she was sweating, Andy walked over and handed her a cup of water. They weren't four feet away. I could hear every word they were saying.

"You haven't been in lately," he said. "Where have you been?"

"My married sister was in town. She lives in Little Rock."

"I dreamed about you last night."

"You did? What did you dream?"

"I was going along a line of girls and talking to each one. You were at the end."

"At the end?"

"Yeah."

"What did I say?"

"You just held out your hands. Like you wanted to be friends."

"No one ever dreamed about me before."

"I bet they did."

"They didn't tell me."

Long, long pause. Doctor Wheeler coughed, then coughed again. I didn't look at him.

"I'm trying to get up to forty-five minutes at level six."

"That's too high. Do it longer at a slower speed."

"Longer than forty-five minutes?"

"No, that's plenty long. You ought to try the new Exercycle. It's a real workout."

"This is all I have time for. I don't have time for this."

"You been busy at the hospital?"

"Have we ever. You know night before last when the moon was so full?"

"It was beautiful, wasn't it?"

"It was the closest the moon has been to the earth in a hundred years. We had twenty-one babies born that night. We had to put beds in the hall and the surgical ward. The whole place was crazy. It was the strangest thing. All afternoon we barely had a patient. There was one girl in labor. Then, about five-thirty, they started coming in. We had interns delivering babies. You should have seen it when it was through. There were twenty-one babies in the nursery. People were taking pictures of it. There was a story in the paper. Did you read it?"

"No. I'm sorry I missed that."

"I'll bring you mine and let you see it. God, this is getting harder." She was pumping her legs up and down. Her black hair was flying. Her black eyes were flashing. Andy stood beside her holding the cup of water. She reached down and took the cup and drank from it. She smiled a smile to light up heaven. I turned to look at Doctor Wheeler. He was shaking his head, his good foot moving on the treadmill, his artificial foot resting on the side. "I have a friend whose daddy is eighty-eight years old," I said. "He's going out with a girl who's thirty-seven. You tell me what is going on in the world and I'll stop being mean. I'll never have another vindictive thought. I'll be for letting the Haitians in. You name it."

"Vast metaphors all around. Fields being sewn. Lilies springing up. Fin de siècle. End of a world. Or else, it's all just funny."

"It's funny all right. It's hilarious."

"What do you do when you aren't in here, Virginia? If I might ask."

"Nothing. I'm married to a broker at Merrill Lynch."

"I'm explicating the cantos." He laughed again and got down off the treadmill and straightened up his tie. Then he went off to the dressing room.

Two weeks went by and Athena didn't return to the center. Andy was asking about her. He asked me several times. "Why don't you call and ask her where she is?" I suggested.

"Oh, I couldn't do that. I don't know her number."

"It's bound to be in her records."

"We aren't supposed to call people. It's soliciting."

"Write her a letter. Tell her we miss her."

"I guess I could do that."

"She could have broken her leg. Maybe she's on vacation."

"That's probably it." He put his hand on the rail of the stationary bike and bent his head to see how fast I was peddling. "That's good. You're going fast."

"One of the old jocks told me the other day he saw a television program and some tacky television starlet said she had a twenty-one-inch waist from doing the Exercycle. I don't want a twenty-one-inch waist, I told him. You know what he said?"

"No. What?"

"He said, Of course you do. The gall of the man. He's the one that always wears the baseball cap. Who is he, anyway?"

"He's a football coach."

"I knew it. They all look alike. Well, listen, are you going to write to her or not?"

"I might. Okay, I will." He walked away and began going from machine to machine talking to the patrons. He was especially nice to anyone who was really old or just beginning. What a darling young man he is. And now Athena has disappeared. "Andy," I said, when I was leaving. "You have the nicest manners of any young man I have met in years. I'd like to meet your mother. Tell her that the next time that you see her, will you please?"

"When I do." He blushed and threw his arms back as he does when he pretends to be astounded that someone has stayed on the treadmill for twenty minutes, getting their pulse up to normal for the first time in twenty years. You see a lot of that at the Washington Regional Medical Center for Exercise. And don't get me wrong, I'm not knocking it.

On Wednesday afternoon the mystery was solved. I got to the Center about two o'clock and was just climbing on the Exercycle when Athena came in the door. Her hair was tied back with a ribbon and she had on black tights and a long white T-shirt that said *Venice, Arkansas* in black letters. On the back were the names of the registered voters of the town. There were forty-seven, including four men who were in the armed services.

"Where have you been?" I asked. "We've all been worried about you."

She climbed on the Exercycle beside me. "I've been working nights, taking care of this nice old lady who's dying. She knows she's dying but she doesn't even care. She's had an exciting life. That's all she says to me, how exciting her life was and how she didn't miss anything. She's over a hundred and all her family and friends are dead so she doesn't care if she dies. She has this nice house on the mountain and she's in this room with paintings all around her." She got down and adjusted the seat on the Exercycle, then climbed back on. "Anyway, she used to run around with painters and she ran the Spoletto Festival in Italy, you know, for music. She's so nice to me I'm ashamed to take the money, but she's loaded. Anyway, I'm staying there at nights only she made me take a night off. She said young people aren't supposed to spend spring nights by deathbeds. She's as clear as a bell. She's over a hundred years old. I feel honored to get to know her." Athena turned up the heat on the Exercycle, bent over the bars. I speeded up beside her. "I'll tell you more about it later," she said. "God, this feels so good. I've been missing this."

"Your parents let you stay there at night?"

"I don't have any parents. I live with my cousin."

"I'm sorry."

"They died when I was four. I'm used to it. They were in a car wreck, coming home from a fair. It's okay." She flashed that smile at me and hard as I tried, I couldn't register pathos or pity. A beautiful young couple late at night on one of our one-lane roads, from Tontitown to Springdale, say, a truck on a curve. It happens every Saturday night up here. It happens still.

"It's really okay," she said. "I can barely remember them. It was my dad's fault. I guess they were having a good time."

Andy emerged from the office and spotted her. His face lit up, and he hurried across the room and put his hand on a StairMaster to balance himself. "Where've you been?" he asked. "I was thinking of calling the cops."

"I've been working overtime. Trying to save some money. I'm losing weight, but don't worry. I know it's just muscle turning to fat." She was laughing. She always started laughing when Andy talked to her. Shimmer, shimmer, shimmer. Like water on a pond. Go on, Andy, I was thinking. Ask her out. Go on and do it.

"It looks good to me, but you're right. It's only temporary. Well, we're glad to have you back."

"I know. The deal is to be healthy, right, not thin." She giggled again. Gave him that Greco-Roman smile. Andy returned the smile. You could have tanned yourself in the radiance.

"Can I get you some water?" he asked.

"He's been worried sick about you," I put in. "You should take him to a movie for all the pain you've caused him."

"I will," she said. "Have you seen *The Distinguished Gentleman*, with Eddie Murphy? It's at the Springdale dollar movie. You want to go?"

"When?"

"Tonight. I was going anyway. You want to go?"

"Sure. I get off at six. What time does it start?"

"Excuse me," I said. "I have to change machines." I got off the Exercycle and went across the room to the rowing machine. Where was Doctor Wheeler when I needed him? Wait till I told him this.

I never found out what happened at the movie. Because the world is full of surprises, pebbles thrown into the pond, concentric circles. It's not just the little surprises either, like my friend Brenda's cherry tree bearing fruit for the first time in years, not just every child that's born and so forth. Take the headline that greeted me the next morning on the front page of the *Northwest Arkansas Times*. LOCAL GIRL LEFT FORTUNE.

Mrs. Rosa Neely Parker, age 102, of Fayetteville and Key West, Florida, died last night of natural causes, leaving four million dollars in bonds and property to a young woman who nursed her in her last days. According to Bass Howard, attorney for the estate, the will is airtight. Miss Parker leaves no legal heirs other than the designee. The young woman, Miss Athena Magni, of Fayetteville, is currently employed by the Washington Regional Medical Center and lives with a relative, Mrs. Stella Magni, of 1819 Maple Street. She is a graduate of Fayetteville High School and the University of Arkansas School of Nursing. Miss Magni told this reporter she didn't want to talk about it. She said she had taken the night off at Miss Parker's request and blamed herself for not being there when Miss Parker died.

Internment will be at Kitchen's Funeral Home on Spring Street with burial Monday afternoon at the National Historic Cemetery on Spring Street. Miss Parker will be buried beside her maternal grandparents. This will be the first funeral at the historic cemetery in many years.

Mourners are requested to send donations to the music department of the university in lieu of flowers.

I called Doctor Wheeler. "What should we do?" I asked. "She lives with a cousin who works for Tyson's. She's not prepared for this."

"Bass is a good man. A good lawyer. I'll call him."

"Ask where she is. They won't answer the phone."

"Maybe she's at the funeral parlor."

"At eight-thirty in the morning?"

"Four million dollars. Rosa owned a de Kooning and an O'Keeffe. I saw them once."

"You knew her?"

"When she first came home to live. At first she traveled quite a bit. Then she stayed alone. No one saw her. I haven't thought about her in years."

"We should go see Andy. He's madly in love, completely smitten. They were going out last night."

"Four million dollars. Even after taxes it will change her life."

Miss Parker hadn't just left Athena money. She had called Paris and told them Athena was coming. She had called Italy and told them what to do. She had called the Emerald Travel Agency and gotten Annie Smithson to make reservations and arrange cars and hotel rooms. She had a young man waiting to meet the plane in Paris.

She had left Athena a letter with instructions of where to go and who would be waiting at each place and assurances of how safe she would be. She had left a package wrapped in shiny white paper with blue ribbon. It contained books to read on airplanes. "This is to ease my dying," the letter said.

> If I can think of you discovering the places I discovered when I was your age, then I am already in heaven. As for death, I do not fear it. I have been practicing sleeping for many years and have always considered it a blessing. When I was young I could not sleep more than five hours a night. Now I will get the rest I lost back then.
>
> You have brightened up these last days. Live a long and happy life. Thank you for sharing a premonition of it with me. Yours in praise and wonder, Rosa Neely Parker.

That was all. We went to the funeral and Athena told us the plans. She kept her hand on Doctor Wheeler's arm, saying, "Well, no more bedpans or staying up all night eating junk food. They didn't bat an eye when I told them I was leaving. They can get plenty of people to work for what they were paying me." She held up her head and I saw the thing that Rosa must have seen, the incipient thing. She would make it in the big world. She was already shedding her provincial manners. What had she dreamed all these years that made that possible? What movies had she seen? What books had she read?

"Take our phone numbers and call us if you need us," I said, and gave her a piece of paper Doctor Wheeler and I had prepared.

"Thanks," she said, and stuck it in her purse.

Then she was gone. It's funny how at a place like the center one person going off can leave such a hole. A couple of chubby girls from the Music Department started coming in and we were all pulling for them as they tried to lose weight for their auditions in the fall. At least they knew about Italian opera and could discuss it with Doctor Wheeler.

The center started a program for nine- to twelve-year-olds and that was a diversion for a while, only most of the kids who came in were morbidly overweight and it was hard to stay interested in them.

It wasn't like having Athena come bounding in, light and youth coming into a place where most of the people were beginning to dim. Even the most brilliant ones like Doctor Wheeler were like flashlights on the last week of camp, like batteries getting damp and undependable. I did the best I could to cheer things up and started wearing bright shirts and even putting on makeup and lipstick before I went to exercise.

As for Andy, he dimmed too, but I thought it was a temporary thing. Soon he'll be starting to make plans for the Fit-for-Life run against Springdale and that should keep him busy. He's like a moon that's good at reflecting light. Sooner or later someone will be coming in that door to illuminate his face.

Joyce

∽

IN 1976 DOCTOR WHEELER TAUGHT JOYCE for the last time. He had sworn never to teach it again but the graduate students begged and pleaded and the dean cajoled and finally, one Sunday morning at breakfast at The Station, with the graduate students all around him and a piece of pumpkin pie topping off his scrambled eggs, he gave in and said yes.

"I will teach it," he said. "If you will read it. I won't lecture if no one reads the books. My notes are not the works of James Joyce. Don't take it unless you're going to read the books."

"We will," they swore. "You can count on us." And all around the long table of young writers and graduate students a great sigh of determination took place and moved from one to the other and rose like a cloud and joined the smoke from Doctor Wheeler's cigarette. Nothing is free. To be in the presense of so much brilliance was also to be in the presense of cigarette smoke. Doctor Wheeler chain-smoked. He smoked because he liked to smoke. He smoked until the very last minute of the clock that ticked away his life. After all, how much oxygen does a man with one leg need?

One of the students at the table was a woman named Rhoda Manning. She was a housewife from New Orleans who was trying to learn to write poetry. All morning every morning she sat at a Royal portable typewriter in a small apartment near the campus and tried to turn everything she saw or experienced into metaphor. She was forty years old and she considered this the time of her life. She had this one semester to be a student in a writing program, with other students all around her and people like Doctor Wheeler to adore. She knew about Joyce. She had tried to read Joyce. She had an old recording of Siobhan McKenna reading Joyce. Now she was going to study Joyce. She stood up. She raised her glass. "Champagne," she said. "Let's order champagne. This demands a celebration. He's going to teach the Joyce seminar. We will read *Ulysses*."

Also at the table was a tall unhappy man named Ketch McSweeney. He had been in Vietnam and had brought his wife and daughter to Fayetteville to learn how to write a book about the war. He couldn't stop thinking about the war. He couldn't stop dreaming about the war, so he thought he might as well make some money writing about the war. Not that he had much in the way of alternatives being offered to him at the moment. He was from Pennsylvania and had come to school to find a way to begin to make a stand. His wife had a job teaching second grade and his daughter was in a cheap Montessori school. He was making twelve thousand dollars a year being a graduate student in the writing program and teaching semiliterate freshmen to read and write the language that they spoke. He didn't mind. He was a good-looking man and the young girls all made eyes at him and he was sure that sooner or later he would make a killing of some kind in the writing business. Meanwhile, he was determined to make the best of it and have all the fun he could while he waited.

"I will teach it in the fall," Doctor Wheeler said. "Sign up now because I'll limit the size of the class."

The next afternoon Ketch McSweeney and Rhoda Manning met at the registrar's office. "You too?" she said. "Jesus, we're lucky. I can't believe he's teaching it."

"I thought you were going back to New Orleans after this semester. You decided to come back?"

"I will now. I can't miss this."

"What about your husband? He's going to let you do this?"

"I'm doing it. I'm going to be a poet if it takes the rest of my life."

"That's how I feel. Only I want to make some dough. There's got to be a way to make some money writing books."

"Well, I'll see you in class then, won't I? If not before."

They didn't see each other again until the fall. But they were thinking about it. Both of them had been on the make most of their lives. Not to feed off other people or do intentional harm. Just to sample the wares of the world, to trade at the fair, to know the mornings, evenings, afternoons and not to hesitate when something fine or plump or juicy was at stake. They both liked excitement and they both knew how to generate it.

Doctor Wheeler thought about them too. He read over the list of writers and graduate students who were signed up for the course and as he read he knew much of what would transpire. He had taught this class too many times not to know its generative power and its dangers. He had taught it the year Amanda McCamey showed up on campus. He had taught it to Barry Hannah and Frank Stanford. He had taught it the year Carolyn Forche was the poet in residence and would come and sit in on his classes and look at him with her wide, beautiful, Eastern European eyes.

He walked out into his garden and thought about it. His garden overlooked the Confederate Cemetery. In it he had planted all the flowers he remembered from his youth. Hollyhocks and morning glories, pansies, delphiniums, foxglove and four o'clocks and bachelor's buttons.

"Virag speaks," he said out loud. "'(Agueshaken, profuse yellow spawn foaming over his bony epileptic lips.) She sold lovephiltres, whitewax, orange flower, Panther, the Roman centurion, polluted her with his genitories. . . .'"

★ ★ ★

The first meeting of the class took place on a warm September night. A new moon was in the sky. A thin silver curve deep in the dark sky. Eight o'clock. The students had gathered in the hall, they milled around and talked about their summer adventures, they looked each other over, they overcame their egos and were kind. "Let's go in," Ketch said. "He'll be here in a minute." Rhoda went inside and found a seat in the middle of the room. He came and sat beside her and propped his legs on the rungs of an empty chair. She laid a notebook on the desktop and turned and smiled at him. Good, there wasn't going to be any pretense. He wasn't going to be coy.

Doctor Wheeler came into the room and sat down behind the desk and lit a cigarette. He adjusted his artificial leg so that it rested against one of the legs of the desk. He looked out across the thirty-two faces waiting to be filled. He took a drag on the Camel and began. "We will begin with *Portrait of the Artist as a Young Man*. This is Stephen's story, the young Stephen who later will be the lover in *Ulysses*, and Leopold's foil. His name is Stephen Daedalus. 'The archaic Greek mind ascribed all things cunningly wrought, whether a belt with a busy design, the rigging of a ship, or an extensive palace, to the art of the craftsman Daedalus, whose name first appears in the *Iliad*. Homer, describing the shield Hephaistos makes for Akhilleus, says that the dancing floor depicted on it was as elaborate as that which Daedalus designed for Ariadne in Crete. This dancing floor is perhaps what Homer understood the Labyrinth to be. Joyce did, for the ground on which he places all his figures is clearly meant to be a labyrinth.' This from Guy Davenport. The book's on the desk. You can look at it when we take a break."

"Now, you won't have to wander into that labyrinth so soon in the fall. Read the first two hundred pages of the *Portrait* for next week. How many of you have a copy already?" He waited while fifteen or twenty students held up their hands.

"Good. How many have it with you?" The same twenty or so held up their hands. Ketch and Rhoda were among these good students.

"Fine; and here are seven or eight copies I brought along from the library. The rest of you can share them." He sat back. Nodded his head. Rhoda opened her fresh new copy of the book and beside her Ketch opened his. "What are you doing after class?" he asked. "Let's go and have a glass of wine."

"Fine. I'd love it. We can go to my house. I have some wine I brought back from New Orleans. Better than anything you can get around here." She smiled and looked him in the eye. Good, better, best, no hesitation, no fooling around or wasting time. She scooted her chair an infinitesimal bit closer to his.

"Take the role of Aristotle," Doctor Wheeler was saying. "He plays in the minds of the characters. He appears over and over. Stephen Daedalus in 'Proteus' is conversant with Aristotle and ponders and tests his ideas. Bloom in 'Lestrogonians' is interested, perhaps unwittingly, in many of the same matters that interested Aristotle, and Molly knows or probably cares so little about him that she turns his name into Aristocrat. Many streams like this flow between the minds of the characters. You can get an A in here if you find one I haven't seen. . . ."

Ketch looked at Rhoda. Watched as her dress slid up her silk stockings when she crossed and uncrossed her legs. He sighed. She turned her head and acknowledged it.

They left the building by the wide front door and walked out onto the main street of the campus. "I wish we could walk," she said. "It's such a pretty night. It's only a few blocks to my house. Want to leave the cars and walk?"

"Sure. Why not?"

"We can walk home through the old cemetery on Spring Street. Have you ever been there?"

"No. Not that I know of."

"It's nice. The old families that built the town are buried there. I used to go up there with a photographer friend of mine and try to make art photos." She shifted her notebook and bag to her other arm and began to walk briskly down the street. "What do you think? Do you think it's going to be good? I think he's a genius. I love to watch him smoke. Sometimes he has two cigarettes going at once."

"I need the credits. I want to get out of here as soon as I can. All I want is a novel and an MFA and I'm gone. I've got to earn a living."

"I don't have to worry about that right now. We can go up there and take the path through the cemetery if you want. Are you ready?" She was walking very fast, and he quickened his pace and caught up with her. They went up a gravel road and came out at the top of a small old cemetery with huge maple trees hiding the sky and walked in darkness past the massive tombstones. "This will put it in perspective, won't it," Rhoda dropped the notebook and the bag on the ground and let him kiss her. Then she took his arm and they walked more slowly down the hill and across the street to her apartment building.

They opened wine and lit candles and then Rhoda went into her bedroom and put on a long blue silk kimono and they took the wine into the bedroom and made love with the window open and the thin moon, now brilliant in a cloudless sky, making their skin luminous and white. They made love out of curiosity and greed, without passion or tenderness or joy. They made love to prove they were mean enough to do it. When it was over he got up and put on his clothes and went home to his wife.

It became a ritual. They went to the Joyce class and listened to Doctor Wheeler explicate the material which they usually had not read, since the semester had heated up and they were busy writing and exploring the world. Rhoda would read the assignment in the car as she drove to class, get there half an hour early, take a seat and read very fast until Doctor Wheeler came in the door. When she met him on the campus she would tell him about it. "I'm behind," she would say. "But your lectures are brilliant. I want to hear them."

"Don't worry about it," he would answer. "Just read as much as you can."

And every Wednesday night after class Rhoda and Ketch would go to her apartment and make love and drink wine and talk about their work and where they were submitting it and what had been accepted where. As the semester wore on they became thinner and meaner. The anxiety of writing and not being published began to wear on them.

"I'm writing a short story," she told him one night. "I know it won't be any good. I'm just writing it to please Randolph. He said I have to write one to get an MFA."

"Oh, what's it about?" Ketch sat up. This wasn't right. She was a poet. He was a fiction writer. On this basis they fucked each other. No, it wasn't right. "I wouldn't waste my time on that if I was you," he said. "You're publishing poems. Fuck Randolph."

"Well, I just want to try. It's pretty funny really. It's set in New Orleans."

"Oh."

"Well, that's where I live. Where else would it be set?"

"I'd like to see it when it's finished."

"Sure. It would be nice if you'd read it." But Rhoda had seen the jealousy. She knew she would never show him a line she wrote after that. Fuck him, she was thinking. His stories aren't that good. They're too violent. No one's ever going to want to read them.

In the middle of November they had come to the "Sirens" in *Ulysses*. "A husky fifenote blew. Blew. Blue bloom is on the gold pinnacled hair. A jumping rose on satiny breasts of satin, rose of Castille. Trilling, trilling; Idolores. . . ." Rhoda's plans had changed. She was going to have to go home to New Orleans and finish the semester by correspondence. Her youngest son was in trouble and her husband had demanded she return. She was glad to go. She was bored with being a graduate student in a writing program and living in an apartment and doing her own laundry. She was tired of going to classes and writing papers and waiting for her poetry to be published. She was bored with fucking Ketch on Wednesday nights. It was so cold, so pointless, so rude. The week before she had been menustrating, bleeding like a stuck pig from her Lippes Loop. They had gotten drunk and made love anyway. In the morning there was blood everywhere, on the carpet, on the sofa, on the lining of her blue silk kimono. She never threw the kimono away. After being cleaned six times it still showed the bloodstains on the hem. She kept it anyway, out of some sort of abandoned rebellion, to remember how bad she had been and how free.

"This is a fugue," Doctor Wheeler was saying. "The sirens sit on a meadow on the bones of sailors. The music is a flight of song. The barmaids are the sirens. Twin sirens, they sing and dance and draw the sailors in. It is one of the most intense parts of the book. Joyce believed he should leave behind him a burnt-out field. . . ."

"I have to go home Friday," Rhoda was whispering. "For good. To see about my son."

"This Friday?"

"As soon as class is out. He's making bad grades, driving my husband crazy. He's sixteen. I shouldn't have left him to begin with."

"What about your classes? How can you leave?"

"I'll do them by mail. Everyone is going to let me. Well, I haven't asked him yet." She looked toward Doctor Wheeler, who was lighting one Camel from another. He was leaned over his desk, his artificial leg propped against the desk leg, papers spread out before him on the desk.

"He'll let you. He's crazy about you."

"Joyce's mother was a pianist," Doctor Wheeler was saying. "His father was a tenor. Joyce himself was both a pianist and a tenor. Everywhere in this chapter, which is a small inset in 'Scylla and Charybdis,' of course, are references to preludes, overtures, fugues. Fugue means flight, by the way. Pound disapproved of this episode, wanted it out of the manuscript, but Joyce insisted on it. As the sailors are taken in by the sirens, likewise the sirens are enchanted by the sailors' voices. It is like a prelude stuck in the middle of 'Scylla and Charybdis.' There are so many nice touches. The piano brings in Bloom, for example. In music you can play two themes at once, of course. And everywhere is blue and white, the Virgin's colors. . . ."

"My short story was accepted by *Intro*," she said. "So that's nice. I didn't tell you that, did I?"

"What?"

"Randolph sent it to *Intro* and they took it. It's going to be the lead piece."

"*Intro?*"

"What's wrong?"

"We better be quiet."

She watched him seethe. *Intro* was the epitome for a writer in a writing program in 1976. It was the springboard. New York agents read it. *Intro* could be the start of a real career. Ketch had five stories on his desk right now that had been turned down by *Intro*.

"This is a song from an opera," Doctor Wheeler was saying. "Oh, my Delores. Later they will toast the thirty-two counties of Ireland. Joyce hated Rome and thought it inhospitable. Rift in the lute. Well, it's getting late. Be sure and get up to page four hundred for next week." He stood up, began to gather his papers, laid a cigarette down on the edge of the desk where it teetered precariously, messily smoking. Rhoda went up to him and began to have a conversation about her leaving and he shook his head from side to side and up and down and agreed that she should go home and take care of her son. "I'll miss you," he said. "I was looking forward to your paper."

"Oh, I'll write it. I can't wait to write it. I can't tell you how much I've loved this. I'll always feel like something passionate and critical was interrupted in my life. Something important." She looked into his thin sweet face, his clear good face. Ketch was behind her, standing near the door. The other students were gone. There were only the three of them. I want to follow you home, she felt like saying. I want to sit up all night and talk to you.

Ulysses had himself tied to the mast not to miss their singing, Doctor Wheeler was thinking. Sound of the sirens, sound of the sea.

"Mail it to me when you write it," he said. "What episode would you like?"

"Oh, 'Penelope.' "

"Of course. You've finished the book then?"

"No, I've always known it. I had a recording of it by Siobhan McKenna when I was young. I may know it by heart."

"Then do that. I'll look forward to reading it." He waited.

"Come on," Ketch said. "We better go."

They went out the door and down the long hall and the marble stairs and out into the parking lot. "Let's walk to my house," she said. "For old times' sake and go up to the cemetery. I can walk to school tomorrow. I like to."

"Okay. If you like." They began to walk down the sidewalk in the direction of the gravel road behind the buildings. It was a cloudy night. A waning moon rode the spaces between the clouds. It was cool but not too cold. Ten o'clock on a Wednesday night. The campus was deserted. They walked without talking up to the cemetery and stopped under a maple tree by a large granite tombstone with a kneeling angel and lay down upon the grave, upon his coat, and fucked each other without mercy.

When it was over he got up and buttoned his pants and stood leaning on the tombstone waiting while she stood up and shook off his coat and gave it back to him. He put it on. She took his arm and they walked down the hill to her apartment.

"Why does this remind me of the poets versus the fiction writers baseball game?" she asked.

"I don't know. Well, I've got to be going now. Joanne's waiting for me." He left her then and she went inside and sat down at her typewriter and went back to work on a poem she had started that morning.

> At any moment you may meet the child you were
> There, by the Sweet Olive tree.
> If you turn the corner by the faucet
> He will come around the other way
> Carrying your old sandbucket
> And your shovel
>
> You may notice the displeasure in his eyes,
> A sidelong glance, then he'll be gone,
> Leaving you holding your umbrella
> With a puzzled look, while the spring day

Drops like a curtain between the clocks
And the dialogue you rely on stops.

Doctor Wheeler walked up the dark steps to his house. His cats were waiting beside the door. "Darlings," he cooed. "Simonedes. Dave. Well, wait a second. Let me find the key." He laid his papers on the wooden porch floor, found the key in the pocket of his jacket, turned it in the latch, and went into the darkened room. The cats followed him. He walked back out onto the porch to collect his papers. Above the house the maple trees stood guard. Doctor Wheeler knew them in every weather. Had seen them bent double by wind. Had known them in lightning, rain, snow, or when fall turned them saffron and gold, as they had been only a week ago. They were fading now. Winter was coming on.

He went back into the house and lit the fire and fed the cats and sat down in his armchair. Homer was on the table by the chair. He picked up the book and held it to his chest, patting it as though it were a child. Finally, when he had almost fallen asleep, he reached up above him and turned on a lamp and opened the book at random.

The old nurse went upstairs exalting,
with knees toiling, and patter of slapping feet,
to tell the mistress of her lord's return,
and cried out by the lady's pillow;
                    "Wake,
wake up, dear child! Penelope, come down,
see with your own eyes what all these years you longed for!
Odysseus is here! Oh, in the end he came!
And he has killed your suitors, killed them all
who made his house a bordel and ate his cattle
and raised their hands against his son!"

He closed the book and pressed it back into his chest. Then he reached into his jacket pocket and took out a crumpled package of cigarettes and turned off the lamp and lit the cigarette and sat in the dark looking into the fire and smoking.

Death Comes to a Hero

⌐♫

THE WASHINGTON REGIONAL Medical Center for Exercise had become the pickup bar for all the old people of Fayetteville, Arkansas. Every health-conscious fifty- and sixty-year-old citizen in town had started going down there, at noon to hear the old forties and fifties music, with its crescendo of "Begin the Beguine." Later in the day, to get serious on the StairMaster and treadmill and Exercycles, while radio station ninety-two-point-four poured out Oldies onto the airwaves. By which the twenty-six-year-old disc jockey meant songs from the 'seventies and 'eighties, music that reminded Brenda Lacey of the years her sons had been into dope. Still, it was nice to exercise to the Pointer Sisters and the Marvelettes and Diana Ross and the Supremes. Brenda was in great shape for her age. Her legs were long and thin and her skin was tight and she only weighed two pounds more than when she had been Homecoming Queen of Fayetteville High. She had lived a lot of history and none of it had gotten her down. She was living in an age of miracles and proof of it was all around her. An elderly man with one leg was working the ski machine with great dexterity. It always cheered Brenda up to be at the center when he was there. He came in wearing a suit and tie and never took them off the whole time he went from machine to machine with his good leg and his other miraculous man-made leg.

Brenda never tired of watching him make his miraculous adjustments. He was plump and had a fine handsome face that was intent on every step of his way. She had seldom seen him smile but he always had a pleasant look on his face.

Another thing that cheered her up was the group of elderly housewives who met each day at noon to do aerobics to the 'fifties music. They told stories as they danced, of wars their husbands had gone to and what the music meant to them. When "Begin the Beguine" came on, a soft dreamy spirit would fill the room and the women's faces would become sensual and tender. Brenda was not quite as old as the women who danced at noon. "Begin the Beguine" reminded her of her young aunts and their friends, who would sit around the living room floor on Saturday afternoons, playing phonograph records and rolling up their hair and writing V-mail letters to their sweethearts overseas. *When they begin the beguine, it brings back a night of tropical splendor. It brings back the sound of music so tender. It brings back a memory, ever green . . .*

The young men and women who ran the Washington Regional Medical Center for Exercise all belonged to a Christian church. They kept everything immaculately clean. They changed the filters on the air-conditioning units. They were polite and kind to the old people who came there to recuperate from their triple bypass operations and varicose veins and gastrointestinal upsets. The old people were remorseful over their old ways. They were sorry they had eaten too much and drunk too much and been too lazy and waited so long to get on the StairMasters and treadmills and Exercycles and weight machines. They were going to make up for lost time. With the help of the young people they were going to learn how to live forever. How to eat, how to do aerobic exercise, how to be healthy, happy old people, how to be thin and get the heartbreaking fat off their buttocks and hips and waists.

It occurred to Brenda that she had never seen anyplace as hopeful as the Washington Regional Medical Center for Exercise. People came in smiling and left smiling. It was a good idea. An idea whose time had come. Brenda smiled at the obstetrician who had come in the door. He was a local hero. The only doctor in northwest Arkansas who was brave enough to do abortions. Once a year for twenty-six years he had examined Brenda to make sure she wasn't getting cancer. She had never had cancer and she thought it was the goodwill and kind nature of Doctor Hadley that made those pap smears come back negative. If she had gone to a mean or stupid doctor there was no telling what might have happened. She smiled and waved to let him know how much she cared. "You've lost so much weight," she said. "You better be careful. You'll be going anorexic on us."

"Not a chance," he answered. "Not as long as they make Häagen-Dazs."

The dean of the Business School at the University of Arkansas came in the door, signed in, and went to work on the free weights. A sportswriter for the *Northwest Arkansas Times* came in the door and took his stack of newspapers over to the Exercycle that had the plastic holder for papers and climbed aboard and began to pedal. The mistress of the richest man in town came in. She looked great from her hours on the treadmill and her plastic surgery. She wore panty hose and makeup when she exercised. She had her hair done and came right over and messed it up.

Brenda climbed down off her machine and went to the heart-rate moniter and stuck in her index fingers. One-forty, which immediately went down to one-ten. She was going to live forever, that much was clear. "Are you finished?" the obstetrician asked.

"Yes, I have to go pick up a child. I'm in the Big Sister program."

"That's nice. That's lovely of you."

"I like to have children around. They cheer me up." She smiled and threw back her head. It was true. Her children were grown and gone and her husband had run off to the Virgin Islands when he had his midlife crisis. All she had was one part-time boyfriend who was out of town half the time selling prefabricated buildings and she sure wasn't going to marry him and nurse him into the sunset. She had all the old men she wanted right down here at the Washington Regional Medical Center for Exercise.

She walked over closer to the obstetrician. She spoke loudly enough for the one-legged man to hear. "I have a cherry tree in my backyard that is full of cherries. I'm going to invite the neighborhood children over to pick the cherries. Who knows, I may make a pie, if I can remember how." The obstetrician beamed. The one-legged man lifted his head and smiled. Brenda took their approval and wrapped it around her like a cloak. She heaved a deep happy sigh and turned and walked out into the summer sunlight. It was true about the cherry tree and now that she had thought of it she would invite all the children over to pick the cherries. They would fall from the children's hands into bowls and pans and saucers. She would stop by the store and buy piecrusts and cream. They would have a party, here on the planet earth, in the summertime, in the only world there is.

II

The one-legged man was a retired professor of English at the University of Arkansas and his specialty was Joyce and Eliot and Pound. He was spending his retirement explicating the *Cantos*, work which he thought would last him the rest of his life.

Brenda found this out one rainy Sunday afternoon when she was at the center and he was the only other person there. The center was only open from two to five on Sunday afternoons so the young people who ran it wouldn't have to miss any Christian church events.

"I hate the way they only stay open three hours on Sunday," Brenda began. The one-legged man was on the biceps press. She was on the inner thigh machine. "It's so inconvenient." He didn't answer. She giggled and tried again. "Still, it's an imperfect world. And we're lucky to have this place. All the other health clubs I ever went to were so dirty. I thought I was catching things all the time. Well, I won't even come here during flu season."

"Ariadne's dancing floor," he said. "The way the machines all spread out from the middle."

"A dancing floor. That's right. I always try to get in here at noon to watch the old ladies do aerobics. Listen, they're really getting in good shape. I was watching them the other day, they're really getting limber. When I used to first watch them I was laughing at them. Now they're getting good. It makes me ashamed of myself. I'm starting to love them."

"You could follow one of them through a day and know the history of our culture. May I introduce myself. I'm Morais Wheeler. I've been watching you. You work very hard, don't you?"

"I've done this all my life. I can't sit still. I have a lot of energy. My name is Brenda, a boring name." She got up and went to the other side of him and got on the StairMaster. "Morais, that's a pretty name. Yeah, that's nice."

"It's French. My mother was French. I keep thinking I've seen you somewhere. Do you work in town?"

"I used to. I was in the courthouse for a while, in the driver's license bureau. But I don't remember you. I would have noticed you."

"Is that where you are now?"

"No, I work for the Organ Recovery Team. I'm the secretary. It's real good hours."

"Joyce would love it."

"Your wife is Joyce?"

"No. Joyce is a writer I admire. I haven't ever had a wife."

"How'd you lose your leg?"

"A long time ago, in another country."

"In a war?"

"You might call it that." He smiled a deep wide beautiful smile that lit up his face and her face and all the space around them. It was a smile full of mystery and excitement. As old as he was, his smile seemed to promise things.

"Oh, God, I'm sorry. I guess you don't want to talk about it."

"I don't actually. Not really." He smiled at her again. He wrapped a smile around her embarrassment and then he got down off the machine and went over to the ski machine and began to make the delicate adjustments that put him in balance so he could exercise his good leg. His tie moved up and down on his white shirt. His coat was unbuttoned.

Brenda moved her legs and feet up and down on the StairMaster. It was divine, amazing. He was someone special. She had known that all along. He had probably been in some secret service in the army. In some code business or some secret thing behind the lines. He couldn't talk about it, of course. Real heroes never wanted to talk about their deeds. Yes, this was just what Brenda wanted. To get to know some people who did something besides watch basketball games. Brenda's boyfriend watched basketball games all the time. Every time he came over it was just to sit in her den and watch basketball games. "Why don't you go play basketball?" she had told him finally. "Why do you just sit around and watch it all the time?"

She climbed down off the StairMaster and went over and stood beside the ski machine and started doing stretches. "Do you mind if I talk to you while you do that?" she asked. "Tell me if you can't talk while you do it. I've been watching you for so many weeks I feel like I know you."

"I can talk. Of course. I'd like to talk to you. Where shall we begin?" The smile again. That great big space-filling smile.

"What did you say just then? About someone's dancing floor? What was that about?"

"Ariadne. The labyrinth. A maze emanating from a center."

"You're a teacher, aren't you?"

"Yes, I am. Retired these last few years, although they still run me in when they're shorthanded."

"I'm going back to college. I want to study French, then I'll go to Paris and parlez-vous. God, it's really coming down out there. I love a summer rain. Well, I'd better go get on the treadmill. We've only got half an hour before they close." She waited. He gave her half a smile. He was getting tired. It was amazing that he could hold himself up on that machine as long as he did. Oh, God, she thought. I tired him out. I'm so inconsiderate. I ought to be ashamed of myself.

She went over to the treadmill and set the speed on thirty-eight to punish herself for being insensitive. Behind her Professor Wheeler bent to his task. He had promised his cardiologist that he would exercise an hour a day and he always kept his promises. Molly, he was thinking. Artless, timeless, the scene is the bed; the organ is flesh; the symbol, the earth; the female monologue. You are Molly. I am Leopold. A marriage bed rooted to the bole of an olive tree. The rain falls on our empty pastures.

I'll make a pie for dinner, Brenda was thinking. If he tries to eat it in front of the television set I won't let him. I'll say, Sit here at this table and talk to me. If you take that cherry pie into that room with that television set, it's over. I'll go out tonight and get another boyfriend or I'll do without. Sit here at this table, David. Sit down and talk to me.

We are all wanderers, Professor Wheeler was thinking, as he got off the machine and straightened up his spine. Everyman is a Jew. But not Molly. Molly is warm from making love. Bloom would create order from chaos. Would create order from Molly, who knows no order.

I am not watching television tonight, Brenda decided. She turned the treadmill up to forty, then forty-one. I want to go for a walk on the mountain and see the vistas. I want to walk until the sun goes down. It stays up so long in summer. We might have to walk for hours. We might just walk along and talk about how beautiful the world is in summer. How long the days, how fine and clear the nights. The stars, how they shine down upon us. Professor Wheeler's right. It is a dancing floor. The best thing to do is dance.

The young Christian boy who tended the machines was standing by the door looking at his watch. Brenda looked in his direction and smiled at him. She felt guilty for keeping him so long. He probably had better things to do than watch old people exercise. He probably had a date.

Think of the courage in all of it, Professor Wheeler was thinking, as he straightened up his tie. What a wrenching it will be to leave this world.

★   ★   ★

On her way out to the car Brenda found a blue and black Monarch butterfly flattened out against a window. She moved in close and studied it. Later, there was a daddy longlegs on the screen door. The next morning she took a piece of coffee cake out onto her patio and a bumble bee came and sat upon it and began to take the honey on the icing. "I feel like I'm getting messages from somewhere," she told Professor Wheeler that Monday when she met him at the center. "It's like everywhere I look something's going on to make me remember nature."

"It hasn't rained in weeks. The creatures are looking for moisture anywhere they can."

"Why do they flatten themselves on windows? The butterflies, I mean?"

"There's a small amount of condensation there. Half a cup of water is a treasure in the desert."

"What did you teach when you were a teacher?" She speeded up the Exercycle to make up for asking him such a personal question.

He stopped his machine and thought a moment. "Poetry mostly. Literature. From all over the world at one time or the other. I know quite a large number of languages. Did you think further about calling my friend, Dan Levine, about your French classes?"

"No. I've been too busy. I'm breaking up with my boyfriend but he doesn't know it yet. I'm giving him tests. He's flunking them." She considered telling Professor Wheeler about the eating-pie-in-front-of-the-television test, then decided against it. It was too crude to talk about to him. "He keeps wearing his baseball cap in the house. I can't put up with that." She speeded up even more. "To tell the truth I won't sleep with a man who wears a hat in the house. My grandmother was a charter member of Chi O. It was founded here, did you know that? Well, that was all a long time ago. My family hasn't done too good since then."

"Families rise and fall, like tides. Only the genes remain. You can breed out a lot of genius in a generation. So, that is why,"—he took his towel and wrapped it around the neck of his coat and shirt and tie—". . . I chose literature. I cast my lot with the muses. Erato, Clio,

Calliope, Euterpe, Melpomene, Polymnia. Of course, I have been lucky. I have had an endless supply of students for children."

"My children live so far away. One's in Seattle and the other one's in Alaska. It's like they're gone forever. So I was thinking I could take up where I left off and go back to school. I was thinking about learning massage therapy maybe. Think of the good you could do."

"I'll bring you some forms for the French class when I come back in. Will you be in tomorrow, do you think?" He straightened his tie. Moved his hand from the StairMaster, waited.

"Sure I will. I'll be in at noon for sure. Our office is just down the street so it's easy for me to come in at lunchtime."

"I'll see you then, if I may."

When he left the center, Professor Wheeler drove over to the university administration building and collected all the admission forms and put them in an envelope for Brenda. He smiled at himself for doing it. It was almost time for a semester to start. Time to believe you could fill one mind with treasure and the world would somehow profit. He left the administration building and walked with his crutch down to the student center and sat at a table eating a piece of devil's food cake and watching the young people going in and out of the bookstore. He had already wandered around the bookstore glancing at the texts of the various disciplines. They were mostly so poorly written and devoid of opinion it was impossible for him to imagine anyone reading them without falling asleep. The language police had triumphed. Every opinion was hedged. Dialogue banished. Argument eschewed. Cant had displaced thought on American campuses. If I had time I could educate Brenda, he decided, and somehow that thought made his cake taste better.

The next day he did not feel well but he managed to get himself up and dressed and to the center by noon. He delivered the forms to Brenda and even exercised for half an hour and then went home and stayed in bed reading and writing letters.

At nine that night she called. "Professor Wheeler, listen, it's

Brenda Lacey. I hope you weren't asleep. Listen, I just filled them out and I'm turning them in tomorrow. I just thought you might want to know."

"That's wonderful. I'm awfully glad. Remember to request Doctor Levine, if you can get him."

"I will. Well, how are you? Are you okay?"

"I'm fine. I was just tired from the heat, I think."

"You looked pale. Does your leg hurt? The one you lost, I mean?" She would never have asked that in person. Over the phone, in her excitement over the forms, it seemed okay somehow.

"No. I just get tired. You couldn't use this old heart at your donor center, I'm afraid. It wouldn't keep a lazy cat alive. Will I see you to-morrow then? I'm planning on going in at eleven."

"Maybe you need a transplant. We can put you on the list. You have to—"

"Oh, no. I'm much too fastidious for that. I'll see you tomorrow then, will I?"

"Sure. I'll be there. As close to noon as I can make it."

He hung up the phone and stood with his hand on the receiver think-ing of how pleased he was, as pleased as a child. He closed his eyes and felt his heart straining to let in so much happiness. Then he walked outside in his pajamas and seersucker robe and sat on the porch for a long time looking at the stars. There was a new moon high in the sky and not a cloud or a streetlight to mar his view. Down in the Tin Cup project, a block below the cemetery, jazz was coming from a radio. How high the moon, he hummed along. A tenor saxophone, a trum-pet, a piano. German instruments found their way into the hands of Africans in New Orleans and voilà, jazz. I do not want to leave this, he decided. I should go back to New Orleans for a week before I die and listen to that music. If Pound heard it, oh, liquid poetry, he might have seen it as a river, a small clear mountain river like the Wind River in Wyoming. But that was another trip, in another place, an-other time.

It was very late when he went back inside and went to sleep.

That was a Tuesday night. On Thursday afternoon, when they happened to finish exercising at the same time, Professor Wheeler invited Brenda to his house to see his flowers. "I could make you a sandwich if you're hungry," he added. "I've been cooking things this morning. I can smell fall in the air, can't you?"

"What flowers?" She was so pleased with the invitation she was blushing.

"The hostas are blooming. And there're still some zinnias. I will cut some for you to take home for your table."

They went to his house and he set the table and fed her soup and a tuna fish sandwich and a glass of iced tea. They looked at the flowers and then sat on the porch and he told her about the young men who were buried in the Confederate cemetery across the street. He told her what states they were from and what they thought they were fighting for. "They were fighting for Missouri," he said. "To save it for the Confederacy."

"I was born in Missouri," she said. "Why didn't they teach us that in school?"

"Did you turn in the forms for your French class?"

"Not yet. I'm going to do it this afternoon. They never are open when I can get away. Not that we're very busy. We mostly just sit around. Or take false alarms. We never know when there'll be someone to harvest."

"Harvest?"

"That's what we call it. Didn't you know that? They've tightened up about what they'll take. And there aren't as many car wrecks as there were last year. Last year we got four hearts. Well . . ." She was afraid she had offended him in some way.

He was laughing. "Actually I have a donor card in my wallet. Not that anything of mine could be of much use, except my liver. I haven't given it much to do for many years." He laughed again.

"When I went to work for them I thought they were going to send me to school to learn how to be on the harvest team but they never did. I'm still the secretary. Mostly I answer the phone."

"You have a nice voice. That's important for work like that."

"Finding people fast is the main thing. You have to break into calls."

"Think of the harvest you could have made out there." He pointed toward the cemetery, where seven hundred and twenty young men lay underneath the maple trees, spread out like a star from a central monument, the dead of Missouri, Arkansas, Texas, Louisiana, and Mississippi.

"Why do you live way back here?"

"Because it's quiet. Except for the project in Tin Cup. Sometimes I can hear the children getting on the school buses. That's always nice. Would you like more tea?"

"No, I think I'll go on. I want to make sure I got all the lines filled out on the forms. I'll turn them in tomorrow. They don't care if I leave as long as I take the mobile phone." She stood up, collected the flowers he had picked for her and put into a Mason jar. He walked her to her car and watched as she backed and turned by the cemetery gates and drove off down the road. The graces all attend her, he decided. Strange how they choose the ones they do.

He walked back into the house and lay down upon his bed to listen to his heart grind and beat. He should have let them implant the pacemaker but he couldn't bring himself to do it. Perhaps he would relent. Who could bear to die as summer dies, with glorious fall only weeks away. He closed his eyes and began to remember a dance at V.M.I. in nineteen thirty-nine. A girl in a Black Watch plaid taffeta formal, her breasts swelling up out of the bodice, her cheeks aflame, her strong arms and laughing face.

Brenda had forgotten her purse. She was almost to the courthouse when she remembered it was hanging on a rocking chair on Professor Wheeler's porch. It had fifty dollars in the billfold. Money she had taken out of the money machine at the McElroy Bank that morning on her way to work. He'll think I'm so stupid, she decided. And just when I finally got a friend who reads books.

She turned the car around in the courthouse parking lot and

started back up toward Tin Cup. There was a construction project going on on Spring Street. A water main had broken and the city was fixing it. She had to wait five minutes while a teenager in an orange vest let the traffic through from the other direction. Then he motioned her on and she picked her way around the machines and up the hill.

Professor Wheeler got up from the bed and sat in his reading chair and opened the day-old *New York Times* that had been in the mail. He opened the paper to the editorial page and began to read Russell Baker, who was in one of his silly moods over American foreign policy. His heart tightened as something made him laugh. He took a cigarette out of a package and struck a match and lit it. He inhaled deeply. His heart contracted. It pulled his chest into a knot for what seemed an eternity. It pulled and pulled and pulled. Then it stopped.

Brenda drove slowly up the gravel road in third gear. She had a recurring nightmare that she was driving her old Toyota up a hill and it wouldn't go. It was her punishment for buying a car with a standard transmission. She had always liked the idea of shifting gears for herself. Now she had to pay for it with this stupid dream. The dream took many forms. In its most terrible form she was trying to get to a seven o'clock movie at Fiesta Square and the car wouldn't go up Township Road. She would be trying to get to the last showing of something she really wanted to see.

She pulled into the parking space before Professor Wheeler's house and saw the chair with her purse hanging on it. She got out of the car and walked up onto the porch and retrieved her purse and put the strap over her shoulder. The door was open. She looked through the screen and saw him lying there. The cigarette was still smoking. It was a few inches away from the day-old *New York Times* and it was smoking.

The sounds of the earth were deafening. A billion cicadas seemed to be singing a dirge. From the maple trees across the road and the gardens and the grasses the small creatures of the earth were singing and calling, mourning a man who had believed in dharma, in dialogue and metaphor, in justice and peace. A man who had outgrown evil. Who had never stopped to have an unkind thought.

Brenda knelt beside her friend and searched for a pulse but the pulse was gone. She ran around the house and found the phone on a shelf in the kitchen. The pulse of the earth kept on beating until it was joined by the sound of sirens.

The Divorce

⌒

THE FINLEYS' DIVORCE has become a legend in this town. Who would have thought a diabetic insurance agent only five feet six inches tall could have soared to such flights of imagination. You should listen to this story. In case someone you trusted and had children with decides to dump you and go on to another life.

You think men have to put up with that, don't you? You think a man has to sit on his hands and keep his mouth shut and let his wife break up his home and send him off to live in a hovel? The moment she wants to, a woman thinks she can quit and expects you to take it like a man. Well, Bobby Lee Finley didn't take it like a man. He fought back. He became a whole new thing, a lesson to us all. Bobby Lee, who couldn't even make the football team, who had to be a cheerleader in junior high, who played saxophone in the high school band. More about the saxophone later. It's going to play a part in this story.

When the divorce began Bobby Lee and Ginger had been living here in Harrisburg, Illinois, for fifteen years, seemingly at peace. She was from Marion, which is only twenty miles away. Bobby Lee met her when they were at Carbondale in business school. She was too pretty for him really, but her father had just died and her mother wasn't well, so when he offered to marry her, she did it. I guess she thought moving to Harrisburg was a pretty big deal. At least it wasn't Marion. Anyway, she married him and two years later they had a baby girl named Little Ginger. Three years after that they had another baby girl. They named this one Roberta, signaling to anyone who was interested that this was going to be *it* for babies for the Finleys.

Little Ginger was an ordinary, normal child, selling Girl Scout cookies to the neighbors, singing in the children's choir, riding her bicycle around the square on sunny Saturdays. But Roberta wasn't well. She was a sickly baby and she grew up to be a sickly child. Nothing anyone could put their finger on. She was just delicate. As soon as Roberta was two years old, Ginger started working as a secretary in a law firm and a lot of people thought she neglected the little girl. If she did, Bobby Lee more than made up for it. He doted on that child. He carried her around. He took her everywhere with him.

So fourteen years went by and no one paid much attention to the Finleys, except to worry occasionally about Roberta, who was wearing thick bifocal glasses by the time she was ten, or to think how nice it was to do business with Bobby, or to wave at Ginger at the grocery store. She always dressed up in high heels to go to work and would come tearing into the IGA at five-thirty every afternoon trying to find something to cook for dinner.

Then the divorce began. It was the year the hospital built the health club in the parking lot by the replica of the Statue of Liberty. Ginger's boss at the law firm had offered bonuses to anyone who would go down there and exercise on their lunch hour three days a week. He got a rebate on their health insurance for convincing them to do it, so Ginger, ever law-abiding and obliging, signed up for an aerobics class. After the divorce began, several people commented on how good she looked and no wonder it ended in divorce.

I want it understood that this is not gossip. I never gossip. I just want to get the facts straight and explain why I am serving fifty hours of community service for contempt of court. People in Harrisburg know how I got caught up in this. But outsiders might not understand, so I have decided to set this down while it's fresh in my mind.

In the first place I work across the hall from Ginger. Also, I have known Bobby Lee since he was a year behind me in Horace Mann Elementary School. I know what happened in this divorce. There may be bigger towns than this, with more excitement and bigger malls, but no one in the United States can boast a more eventful divorce or one more tailored to the expanding horizons of the nineties. Beware the fin de siècle, my German grandfather used to say. It is always a time of decadence.

The divorce started off simply enough. One weekend Ginger went off to Marion to meet her two best friends from high school. That's a normal thing to do. Lots of wives around here do that sort of thing, go home and visit and leave the children with the father.

The first thing I knew about it Bobby Lee called me at ten o'clock on Saturday night and asked if I had the number of Ginger's boss. It's unlisted. I did happen to have it in my address book and I gave it to him. "What's wrong?" I asked, just trying to be polite. You could tell Bobby Lee was mad. Beware a short man when he is angry, my mother always said. Banty rooster syndrome and all that.

"I'm looking for my wife," he answered. "She was dancing at the Krazy Cat last night with Eugene Holcomb. How do you like that, Letitia? I'm baby-sitting and my wife's in Marion dancing with her boss."

"I don't believe it," I answered. "Calm down, Bobby. Ginger isn't having an affair with Eugene Holcomb. Eugene weighs two hundred and fifty pounds. He's too fat to have an affair. Why are you calling him? You'll be sorry you did this in the morning. Call Ginger at her mother's."

"I tried that. Her mother said they'd gone out again. That's two nights in a row. I bet they're back at the Krazy Cat."

"Bobby, are you drinking? This doesn't sound like you."

"I am not drinking. I'm trying to find my wife. Last night she was dancing with Eugene Holcomb. Tonight they've gone out again."

"Then drive over to Marion and find her. It's only fifteen minutes away on the bypass. Calm down, Bobby Lee. I've never heard you sound this way."

"I've never been left to baby-sit while my wife dances in a road-house with her boss. I've never been left alone while she flaunts herself all over Marion, Illinois."

"Go over there and find her. It won't be what you think."

"I can't leave the kids."

"Bring them to me. I'll take care of them."

"Little Ginger's at a movie with her friend. She isn't home yet."

So he raved some more and then he hung up and I made a peanut butter sandwich and went to bed with a book. I've been reading about the twelfth century in England and in France. A biography of Eleonor of Aquitaine. Back then no one thought a thing about adultery. No one expected people to be faithful if they had any power in the world. They didn't act all shocked if the king had a girlfriend in every hamlet or the queen ran in some poets to shore her up as she grew old.

I didn't expect to hear any more about Ginger and Bobby Lee, but by noon the next day Ginger had me on the phone. "What did Bobby tell you?" she wanted to know. "He told me he called you for Eugene's number. I'm mortified, Letitia. I've never been so embarrassed in my life."

"What happened?"

"He came over to Marion in the middle of the night and dragged me home. He came to the Krazy Cat at eleven-thirty at night with my girls and made me leave with him. He wouldn't even let me go by mother's and get my clothes. Who else did he call? Who else knows about all this?"

"I don't know about it. All I was doing was reading a book when the phone rang. What's going on, Ginger? Were you and Eugene dancing at the Krazy Cat?"

"His wife was there. Janet Holcomb was right there with us. We were all there together. Then Bobby came barging in with Little Ginger and Roberta and dragged me home. I will never forgive him, Letitia. I will never forget this as long as I live. I shouldn't have married him in the first place. Never marry anyone who can't make the football team. My daddy taught me that." She had this icy tone in her voice, like whatever she had been keeping inside for years had finally found an outlet.

We hung up and I was left trying to decide how I'd been dragged into this domestic crisis. I'm the director of the Harrisburg EOA and president of the Literacy Council. I don't get involved in people's lives. I have all of that I want at the office.

The next thing that happened was that Ginger took the girls out of school and went to Marion to stay. She left her job and kept them out of school for seven days until Bobby Lee agreed to vacate the house and let them move back in alone. It was the last concession that he made. What happened to him between the time he moved out of the house into a messy little apartment near the railroad tracks and a week later when he went on the offensive is something we will never know. I think he went to Chicago to see a psychiatrist or a marriage counselor, but other people think it was a witch doctor or some dark, demonic force. The Bobby Lee who emerged from hiding that third week was someone we didn't know. In the first place he was letting his hair grow. It was down to his collar by the time Ginger returned to town. In the second place he changed his hours of business. From now on, if you wanted to talk to Bobby about insurance you had to call before two in the afternoon. After two, all you got was voice mail.

"He's completely nuts," Ginger said. She was out in the hall when I got to work on Monday. "He's supposed to take the girls to dinner tonight. He'd better behave. This is his chance to show he's going to be civilized."

"He'll be fine," I answered. "He's always been a model citizen. What makes you think he won't be fine?"

"He says he's going to start a soup kitchen." She giggled. How could she help it? "He says now that he knows what loneliness is he wants to stop it for other people. He says he's going to turn his apartment into a place where anyone who's lonely can find someone to talk to and have something to eat. What if he does it? What if he takes Ginger and Roberta to his house and there are homeless people there?"

"We only have two homeless people. That man who stays on Hill Street and the one who walks around the park."

"He's picking the girls up after school. They're going to spend the night with him."

That evening went all right, Ginger reported the next day. The girls helped him cook dinner and the only funny business he tried to pull was questioning them about their mother's whereabouts. "He isn't supposed to talk to them about me," Ginger complained. "My lawyer said he would cite him for contempt of court if he asked them questions about me."

"That might be hard to prove." We were out in the hall, balancing coffee cups on our break. Everyone in our building used to hang out there when it was too cold to go outside. That was before we had the new café.

"He let me have the good car," Ginger continued. She smiled and licked her lips. To tell the truth she was acting like a schoolgirl who was delighting in the pain she was causing some poor boy who had a crush on her. I couldn't help thinking she was enjoying it. And why not? What excitement had she had for the last fifteen years? Typing up Eugene's briefs? Throwing away junk mail? Trying to figure out why Roberta caught every cold that came along?

"Bobby's a nice man. You better think twice before you let him go."

"After what he did to me? I'm afraid of him, Letitia. I changed the locks on the doors. You didn't see him that night in Marion. He's lost his mind. His hair is down to his collar. Have you seen his hair? He's taking the girls this weekend. I'm worried sick about it."

"What will you do while they're gone?"

"Oh, I'll be busy. Little Ginger's coming back on Saturday afternoon to get dressed for her freshman-sophomore dance. I'm going to chaperone. I'll be plenty busy." She swished back into Eugene's office and I watched her swish. She's lost ten pounds since this began. I've never seen her look better.

★ ★ ★

At five-thirty on Saturday afternoon she called me. "I have to talk to someone. You won't believe what he's done to me."

"What did he do?"

"He rented a tuxedo. He's going to the dance with us. He had Little Ginger call and tell me. I got him on the phone. I said, 'Bobby, if you go, I'm not going.' So he's going anyway. Ginger's going to be so disappointed. My oldest daughter's first dance and I can't go."

I didn't say a word to that. I didn't say, She's his oldest daughter too. I didn't say, Leave me out of this. Perhaps I didn't want out. There isn't much going on in Harrisburg that time of year. I guess I liked the excitement of being the first to know each new development.

"You better not go," I said. "That's playing into his hands. That's what he wants you to do."

"But what about Little Ginger? She'll die if I'm not there. I'm supposed to chaperone."

"Do what you want to then."

"I might go and then I might not."

I hung up and went back to my reading. I had finished the twelfth century and started in on *Little House on the Prairie*, which my book club is reviewing. I read it straight through without stopping and went to sleep and dreamed of pioneers and men fording rivers with Christmas presents for little girls on their heads.

At nine the next night Ginger called me in a rage. "You sound terrible," I said. "What happened? What's going on?"

"He bought them a dog," she screamed. "He delivered them home with a half-grown collie he bought from some white trash in Shawneetown. He dropped them off outside the house in the rain with this dog. I don't even have a fenced-in yard. The gate's been gone for years."

"That's brilliant," I couldn't help saying. "A dog. My God, that's a move by a master. I didn't know Bobby Lee had that in him."

"It isn't funny, Letitia. I'm going to call my lawyer in the morning and have him cited. This wet dog in my kitchen. What will I do with it?"

"Find out where he got it and take it back."

"But Roberta loves it. She's been hugging it ever since she got home. I've never seen her so happy. She loves this dog."

"Then keep the dog."

"I haven't told you what he did to me at the dance, have I?"

"You went to the dance?"

"I had to go. I couldn't let Ginger down."

"Where was Roberta while you were all at the dance?"

"With the dog. It's Roberta's dog. When I got to the dance he was standing there in his tuxedo with a video camera. He videotaped me. Every time I looked his way he had this camera turned on me. I don't know what to do. Do you think I should call my lawyer now or wait until the morning?"

"It's clear he doesn't want this divorce."

"Well, he's going to get it. I'm not going to put up with his jealous rages. I'll never forget that night."

I hung up. I couldn't help thinking that maybe all of this was lost on Ginger. Maybe she didn't have a high enough IQ to understand what was being lavished on her. Didn't she know she was going to start wanting to see that videotape?

On Wednesday of the following week she filed formal charges and a date was set for the divorce proceeding. On that same day an ad appeared in the *Harrisburg Sentinel*. Opening November 1st. ONLY THE LONELY CAFE. Modeled on the famous coffee shops of San Francisco. We will feature Cappuchino, Espresso, Latte, Café Au Lait and cakes of many kinds. Homemade cakes, cookies, muffins, scones, and Southern sweet rolls. Bookstore and Art Gallery opening soon. Dance Floor and Band to follow. Twelve Seventy-Five Maple Street. BOBBY LEE FINLEY welcomes you to a New Highlight in Harrisburg History. Free Refills.

I should stop a minute and describe our town to you. It's a sweet-smelling town, situated in the bootheel of Illinois, thirty miles west of the Ohio River and twenty-five miles north of the Shawnee National

Forest, home of Mammoth Cave. It is the county seat of Saline County, a clean, simple city of maple trees and sycamores, brick buildings and neat lawns. We boast a Carnegie Library that looks like a temple. We are twenty thousand souls, give or take a hundred. Our streets meander up gentle hills. Glaciers crossed this country. There are limestone formations outside town and abandoned strip mines. There are pastures with neat fences and houses where the James gang holed up one winter. Our high school has a thousand students. We are law-abiding church-going people who like hobbies and hard work and minding our own business. I used to mind mine. Until I got sucked into the vortex of Bobby Lee and Ginger's divorce.

You probably wouldn't think a town like the one I have described would be a good place to open a San Francisco–style coffee shop, but you would be wrong. From the first day it was packed and it stayed packed. Bobby had torn out the insides of his grandfather's old office beside the Quorum Court Building off the square and completely re-built it. It looked like something from old Vienna, with wrought-iron tables and chairs he ordered from California and a curved wooden counter he salvaged from an old hotel in Eldorado. The inside was painted white and green. There were green and white tiles on the floor and a baker's rack holding copies of exotic newspapers and magazines. (He had a friend in Chicago who sent them down.) *Harper's* magazine, the *Atlantic Monthly*, *The Economist*, the *Village Voice*, the *Prairie Schooner*, the *New York Times*. Every week a bundle arrived from Chicago with new magazines and newspapers you can't get in Harrisburg. A certain segment of his clientele was coming in just to read the papers. That was my excuse when Ginger cornered me and suggested it was disloyal of me to spend so much time at the Lonely, as it was being called in Harrisburg. Of course, she couldn't keep her kids away. Little Ginger and Roberta were there every day after school, helping out their father and eating cake.

It was a complete success from the word go. In the first place the food was good, always an important consideration in southern Illinois, where people make no bones about their appetites. At first

Bobby Lee had Mrs. Saxocorn baking for him, but the demand outgrew the supply and he began to spend his evenings baking.

He bought a copy of the Garden Club cookbook and called up the contributors for tips. Pretty soon the glass windows of the stand by the cash register were filled with pieces of Mrs. Hancock's Poppy Seed Cake and Mrs. Kalicha's Pecan and Marble Delight. He was selling slices of cake for one dollar and fifty cents apiece, and the young people of Harrisburg were forking over their allowances with abandon. Bobby Lee stood behind the counter in an apron, serving Café Au Lait and Hawaiian Mocha Dreams and Sports Tea and Cappuchino. He soon had two or three of the young people working for him. He spent from eight to two in the insurance office and the afternoon in the café and the evenings baking. He wasn't sleeping much, I heard.

"He drives by our house every morning and puts the paper on the porch," Ginger told me. "Eugene said I could cite him for contempt if I wanted to but it probably isn't worth the trouble. At least he hasn't gotten them any more animals."

"What happened to the dog?"

"Oh, we still have it. Roberta is so attached to it. It isn't a bad dog. I don't let it in the house, of course, but I let her keep it in the yard. They're building it a doghouse."

"Who is?"

"Bobby and the girls. They work on it in his backyard when they go over for the weekend."

"Where is the dog sleeping now?"

"In the kitchen. Just until the doghouse is finished. It's still cold at night, Letitia. I can't let it stay outside and freeze."

The next thing Bobby started were poetry readings. He started paying people to come down on Wednesday afternoons and read their poetry. He brought in a poet from the University of Southern Illinois at Carbondale to start things off. After that they were mostly local people. Even old Mr. Aaron, who is eighty years old and used to be in a group of poets in Chicago, came down. No one has seen him in years. We all thought he was dead and all of a sudden he shows up at the coffee shop wearing a tweed suit and a lovely new tie and reading his poetry out loud. Most of the poems were about when he was overseas during the Second World War. Several were about going to Italy after the war and falling in love with a beautiful young girl he couldn't marry.

I had a talk with Bobby Lee around that time that surprised me. I ran into him in the post office a few days after the poetry readings got started. We were waiting in line to get our packages mailed. He had three manila folders in his hands. I was holding a large package containing a pocketbook I was mailing to St. Louis to have restored.

"Let me hold that for you," he said.

"It's not heavy. It's a frivolous mailing, to tell the truth. I'd hate for anyone to know how I was wasting time."

"I'm sending poems to a magazine." He laughed and smiled a truly childlike smile, charming, unashamed. His hair had grown so long he was tying it back with a leather thong. I have to admit he has pretty hair for a man, soft and brown and wavy. His mother was a pretty girl, rest her soul, dead in an automobile accident about the time Bobby finished high school.

"Good for you," I said. "I used to write some poems now and again. I heard the young people read last Wednesday, Bobby. That's a fine thing you have going down there. Keeping them out of bars and pool halls." I lowered my eyes. I didn't want to imply I was thinking about the Krazy Cat in Marion.

"Oh, that isn't why I'm doing it." He laughed again. "I have darker designs than that." The man in front of me finished his business at the window and I stepped up to mail my pocketbook. Darker designs? Was Ginger right? Was all this just to get her back? Is everything we do on earth about love and only love? I have hit on this idea before and pondered it. Not the electric light, I always tell myself. Benjamin Franklin didn't go out in the backyard and attach himself to lightning by a kite string just to get some woman to like him better, did he? I think not. I am of the school of thought that says we are more complicated than that.

★ ★ ★

As soon as the poetry readings were established, Bobby started his jazz band. Remember I told you he played a saxophone in high school? Well, it turned out he had never forgotten how. He had kept that old saxophone all those years while he worked to make a living for his family. Now he got it out and polished it up and started practicing. In a month's time he had a band together, two electric guitars, a bass player, a drummer, a keyboard player, and himself. On Friday and Saturday afternoons they started having Happy Hour at the coffee shop and playing music. When spring arrived Bobby closed the shop for three days and built a patio in the empty lot behind the building. As soon as the concrete was poured he drove to the Wal-Mart in Carbondale and brought back six large white canvas umbrellas and set them up on tables around the dance floor. Mr. Aaron was advising him by now and you could see the Italian influence. That Friday afternoon, with the concrete barely dry, they started the outdoor concerts. Fifty people came the first afternoon. By the next afternoon two hundred were there. It had snowballed. The height of the weekend here in Harrisburg became going to the Lonely to hear music.

They named the band Father Bobby's Raiders and they had these outfits that looked like the undershirts of priests and nuns. Oh, yes, there was a woman in the band. A woman dentist who moved here from St. Louis. A beautiful unmarried girl who plays bass guitar.

Nothing this sacrilegious had ever been done in Harrisburg before, but no one complained. Bobby Lee's refusal to take his divorce lying down had caught the imagination of the people. The men liked it, of course, but why did the women like it? Well, to begin with, Ginger. A new divorcée in a town this small is always a danger. Plus, the children start goofing up. It makes extra work for teachers, work for school counselors, the bills don't get paid. There are reasons society is on the side of order.

The Raiders also played concerts in the park. They played for the Half-Centennial in June, they played at the high school for the Halloween dance. They played old favorites at first, "My Girl," "Earth Angel," "All You Want to Do Is Ride Around, Sally," "The Tracks of My Tears," "Harrisburg Fight Song."

Then they moved on to real jazz, with Bobby Lee doing solos on "The Old Rugged Cross," "If I Loved You," and "The Entertainer." We had never had music like this in Harrisburg and the *Harrisburg Sentinel* did a special section on the café, calling it a Renaissance and Bobby Lee a Renaissance man.

Shortly after the band began, Little Ginger and Roberta started to show an interest in music. Instead of goofing them up, this divorce had opened new horizons for them. Little Ginger started playing the piano and clarinet and Roberta turned out to be some sort of undiscovered instant genius on the trumpet. By the time the second spring arrived and the outdoor bandstand reopened, Bobby Lee was letting them play with the band anytime they wanted to. Little Ginger only played with them occasionally. She was sticking to classical music, but you couldn't keep Roberta off the stage. Bobby bought her a pair of cowboy boots and a fringed and beaded skirt and blouse and she would get up on that stage and play her little heart out. You would never believe she had been a sickly child to hear the power her twelve-year-old lungs could muster. She took the band to new levels. She could play "How High the Moon" or "Chase the Clouds Away" to break your heart, holding the high notes until the crowd would scream for mercy.

The woman dentist began to take an interest in Roberta. You could see the two of them with their heads together before performances, planning new assaults on our senses.

What was going on with the divorce at this point, you well might ask. Well, Ginger kept changing lawyers. Finally she settled on a lawyer in Marion who was said to be the meanest man around. Not that he was having much success. Bobby Lee was into delaying tactics. He wanted his home back. Even though he was creating a perfectly grand new life, he still wanted the one Ginger had taken from him. Of course, she was in a bad mood all the time now. In the first place she had no one to talk to on coffee breaks. Everyone in our building went to the Lonely.

I tried once or twice to get her to go with us. "You ought to at least go look at it and see what he's done," I said.

"Absolutely not."

"Ginger, what is this divorce about? It's been two years since you started this. Do you remember what you were mad about?"

"It's about him being jealous of me. Dragging me out of the Krazy Cat. Don't you remember? It's because he's crazy. He's crazy as a loon. Have you seen his hair?"

"Ginger." It was her boss, Eugene, calling her. "Ginger, come on in. I need you right away."

"I have to go." She snuffed out the half-smoked cigarette in a little tin ashtray on the windowsill and tossed her head and sighed. "I have to type a brief." She turned on her heels and went into the law office, and, I suppose, spent the afternoon typing up things Eugene had marked for her in law books.

As for me, it was Friday afternoon. At five o'clock Happy Hour started at the Lonely and I wanted to go home and put on my long cotton skirt and sandals. It is hard getting one of the umbrella-covered tables on weekend afternoons. I have a group of friends who take turns getting to the Lonely early to grab a table and today it was my turn.

I told my assistant to close up and walked out of the building into the March day. Harrisburg was getting ready for spring. The grime of winter had been washed off the streets by spring rains. Window washers were at work on ladders at the courthouse. The baseball diamond behind the high school was loud with batting practice. Down at the Lonely Bobby Lee would be wiping off the tables, straightening up the bandstand, making fresh coffee and Sports Tea.

I stopped by the courthouse and thought it over. I was trying to decide what blouse to wear. The past Friday Judge Watts and I had done a mean jitterbug to "All You Want to Do Is Ride Around, Sally." If he was there again this week I had resolved to really cut loose. I believe it is good for young people to see old people having fun. It keeps them from believing that hard work makes everyone as sad as their parents.

I decided on a white peasant's blouse. And of course Judge Watts was there. As soon as he spotted me he came over and took a seat beside me underneath the umbrella. "You ready to teach them how to dance?" he asked.

"That's why I'm here," I answered, and we went out onto the dance floor and began showing off. We had the floor to ourselves for a few minutes. Then a good-looking carpenter led his partner out onto the space beside us. He was wearing a black T-shirt that said, OFF DUTY, and his hips were moving like he meant it. I started copying everything he did and the judge copied me. To be a good dancer at the Lonely you have to move into the zeitgeist of the afternoon. If someone hot comes on the floor, move into their energy. Anyway, that's the theory Judge Watts and I were working on that afternoon.

We had not been dancing ten minutes when Ginger appeared in the door. She still had on her suit and heels and she just sort of stood there, looking around and trying to take it in. "That's Bobby's wife," I whispered to Judge Watts, and we started in her direction. Bobby beat us to it. He laid his saxophone down on the stage and climbed down off the bandstand and started walking toward her. The crowd of dancers let him through. Behind him Roberta stepped up to the mike and raised her horn. She broke into her famous rendition of "Chase the Clouds Away." The audience cheered. A few people were staring at Ginger and Bobby Lee but most of them pretended not to notice. This is a polite town. A town this size has to be.

"You'll have to recuse yourself if the divorce ever gets to your court," I told the judge, thinking I was joking.

"You know I can't talk about that," he answered, and we broke into "The Statue of Liberty," a special dance we have created here in Harrisburg for Friday afternoons at the Lonely.

You put one arm up into the air and try to stay as straight as you can from the waist up and only let your hips and legs move.

The next week new evil began. Ginger's trip to the Lonely had only served to make her madder. In the first place she was annoyed to see how well Bobby Lee was doing and it made her greedy. In the second place she had only gone down there, she said, to ask him to sign the divorce decree. When he refused on the grounds that he still loved her, she went into attack mode. She decided to draw blood. She got her mean lawyer to draw up papers demanding twice as much alimony as before and complete custody of the children, including the right to take them out of the state without asking permission.

"Has she gone insane?" my best friend, Cynthia, asked me when she heard about it. "Everyone knows she's sleeping with half the men in Southern Illinois. If she drags this into court, she's the one who will suffer."

"Who is she sleeping with? How could she be sleeping with anyone? Oh, well, the girls are gone every weekend, aren't they?" We were transplanting daisies in my backyard beds. Cynthia was squatting beside the new-turned earth, looking up at me. The sun beat down. Nature was by our side on this clear spring day and here I was, being surprised by nature.

"She's sleeping with her boss, everyone knows that. And she's sleeping with Harlon Davis over in Marion. He was in her class in high school."

"Where'd you hear that?"

"I saw them in Marion a couple of weeks ago. They were out at the mall together. They were holding hands in the B. Dalton Bookstore. They kept on holding hands the whole time I talked to them."

"Cynthia! Are you sure?"

"Sure I'm sure. Now look here, Letitia. Either we have to bunch these up or we have to make another bed. There's not enough room for all of these. Where did you get all these daisies?"

"I started them in the kitchen during that snowstorm. How many people know this, Cynthia? About Ginger and Harlon Davies?"

"How would I know? Well, now you know."

Yes, now I knew and I would live to regret knowing it. Even as we put those daisies in the ground I was regretting knowing it. My mother's warnings about gossip all came back to haunt me. Mind your own business. Stay out of other people's lives.

"Not to mention she's flirting with every man in town," Cynthia continued. "I wouldn't let her near my husband. I can tell you that."

★ ★ ★

Ginger's new demands were the last straw for Bobby Lee. Now *he* changed lawyers. Fired darling Mr. Harrison, whom we all adore, and hired a slick young lawyer who had just come to Harrisburg from Chicago. His name was Mr. Petronilla and it turned out he was even meaner than Ginger's lawyer. If Ginger wanted blood, there would be blood. Bobby Lee counterfiled, charging Ginger with adultery, and we were all subpoenaed. Every single person she had talked to about the divorce. How I regretted that conversation with Cynthia. How I regretted everything I had heard. With the threat of being sworn in *under penalty of perjury* hanging over my head, I began to regret every word.

Also, I was appalled at how well I remembered every conversation and who said what to me. So powerful and wicked is gossip. So fertile and unforgettable is rumor.

My subpoena was delivered to my office on Monday morning. The trial was set for the third of May. I had planned on taking that week off to work in my gardens. Now, instead, I would be down at the courthouse, locked into the witness stand, with mean lawyers making me repeat things said to me in privacy by people that I liked.

The worst divorce in the history of Harrisburg, Illinois, was about to commence.

The day after everyone was subpoenaed I saw Little Ginger and Roberta riding their bikes down Maple Street. There was a pall around them. They looked like girls no one would want to know. The bloom had left their cheeks.

The trial drew near. Those of us who had been subpoenaed were afraid to discuss it even among ourselves. I was afraid even to talk to Cynthia. At any moment I was going to have to drag her name into court or go to jail. Who told you that? the lawyers would ask. My best friend, Cynthia, I would be forced to reply. We were transplanting daisies.

To add to the complications, the court responsible for divorces in Saline County is Judge Watts's court. *My dancing partner* at the café of one of the litigants. In my worst fantasies Ginger's lawyer would be leaning over me, his foul breath breathing cold germs down into my face, the dust in the courtroom making me sneeze. "Are you the woman who has been seen doing immoral dances with the judge? Immoral and unpatriotic, I might add?"

"The Statue of Liberty is not unpatriotic," I would defend myself. "It is a paean to liberty. Land of the free, home of the brave."

Well, of course that part didn't come true. Judge Watts recused himself and a judge from Centralia was brought in. Judge William Watson, who is a first cousin of our beloved Judge Watson, whose daughter is my best friend. I gave my depositions to both lawyers, mumbling and saying yes and no and I don't remember and pretending to have to blow my nose every time they made me mad.

The day for the trial came. We all assembled in the smaller courtroom at the courthouse. Judge Watson presiding. I was sitting with my hands in my lap. Outside the sun was shining. A fine day for anything but what we were doing.

"Call your first witness," the judge said.

"Miss Letitia Scofield," Bobby Lee's lawyer said.

I got up and walked slowly to the witness chair. I sat down. "Raise your right hand and swear after me," the bailiff said.

"No," I answered.

"What?" said the judge.

"No," I answered. "I am a tax-paying citizen of the United States of America, the state of Illinois and the county of Saline. This is my courtroom. Your salary is paid by me. I have a right to speak in this court of law and I demand that right."

The judge only nodded, his gavel in his hand. I had caught him off guard.

"I am acquainted with Mr. and Mrs. Finley," I began. "But I don't know what is going on in their minds that they would drag us all down here to be involved in this.

"What is this trial about, Your Honor? If I thought it was about the welfare of their little daughters who they brought into the world, I would agree to waste a day of my vacation helping them decide what to do. But this isn't about the welfare of children. This is about ego and money. About greed and cruelty and revenge. About two people who want to make each other do things. About a woman who likes money and wants to make a man give it to her. About a man who is jealous and will do anything, no matter how insane, to make the object of his jealousy uncomfortable and unhappy.

"Yes, I know about this divorce. And I am guilty of gossiping about it and listening to the gossip. But I will not lay my hand on a Bible and agree to repeat that gossip in this court. Bring out the handcuffs. I will not be part of this."

I stood up, clutching my pocketbook. I looked from Ginger to Bobby Lee. "You ought to be ashamed of yourselves," I added. "How dare you do this to all of us. I was supposed to be putting in tomato plants this morning."

So the court was recessed and I was taken into Judge Watson's chambers and given fifty hours of community service, which he is allowing me to serve in my capacity as head of the Literacy Council.

Of course, my leaving would not have stopped the trial. It took an act of karmic retribution to do that. While we were in the judge's chambers Ginger's baby-sitter called the bailiff to say that Roberta was having trouble breathing. Bobby Lee beat Ginger out the door but she was right behind him, with half the courtroom trailing in their wake. Bobby Lee and Ginger jumped into his Isuzu and took off for the hospital emergency room. Everything that happened that afternoon I had to hear over the phone later in the day. Roberta's asthma had returned. She was so dismayed over thinking about what was going on down at the courtroom in front of everyone in town (those people she had striven so hard to win on Friday afternoons blowing her little lungs out on that trumpet) that her breathing apparatus had seized up like a fist. She had been at home with a baby-sitter because she was too upset to go to school. As soon as she decided the trial had begun she had started wheezing until she could not talk. The baby-sitter had called an ambulance and then the courtroom.

Bobby Lee and Ginger stood beside her bed (so Cynthia told

me—she is head nurse on that ward and was right there for every minute of it), looking down on their daughter but not at each other. Ginger was not going to back down, even if her daughter died to punish her. It was Greek tragedy, Cynthia said. (She is an actress with the Harrisburg Little Theater and this is not the first time I have heard her say something right here in Harrisburg was Greek tragedy.) "It is tragedy because Ginger refuses to compromise," she went on. "Bobby would have been on his knees in an instant but she just coldly looked from Roberta to the wall."

I got my first report at six in the evening. That night Roberta grew worse. What had started off as a simple asthma attack became critical. They moved her into the intensive care unit, hooked her up to the heart-lung machine. She had a weak heart when she was born but Bobby Lee and Ginger had kept that quiet, thinking someday a boy might not marry her for fear she could never bear him children.

By eleven o'clock the news was all over town. Preachers were writing sermons. Kind heads were bowed in prayer. I was watching the *Tonight Show* when Cynthia called me back. "The joke is over," she said. "They have killed their child. I heard Judge Watson ruled a mistrial."

"Does that mean I don't have to serve my community service?"

"This is serious, Letitia. There were four doctors in conference when I left the hospital. They aren't sure what to do."

"What do they think is wrong?"

"She's lost the will to live. I've seen it before but never in a little girl. She's always been fragile, more fragile than we know."

"Where is Bobby Lee?"

"They're both there. Sitting in the waiting room."

"I'm going there. I can miss work tomorrow if I need to."

"Then go if you think you should. What harm can it do. I've got to get to bed. I'm beat. I'm going back in at seven."

I put on my shoes and found my pocketbook and drove down to the hospital and went up on the elevator and found them there, in the hall outside her door. They looked like hurricane survivors, like people who had been through a flood.

"What can I do?" I asked. "Is Little Ginger in good hands?"

"She's with Ginger's mother." Bobby Lee stood up straighter, took my hands. "Thank you for coming down, Letitia. Stay with us awhile. You were magnificent this morning," he added. "I was so proud of you."

"I have to serve fifty hours of community service thanks to you. Why did you do this to all of us? Subpoena us like that."

"I don't know," Ginger said. "Something just came over me."

"And me," Bobby added.

"We told her we'd make up if she'd start breathing," Ginger added. "But she won't start. Maybe she's forgotten how." She began to weep. It was not the first time she had cried today, that much was clear. The front of her sweater was stained with tears. Tracks of my tears, I was thinking. It is a song the band has been playing.

"Play music for her," I said at once. "Go get a tape player and some music. What does she like to hear?"

"She loves Miles Davis," Bobby said. "It's all she's been listening to for weeks."

"Where's a tape player? I'll go get it. You can't leave."

"Will you?"

"Sure. Tell me where to go."

Bobby gave me a key to his house and I tore out of the hospital and drove over there. A little blue house on the wrong side of the tracks. At least it wasn't that filthy apartment he had at first. I opened the door with the key and found the tape player. It was one of those big heavy things teenagers carry around. I think its called a Bomb Box or something like that. I found the Miles Davis tapes and some of Gato Barbieri and John Coltrane and took them to the hospital as fast as I could go.

It was one-thirty when I got there but of course time has no meaning in an intensive care ward when a child has decided to stop breathing.

Bobby plugged in the Bomb Box and turned it on. We all stood around the bed watching to see if Roberta's eyes would open or her hands move. Nothing happened that you could see, but the music seemed to lighten up the room and the sickbed with it.

"You go on home, Letitia," Bobby said. "Take Ginger home too. I'll stay tonight. I'll sit here and change the tapes."

Which is what he did. In the morning Roberta began to listen to the music. In a week she was home. In ten days she was back in school. The doctors told her not to play the trumpet for a while but Ginger told me in the hall one day that she was playing it anyway. "How High the Moon," "Viva Emiliano Zapata," "My Funny Valentine." Her breathing is doubly precious to me, since she may be the only child her age in the United States interested in preserving the great jazz music of the past.

Nothing much has changed in Harrisburg since then. Except that people have gone back to taking marriage very, very seriously. If it's going to be that hard to get out of marriages we are going to have to be more careful about getting into them.

Remember Ginger and Bobby Lee. That's what parents around here are telling their children. Leda and the swan, Romeo and Juliet, Burt and Loni, Woody and Mia, Prince Charles and Princess Di, Bobby Lee and Ginger, whatever it takes to get the point across.

Aside from that, summer is here. The woman dentist has taken up with the carpenter in the OFF DUTY shirt. We all go down to the Lonely and read foreign newspapers and eat cake. The band plays on. As for me, I'm a heroine in certain circles now and will always be. I wish my mother could have seen me at that trial. She was the newspaper editor in this town and a free-thinker from the word go. I think she would have been proud of me. And the first to warn me about pride.

The Uninsured

August 1, 1993

Dear Blue Cross, Blue Shield,

I got your letter advising me that you are redoing our health insurance plans. I guess this means you are going to be raising our rates again. I know you *want* to raise my rates since for the past ten years it has cost you more to pay my psychiatrist than you have collected from me. We may be getting tired of each other. It may be time to sever our relationship especially since I am about to cut down on the number of times I see him each week and aside from that am in perfect health.

Yours most sincerely,
Rhoda K. Manning

September 3, 1993

Dear Blue Cross, Blue Shield,

While I wait to see if you have figured out a way to make money from me instead of me making money from you I have done the following at your expense. Had a mammogram and Pap smear. Had a bone density evaluation and scan. Had an AIDS test. Had a blood profile and blood pressure check. Had ten small skin lesions removed from my hands and arm and lower legs. Had all my prescription drugs filled.

I have also driven up to Jackson, Mississippi, to visit my eighty-six-year-old parents and found them both in perfect health. From all these tests and the evidence of my genes it is clear that, barring accidents, I will live to be about ninety years old with no bone, heart, liver, lung, or brain disease. My blood pressure is ninety over sixty. My bone density is that of a thirty-year-old woman. It is obvious that if you raise my rates I will have to consider bailing out of your Flex-Plan.

Yours most sincerely,
Rhoda K. Manning

October 10, 1993

Dear Blue Cross, Blue Shield,

I have applied to the John Alden Insurance Company of Springfield, Illinois, for inclusion in their Jali-Care Program. I am going to let the two of you bid for my healthy body. A healthy body, I might add, that has been shored up by twenty years of psychotherapy which has taught me to love, care for, and value myself.

The John Alden representative in our area has come to visit me. He is a very nice man about my age who once was a forest ranger in Oregon. We chatted and drank bottled water and he took my medical history. He said that, with the exception of my twenty years of psychotherapy, he was certain my record would be well received at the John Alden Jali-Care Evaluation Center. "I am not mentally disturbed," I told him. "I am a writer. The reason I have never been blocked is because I have been in psychotherapy and therefore able to withstand the pressures of society upon my artistic nature. It is also the reason I have never been depressed or had accidents."

You people at Blue Cross may think the four hundred dollars a month it has cost you to pay my psychiatrist is a lot of money but think of what it might have cost you if I had harmed myself with food or drink or drugs or unhappy love affairs. You are coming out ahead, I assure you.

Well, this is just to keep you updated while I wait for my letter telling me about the restructuring of Farm Policy Group Seven's Comprehensive Major Medical Coverage for the Future.

Yours most truly,
Rhoda K. Manning

November 7, 1993

Dear Blue Cross, Blue Shield,

I just got my flu shot. I didn't charge it to you since I just ran by the Mediquik and it only cost five dollars so I thought it wasn't worth the paperwork. I have been racking my brain trying to think of something else I can have done to myself before I bail out of the health insurance business and devote myself to staying in perfect health until I am sixty-five and can get some of my tax dollars back in Medicare.

The John Alden Insurance Company sent a sweet young woman out to do a medical check on me. She called one afternoon at four and asked if she could come the next day at noon. I guess that was to make sure I wasn't forewarned in case I secretly smoke or drink. I told her to come on and she said I had to fast from eight that night until noon. That was the hard part. I never go eight hours without food as I believe in controlling the blood sugar levels at all times.

She arrived promptly at noon. It turns out she lives in my part of town. She said when she was ready to buy a house she asked a policeman where the safest place in town was and he said these old neighborhoods on the mountain. The houses were built in the 'sixties and look like there would be nothing here to steal.

She came in and weighed me on a pair of scales she carries with her in a carpet bag. Then she drew blood and separated it in various little cylinders and sealed them up and put them in a pack to be taken by Federal Express to a lab in Kansas City. I had to sign a paper saying they could do an AIDS test. That's two in two months' time. I was glad to do it. As I told Sharon Cane, that's her name, if you aren't part of the solution, you are part of the problem. A gay friend of mine tells that to anyone who won't be tested for HIV.

Next I gave Sharon a urine speciman. She explained to me that they could tell from it if I had smoked a cigarette in the last ten days or had a drink. I have not had a drink in twenty years. A hypnotist in New Orleans talked me out of that years ago.

The way I feel now is that if the John Alden Jali-Care people don't have enough sense to want my $157.69 a month after all of this they can go to hell.

You may think from the tone of this letter that I am getting mad at you, but you would be wrong. I have appreciated all those checks for fifty percent of my psychotherapy. I don't blame you for trying to figure out a way to get your money back but I don't think there's any reason for me to give it to you.

Yours sincerely,
Rhoda K. Manning

December 4, 1993

Dear Blue Cross, Blue Shield,

John Alden Jali-Care is considering my application. I passed all my physical tests with flying colors but they are worried about the years of psychotherapy and have requested a letter from my psychotherapist, which he is drafting now.

I assume that the reason I haven't heard from you about my policy is that you have been busy with the lawsuit the Arkansas Senate is bringing against you for raising all the rates of people with preexisting conditions to such exorbitant amounts that they (we) are all going to have to quit. In the meantime I am pursuing other options as I have told you in our correspondence.

It said in the paper today that you had begun all this in order to get ready for the great Health Care Debate of 1994. Well, all I can say is I am losing interest in the whole thing. I have always paid for the things that made a real difference to my health, like eyeglasses, running shoes, good books, good music, movies, food. I know how to go to Mediquik and get shots. Not to mention the dentist, which you do not cover either.

Good luck with your lawsuit.

Yours sincerely,
Rhoda Manning

December 5, 1993

Dear John Alden Jali-Care,

Here is the letter from my psychiatrist which you requested. From it you will see that the only reason I have been going to him all these years is because I am a writer. It has nothing whatsoever to do with health problems. It is preventive medicine, and besides, I'm cutting down on my sessions and you won't be responsible for them anyway as they are a preexisting condition. Hope everything is clear now.

Yours most sincerely,
Rhoda K. Manning

December 15, 1993

Dear Blue Cross, Blue Shield,

I received your offer to continue to provide me with health insurance for $567.69 a month with a three-thousand-dollar deductible and a fifty-thousand-dollar stop-loss. I have decided to decline this offer. It's been nice doing business with you but I think I'll quit while I'm ahead.

Stay well,
Rhoda Manning

January 1, 1994

Dear Blue Cross, Blue Shield,

This is my first day of being uninsured. It feels great. I have had the snow shoveled from my sidewalk, am wearing my seat belt at all times, and have invested two thousand, three hundred dollars in a new Exercycle from the Stairmaster people.

If I subtract the one thousand, six hundred and seventy dollars quarterly payment I would have sent you that is only about seven hundred dollars for the Exercycle.

Looking ahead to the second quarterly payment I have bought a new fur jacket to keep me from catching cold. With the two hundred dollars I saved by having all my prescriptions filled in 1993 I bought a matching hat and muff.

Yours for a happy and healthy new year,
Rhoda Manning

February 1, 1994

Dear Blue Cross, Blue Shield,

Now that a month has passed and all is well I have decided to look ahead to the money I would be paying you the next few years and put in a lap pool. The pool people don't have much to do this time of year and have given me a twenty percent discount.

February 27, 1994   Sorry I didn't get this off sooner but they came and started digging the hole for the pool and it's been chaos around here. All is well now. The pool is nine feet wide and sixty-nine feet long. It has an electric cover that can be opened or closed from a switch in the kitchen. Talk about high technology.

Do you remember Sharon Cane, who came to draw blood for the John Alden Jali-Care Evaluation? Well, she is swimming with me three days a week. She starts at one end and I start at the other to make waves for each other to swim against. We usually bet five dollars on who can swim the most laps in an hour. A lot of times we lose count because we are having so much fun. I am down to seeing my analyst three times a month now that I have to pay for it. No ill effects so far, only I can tell I am not working as hard as I was when I had him to drive me to it. Why should I work seven days a week? It's almost spring. The long winter is over and I didn't catch the flu. That five-dollar flu shot may be the best money I spent all year.

Yours for a healthy America,
Rhoda Manning

March 19, 1994

Dear Blue Cross, Blue Shield,

I had a long talk with my ninety-year-old neighbor, Kassie Martin, yesterday. She praised me for letting my insurance run out. She said that if I have a stroke or a heart attack it is best to arrive at the hospital uninsured as that might lower the chances of them putting you on a life support machine. She has seen many unpleasant things happen to older people who arrive at the hospital fully insured. Greed is nothing new in the world but why should we be victims of it?

On another note I have only had one prescription filled since I left you. I drove around town doing some comparison shopping. That pharmacy that used to fill my prescriptions is twice as high as the one at Wal-Mart. You should look into this.

Yours in spring,
Rhoda Manning

March 21, 1994

Dear Blue Cross, Blue Shield,

Well, it looks like John Alden Jali-Care is going to come through with a cheap policy for me. Their representative called this morning to say all they needed now were some copies of my books with pages marked showing them where I used the information I got in psychotherapy to help my writing.

It's difficult to believe that health care professions could be that unlettered and that dumb, isn't it? Now that I have gotten accustomed to being uninsured and dependent on myself it is going to be hard for me to pay anyone anything for health insurance. I'll let you know what I decide.

Stay well,
Rhoda Manning

March 26, 1994

Dear Blue Cross, Blue Shield,

I can't bring myself to take John Alden up on their offer. Why would I want to do business with people who are dumber than I am?

Instead, I have decided to go to Italy. A hotel near the Ponte Vecchio. I don't know where that is yet, but I will soon. A young man of my acquaintance who speaks perfect French and Italian is going with me. We are going to stay at a hotel in Rome where Sartre and Buckminster Fuller and Isamu Naguchi and lots of other artists stayed. If I get sick in Italy, who cares? What could I have that Italian pasta and Italian men couldn't cure? We are going to Rome for twelve days and then to Florence for seven.

> Arrivederci,
> Rhoda Manning

April 10, 1994

Dear Blue Cross, Blue Shield,

Well, here we are in Florence after a heavenly time in Rome. The sun is shining and the world seems "to lie before us like a field of dreams, so various, so beautiful, so new." We arrived yesterday morning and walked around for a while. Then we slept awhile and ate dinner in a piazza. Tomorrow we will go to see the Uffizi Gallery. There are paintings there by Botticelli, Titian, and Raphael, to name a few. I'll probably faint, but don't worry, it won't cost you any money.

It's pretty amazing to step off an airplane and be in Italy. Thanks so much for making this possible by raising my rates so much that I couldn't keep my insurance.

I picked up a paper as I was leaving Fayetteville and noticed that you had made a deal with State Farm to keep everyone's group policies in effect another year with only a twenty percent increase. I started to call my insurance agent and see if I could get in on that but then I decided to hell with it. Why should I pay you three thousand dollars a year? That's ten more nights in first-class hotels in Tuscany. Well, stay well. This is the last letter I am going to write to you. I'm going to see paintings, eat Italian food, then rent a sports car and drive up to the mountains to go skiing. My young lover and I have a motto. We'll take today. I know we aren't the first to think of that but it still works.

Arrivederci,
Rhoda

Love of My Life

♂

AN AFTERNOON in August. I am in my kitchen in the little frame house on Colonial Drive in Jackson, Mississippi. I am separated from the father of my children. They are six and five and two years old. I am five feet four inches tall. I am muscular and strong. I have strong bones and red hair and straight legs. I am very, very tan. I am wearing sandals, a pair of blue cotton shorts, a tight blue-and-white-striped blouse. I have been taking Dexedrine. I take it three or four days a week. I take Dexedrine and diuretics. I never eat. Food is the enemy of what I want. I don't know what I want but I know how to get it. If I am beautiful, the thing I want will show up. I've been waiting since I was fourteen years old for the thing I want. Once I thought it was the father of my children. Once I thought it was a federal judge my father's age. I never thought it was the children. They are the price I have to pay for looking for it. I don't have to pay anymore. I had a tubal ligation. I don't have to worry about getting pregnant anymore but still I worry.

I am getting closer to what I want. I can feel it in the hot August air, in the sunlight beating down upon the sidewalk and the two-car garage and the heads of the children. I can taste it in the gin I drink. Can hear it in the music on the phonograph. My daddy is a rich man. My husband worked for him. I have a new house, a new car. I'm at home. No one can hurt me now. My father will not let them. My brothers will not let them. I am safe now. I am almost where I want to be.

Outside, in the fenced-in yard, the five- and six-year-old are playing in the water. They have a plastic pool filled with water and a hose and a Slip-and-Slide. They are happy. They've been playing for a long time without having a fight. In a few minutes my mother will come and get them and take them off to spend the night. The maid left at four and Mother's coming at five to pick them up. The only one I have to take care of is Teddy and he's asleep. I walk around my kitchen cutting up vegetables and cooking things. It is safe to cook. I took a Dexedrine this morning. You couldn't push food in my mouth.

I have a new record on the record player. Johnny Cash singing about his Indian blood. I'm into Indians today. I feel their pain, know their sorrow, ride the plains with the braves, wait for them to come to me at night. I've had the record for two days. I play it over and over. It has become me. I know the words by heart.

I put a tray of biscuits in the oven. I turn the water on to boil beneath a pan of new potatoes. I have been separated from my husband for a week. It's wonderful. I am free, and I cannot have another baby no matter what I do. I can fall in love with anyone. I can have a lover, or two lovers, or maybe three. My brothers and my daddy will let me do anything I want to do.

I stop. A dark thought has entered me. I might not get into the Casual Club, the luncheon club my mother wants me to get into. I am waiting for an invitation. Well, surely they will want me. I am so pretty. My daddy is so rich.

A car drives up. It is my mother. We round up the boys and pack their bags and put them in her car. "I wish you'd come out too," my mother says. "When the baby wakes up get dressed and come to dinner." She stands at the door. She is wearing her suspicious look. She doesn't like the way I look. She wants to know what I'm up to.

"I might. I don't think I can. Avery might come over." It's a lie. Avery is the daughter of her best friend who is married to the mayor.

Avery is the president of the Casual Club. Mother wants me to be friends with Avery.

"Oh, that's nice. Well, call in a while. Call and let us know what you're doing." She is smiling, almost smiling. The boys are fighting in the backseat of the car. "Well, I'd better go on and take them. Call us, Rhoda. Call and let me know where you are."

She drives off. Malcolm and Jimmy are fighting away. It is nineteen sixty-three. There are no seat belts. It has barely begun to dawn on us that we need them. Children fall against dashboards, cut their heads, we tell them not to stand up on the seats.

I think I am barefooted now. The baby is still asleep. As soon as mother leaves I go out onto the patio to clean up the mess the children made. I open the drain on the plastic pool. Water spills out on the patio. I walk around in it. I pull the ugly plastic Slip-and-Slide over behind the air-conditioning unit so I won't have to look at it. I have a photograph of myself at this time, in this place. I am very very thin. My half-wet shirt sticks to my ribs and breasts; beneath my shorts my tanned legs are straight and shapely. I am so young. I am twenty-six years old. My hair is cut in a chin-length bob with a part on the side. I wear a barrette in my hair. If I am wearing blue, the barrette is blue. On this day, the day I met my one true love, the Indian man, the man who was my equal, who was good enough for me, on this day I think the barrette was blue. It must have been blue because my shorts were blue.

I walked back into the kitchen from the patio, making wet footprints on the waxed floor, singing along to the music. I started the record over. I strummed the air. It was my blue guitar.

Dudley's black Pontiac pulled up into the driveway behind my new black station wagon. I saw him get out, laughing and talking to his passenger. His passenger got out and they came into the kitchen through the screen door. "Come listen to Johnny Cash," I said. "God, it's so good. I just adore it. What are you doing here?"

"We're playing in a tournament at the club. This is Raine Matasick, Rhoda. My sister, Raine. He's my partner." I shook his hand. I took him in. Too ugly. Too foreign. Too dark-skinned. Not fat, but big, so big. Too big. He kept on smiling. He waited with his smile. He stood back while Dudley and I talked.

"What are you doing later?" Dudley asked. "There's a party at the club. They're going to raffle off the players. It's a Calcutta. You want to go with us? Sally's going."

"You can buy us," Raine suggested. "Dudley and me'll come cheap."

"Don't let him fool you," Dudley said. "He won the state tournament last year."

"Oh, yeah." I was getting interested. Not in Raine, but in the Calcutta, whatever that turned out to be. A party at the club. I could wear my new mauve linen dress. "God, my hair's a mess. You want a drink?"

"Not now," Dudley said. He put his hand on Raine's arm. "You ought to go with us, Sister. Everyone in the state's there. This is a big tournament."

"I'll have a glass of water," Raine said. He followed me to the sink and stood beside me while I filled the glass. I had a sense of the immensity of the man. Not that he was that tall or big. He was six foot three or four. It wasn't that. It was something else, a sense of mass or power. A smell that didn't belong in the same world with the Casual Club. Too dark, too big, too foreign. I looked up at him while I filled the glass. His eyes were dark, like mine. Dark sweet eyes. I would take him for an admirer. I wanted plenty of admirers. "I wish you'd sit down and listen to this music," I said. "I'm just crazy about it. I don't listen to another thing."

Teddy came walking into the room. He was wearing a wet diaper and carrying his bottle. He was still half asleep. He stopped in the middle of the room and looked around. Raine went over to him and knelt beside him and began to have a conversation. Teddy smiled. He pulled the bottle out of his mouth and hit Raine with it. They laughed together. Then Teddy came over and grabbed me around the legs. "I'll have to get a baby-sitter," I said. "I don't know who I'll find this late."

"Call Sally," Dudley said. "She's got a list. Well, listen, Sister,

we've got to go. We have to meet some people down at the Sun and
Sand and then we've got to go change clothes."

"My clubs are still in my car," Raine said. "I need to put them in
my trunk."

I picked up Teddy and held him while they left. I was still so un-
interested in this man I could pick up a child in a wet diaper and hold
him against my half-wet blue-and-white-striped cotton shirt and
stand in the carport barefoot and wave as they drove away. I pulled
Teddy's diapers off and left them in the carport and took him inside
and put him in the tub. While he played in the water I called a baby-
sitter. I walked back into the kitchen and turned the record over and
played the other side.

It was exciting to think of going out alone. When I went out with
my husband I had a horrible time. No matter how many martinis I
drank it was always an awful time. Now I was separated. Now I could
go out somewhere and have a good time. Even if it was only my
brother and his wife and this big, dark man who was a champion
golfer. Still, I had a funny feeling. I was very excited about this
evening. As soon as I had a baby-sitter lined up I got Teddy out of the
tub and dressed him and gave him some biscuits to eat and then I
went into the bathroom and washed my hair and rolled it up. I took
my new mauve dress out of the closet and laid it on the bed. I took
out earrings and a gold bracelet. I gave Teddy some cold fried chicken
and a bowl of cereal and some toys to play with on the kitchen floor.
I started getting dressed. I put on my new perfume, Jungle Gardenia.
I put on makeup. I dried my hair and combed it. As soon as the baby-
sitter arrived and took Teddy off to the backyard, I put on the dress.
I looked at myself in the mirror. I was beautiful. More beautiful than
I had ever been in my life. They had tried to kill me with the babies.
They had tried to ruin and kill me and make me ugly but it had not
worked. I had outwitted them. I was separated now and I was going
out to the Jackson Country Club and find out what I wanted. I
didn't know what I wanted but I believed it existed. It existed and
when I saw it I would know it. I took an ice-cold glass out of the
freezer and filled it with vodka. I stood in the kitchen looking out to-

ward the carport. Soon they would come to get me. They would take me to the place where my life would begin.

After a long time he came. It was dark when he came so it must have been very late. I must have had another drink and played the Indian recording many times. The baby-sitter must have taken Teddy to his room to read to him and I must have gotten tired of waiting and finally a car drove up in the carport and I went out the screen door to yell at my brother for being late. Only it wasn't my brother. It was Raine and he was alone.

Many years later, after it was over, after he had come into my life and changed it, wrecked it and emblazoned it, after I had married a rich Jewish lawyer and made him miserable, after ten years, after I had divorced the lawyer and gone off to live in the Ozark mountains to write my books. After the marriages and the divorces and the beginning of the books. After the week Raine drove me to Arkansas to begin my writing life. After I left the lawyer and took up with Raine again, after so many strange and eventful years. After all of that I heard the rest of the story of that day. I heard it from Dudley on his sixtieth birthday. At his birthday party, late in the evening, beside the lake, at the borrowed river mansion. "We were driving home from the first day of the tournament," Dudley said. "We'd been hitting so well we thought we were going to win. It was the state team tournament. You never did pay much attention to sports unless you were playing, did you, Shortie?"

"No. Go on. So what happened then?"

"We were going by your neighborhood and I said, 'Raine, what would you rather do? Go down to the Sun and Sand and find some working girls or meet my sister?'

" 'You and Ingersol have a sister?'

" 'She just moved back here. Her crazy little husband was working for us for a while. Then she ran him off. You might like her.'

" 'You and Ingersol have a sister. I don't think I can take it.' Then we started laughing and I slowed the car down.

" 'She lives over by the Colonial Country Club. Which will it be?'

" 'If you have a sister I want to meet her.' Raine sat back in the seat and I turned off the four-lane into your neighborhood and brought him to you." Dudley was holding a glass of wine. We were sitting on a double bench on a bluff above the river. He looked at me out of his one good eye and his face got the soft, puffy look it wore when he desired me. When he used to come to the door of my room when he was fifteen and say things to me and offer to give me things and take me places. Get out of here, Dudley, I always answered. Later, when we were older, one night he offered me fifty thousand dollars to sleep with him and I still turned him down. The pleasure of denying him something that he wanted was worth an empire of gold. "Are you glad I did?" he ended.

"It's a good thing I was listening to Johnny Cash that week. I was in my Indian mood. I wanted to meet an Indian. Yeah, I'm glad you did. He was the love of my life. The only man I ever loved that I thought, really believed, was good enough for me." I stared into Dudley's good eye. I guess he is my brother. I know he is my brother. There but for the grace of God and one X chromosome and the fact that he was born first, go I.

"I love you, Dudley," I said. "I'm glad you are my brother."

So Raine got out of his Lincoln Continental and came into my kitchen apologizing for being late and not blaming it on Dudley although, since I always blamed everything on Dudley, I'm sure I did. Then I told the baby-sitter good-bye and gave her the phone number of the Jackson Country Club and we went out and got into the car. I think it had already started. Before I noticed how other men treated him. Before Dudley or one of them or maybe Raine himself told me he had been the best football player in the South. Since I knew nothing about football except the clothes I wore to games and the parties afterward and cared less. Since I never could remember what position he had played. Since only when I saw his name on the back of the program at an Ole Miss game, with his records still intact after seven years, or when men would talk about him and games he'd played and runs he'd made and touchdowns he had scored and passes he had caught, did I begin to envision him playing football. What I envisioned suited the image of the body that lay by mine, that will always be the yardstick against which I measure other men, and because of which I understand when I see love or read about it and say to myself, I had that, I was not stinted, my own true love, my one and only own true love.

And I was his. But that was later. On this night, when I entered the ballroom of the Jackson Country Club on his arm I may have thought that the obeisance was for me. I was so stuck on myself, on my daddy's money and my newfound freedom and my thin tan body in my new mauve dress, I may actually have thought that feeling of waters parting was about me. All evening I kept going away from him and flirting with other men and then going to find him again. He was so solid, it was like going to Hercules or Odysseus, so solid, so still. Going into his presence was not like anything I had ever known. Except, perhaps, my father, when I was young.

I don't think we stayed long at the party. We stayed for the Calcutta and there was a large blackboard and everyone was very drunk and bought the players for ridiculous sums. Dudley bought himself and Raine. Either Dudley did or a rich girl from the Delta did. After that Raine and I went out a side door and got into his car and went to a motel. It was pretty simple really. We got into his car and he took me in his arms and began to kiss me. Devour me. Gently, gently, tenderly, almost in tears. I will fall in love with you, he said. He had not had a thing to drink. He never drank. Since he was eighteen years old and got drunk one night and tried to kill a man he had never had a drink. I was drunk but I was also sober. The enormity of what was happening sobered me. I can remember every moment of that night. I can remember him rising above me on the bed and telling me he would never fuck me again when I was drunk. I can remember him taking me home. Late, very late. The baby-sitter had called my mother and her mother and the country club. I remember him saying that he loved me. I remember the way he smelled. The next day my skin smelt of him. My left and my right arm. I did not take a bath until late in the afternoon. Until after he called and said he had to see me.

★ ★ ★

"We lost the tournament," Dudley was saying. Sitting on the bench by the river looking at me with his one good eye. "I guess that was your fault, Shortie."

"You were pimping for him. You set me up."

"You said you weren't sorry."

"I'm not," I answered. "I just want to get the story straight."

I didn't see him the next day. It was the second day, while the maid was at my house, he came and got me in the Lincoln and we drove somewhere, I don't know where, perhaps along the new four-lane highway that my father had built. "I've never felt this way about a woman," he said. "I don't know what to do." He stopped the car and kissed me. Then he drove to a park and we talked like generals planning a war. Staccato, fast, intense, the terrible intensity of desire. "I'm still married. I don't have a divorce."

"So am I. My wife's crazy."

"Where do you live?"

"In an apartment."

"We can't do it openly. He might take my children."

"She'll take mine."

"Where will we go?"

"Now?"

"No, all the time."

"We'll get an apartment."

"Okay, let's go get one."

Perhaps we didn't say all that that day. Perhaps all we did that day was go downtown to a hotel and make love until the sun went down. I called the maid and offered to pay her three times the amount she made. I bribed and begged her. I was two hours late. We gave her all the money that we had. We gave her too much money and she looked him up and down and shook her head. Even the maid understood. The children were there when we got home. He didn't bribe them. He sat down in a chair and let them come to him.

They didn't care. They were lonesome for their father but they were too young to know that Raine was part of that. They liked him.

He went out into the backyard and threw balls to them. We got a baby-sitter. We went out to dinner and went back to the hotel and made love some more. My mother called me about fifty times. The maid and the baby-sitter wrote the messages down. It was nineteen sixty-three. There weren't any answering machines.

While we were at the hotel my mother and father came and got the children and took them to the country. They paid the baby-sitter. They called Dudley and asked him what was going on.

In the hotel room I lay upon his body and told him the story of my life. He told me how he had acquired the different scars. The worst scars were on his legs. He didn't get them on the football field. He got them in an automobile accident when a drunk man was driving. He had not thought it could happen to him. After it was over he couldn't play football anymore. He had to learn to sell insurance and municipal bonds. He learned how to play golf. He put his trophies away. He wasn't a has-been. He was a great athlete who had had a bad break. It didn't matter. In a year he was the golf champion of the state of Mississippi. People bowed their heads when he came into a room. He was the quietest, gentlest man I have ever known. He had the softest skin. He had the strangest, most unforgettable smell. He was half Italian and half Cherokee Indian. The love of my life. The one and only love.

Even long ago, when it was nearer, I could never remember making love to him. We would enter a room and our bodies would meld. It was absolutely simple. It had a beginning and a middle and an end. I smelled like Jungle Gardenia or Estée Lauder or L'Heure Bleue. He smelled of shaving cream and the wild terrible smell of his body, of physical power and cunning and coordination that was unlike any-thing I had ever known. Except for my father. My father was that strong, his shoulders were that powerful, that wide, that still. Maybe this man was my father to the tenth power. I lay upon his body and talked to him. Later, I would lie upon his body and cry and he would pat me like a child. He was never in a hurry. He never made a mis-take or wasted a motion or dropped anything. He never stopped saying he loved me and I never stopped believing it. Wherever he is, until my death or his death, that time is always there, indelible upon my brain and his brain. My own true love. The man with the Indian blood and the dark skin and the gentle eyes. The uncircumcised man. Because of him I know what books and stories mean when men and women love each other without stint or question, in defiance of order, in defiance of self-interest or knowledge or pain. Sex was only part of it. Sex was where it took place, as on a stage. But sex was not what it was about. It was because I thought he was good enough for me. Because he believed I would one day be his equal.

I can hear his voice. So deep and rich and slowed down to a Southern cadence. Full of humor and pathos. A black man's voice, a foreign voice. It was not the voice of men who married the ladies of the Casual Club or escorted their daughters to the debutante balls. Although his family would come to that, because of him, because he was a hero and they were the sons and daughters of a hero and could get soft and still be safe.

Then it was fall and we had found an apartment and I lived in it with a roommate and he only came there. He didn't live there because his wife was pregnant. When I found out about it I went crazy. I beat upon his shoulders. I got drunk and yelled at him and woke the neighbors. I called him in the middle of the night and he would get into his car and come to where I was and say he loved me and cry. Lots of times he cried. He cried because he loved me. He suffered because of me. I loved to make him suffer. He brought his children to see me and I was nice to them. They sat in my apartment being very polite and drank the Cokes I gave them and told me about their schools. I thought they were ugly children. He must have known I thought that. After that evening I never had to see them again. Instead he came and got me and took me to the airport and we flew off to North Carolina in his plane. We rented a car. We drove around North Carolina and I waited outside offices while he sold municipal bonds to men.

★ ★ ★

We took long trips together while he sold these bonds. He had several offices around Jackson. And several business partners. They were massive quiet men who had played football with him. Some were men who had thrown passes to him. Others were men who had made holes for him to run through. I didn't know how to talk to them. They were too far away from what I knew. But Raine was not. He could be anything he wanted to be. He made people like him. He was likable and kind, quiet and dependable. Until me he had not been crazy.

I wondered if he only liked my daddy's money. But he knew it was not mine. Later, after I left him and began to find other men, he took one of the men out to lunch one day and told him the money was not mine, would not ever be mine because women didn't get to have the money in my family.

It was me he loved. Because he thought I would someday be his equal, was already his equal because of something in me that did not give up, never stopped looking, never stopped wanting, never gave in or compromised. Later, when I had my books and my name in the papers, he would call and tell me he was proud of me, would show up at my autograph parties and stand against a wall and look at me.

II

I had found something worth wanting, worth suffering for. With this blood in me that came from my daddy and liked to fight, I had found something worth fighting for. But who was I to fight, his broken-hearted wife and her children and her unborn baby?

At Christmas of that year he had to go to Chicago to a reunion of his old football team. He had been Rookie of the Year. Had scored the most points of anyone in the backfield. Then he had the accident and it was over. But these men did not forget. Life did cruel things to men and men could bear it. Could go on loving each other in this strange fraternity of professional sports, where they did for a living what lesser men dreamed of doing, outran, outlasted, outwilled each other on a playing field. Anyone could have bad luck. They loved Raine for taking the bad luck away from them. They asked him about his knees.

We had gone out to dinner with these men when they passed through Jackson, Mississippi, or when they lived in one of the towns we flew to in the airplane or drove to in the Lincoln. So now, to make me feel better about Christmas, we were going up there together to join their annual celebration.

This was the first time I knew how much he lied to me. He had lied to me all along but I had not really understood it. I was vain and I had not been lied to before. The men who marry girls whose mothers go to the Casual Club don't lie to people until they are middle-aged. They have a code. They marry you and tell you the truth until the time when they really fall in love. Then they lie to spare your feelings. They take upon themselves the burden of the lie to spare you pain.

The world that belonged to this Indian-Italian man was not that world. In his world you took what you needed no matter what the cost. If the woman yelled at you and threw things across the room, you put your arms up before your face and took the blows. Then you begged and said you loved her, you cried if necessary, you bought her sofas and cars and rings with large stones your friends got for you on the black market.

So I bought a beautiful new evening suit I saw in *Vogue* magazine and packed it in a suitcase and counted off the days until I flew with him to Chicago.

Where were my children while this was going on? I had forgotten them. My brother Dudley told my father I was going to bring Raine in and marry him. Take care of the kids, he might have said. Let Rhoda capture him.

Even my father was not immune to Raine's glory, his picture in the Hall of Fame, his name on the back of programs, his gentle manner when he came into my parents' home. Yes, my mother had seen him now. My mother knew I went to rooms and took off my clothes and lay down with this huge Indian-Italian man. She wore an expression that said this was the worst thing that had ever happened to her.

Still, she paid thousands of dollars every year for fifty-yard-line seats in the stadium where he had been the hero. She read the programs too. She was not immune. Then too, he courted her. Looked up at her with his dark sweet eyes and told her that he loved me, that I was the love of his life, that he would never harm me in any way.

I enrolled in a college in the town. A small, private college in the old part of town. I went to classes when Raine wasn't around. It was the excuse for the apartment. It was what my mother told her friends at the Casual Club.

I remember packing a suitcase to go to Chicago. I remember putting my beautiful black pantsuit with lapels of black satin and the little white satin blouse into the suitcase and closing the top. I remember the drive to Nashville where we caught the plane to Chicago. I remember the drive home on the eve of Christmas Eve and how we saw the dark shape on the horizon, just at dusk, halfway between Nashville and home. I thought it was a flying saucer. I told everyone I had seen a flying saucer and Raine always said he saw it too. But I would remember anything rather than remember what happened in Chicago.

We went to the Palmer House Hotel where he had been staying on the night he had the accident that ended his career. He stayed there out of some perverse desire not to shield himself from unpleasant things. I had never stayed at a hotel that fine with a man who could pay for it with his own money. But I did not notice the hotel. All I knew was that on that night after we arrived I would put on my new dress and go to the banquet with Raine. As though I were his wife, in place of his wife, he would take me to the place that meant the most to him.

We arrived late one evening. It was bitterly cold outside. I have never been that cold in my life. The wind came around the corners of the buildings and made you run back inside. We left the hotel and he shielded me with his body and we went to a bar where pictures of him were on the walls. His friends were there and we sat at a small table and had dinner with two men who had been referees at the games. They told me stories of his glory. They walked around the bar with me. They showed me pictures of him. Young and sweet and dark, in his football uniform, holding the ball cradled in his arm. I held his hand beneath the table and thought how big it was, how perfectly designed for this football that had given him his power in the world.

He brought me here to see these pictures, I decided. But I came to go with him to the banquet as his wife. First this banquet, then he will get a divorce. As soon as this unnecessary baby that she had only to keep him gets here. As soon as that is over I will take him away from his ugly children and his ugly wife and give him to my sons for their father. To my father for a son, to my brothers for a friend, this man I love, this man who is strong enough for me, who can dodge the things I throw at him, who can bear the pain I cause him because I am his one and only love, the one he cannot bear to be without.

The next day there was a football game in the stadium where he had played. We sat on the sidelines on folding chairs. Other men and their wives were there. It was so cold they had to bring me a cape like the ones the players wore on the bench. They draped it over me. A boy brought paper bags and put them on my feet. I was a geisha at a football game, being cared for by men who could withstand the cold.

A thin black man kept running down the side of the field and making touchdowns. Raine was like that, the other men said to me. Until the black man no one has done the thing he did for us. I held his arm. I watched his face as they said these things to me. I had never seen him happy. Until this day, sitting on those folding chairs in the cold I had never known him to be happy. With me he was in such sadness, such pain. He knew he could not keep me and it made him sad. My beauty vanished when we were together. There was no beauty in me now. Only this terrible Dexedrine thinness and this will to keep and overcome him.

★ ★ ★

Think how desirable it was to him. This young girl from the Casual Club who had been turned into a tiger. Later, back in our room, we fucked each other without mercy. We beat upon each other's body, taking all the pleasure that we could, giving nothing away, taking, taking, taking.

At five o'clock he dressed for the banquet. He went downstairs to meet someone. He said he would come back for me at six. I dressed in my new dress. I ordered a martini from room service. Then I did not drink it. Six o'clock came. He was not there. Seven o'clock came. He did not come. The banquet started at seven. Something terrible must have happened. I called the banquet but they said he was not there. I drank the martini and ordered another one. Eight o'clock and nine o'clock came and went and still he was not there. I called the banquet over and over again. Finally a waiter told me Mr. Matasick had been there but he wasn't there anymore. The banquet was over. They had all gone home. I sat on the bed in my dress. Beware of all enterprises that require new clothes.

At ten-thirty he returned to the room and let me yell at him. I screamed at him. I beat upon him and tore him with my fingernails. He begged me not to hate him. He said he loved me until death. He said he brought me here because he loved me. I cried myself to sleep on gin.

Driving home was when we saw the flying saucer. Coming home on the eve of Christmas Eve. The Christmas before the New Year's Eve when I took the Antabuse and drank on it and almost died, begged to die, wanted to die to punish him.

Money was part of it. That Lincoln Continental with its seats of whitest leather. My father's money, whether I would have it or not. He had never had a poor woman in his life. They were all wealthy women, the ones before me and the ones who followed. The ones who didn't count. He said they didn't count and I believed him.

There is only one love like that, one white hot moment when a man and a woman ask everything of each other, ask sacrifice and pain and dishonesty. Mostly pain. Alone with him in rooms, in my apartment in the afternoons when my roommate wasn't there, beside him or on top of him with his dick buried deep within me. My body pulling on him to empty him and make him suffer.

James Rainey Matasick, the name is enough to make men feel inferior. Now, in my old age, sometimes I drop it in the lap of a man if he tries to flirt with me. If he's the right age, if he looks like an old high school athlete, if he dreamed of glory, I let him make his move and then I ask him if he saw Raine play. He was my lover, I say. My one and only love.

It would be nine years before I needed him again. Before I called and told him to come save me. Only this time I would be richer, surer, older. I don't know why I called him then, only I had some Dexedrine for the first time in several years and I wanted him to take me to a place he knew about, a place that once he had taken me to. I wanted to go to Arkansas. The only time I had ever set foot in Arkansas was when Raine took me to Little Rock to visit his sister who was dying in a veterans' hospital. He had cried in my arms after he saw her and on the way home we ran out of gasoline outside of Dumas and had to walk a mile to catch a ride to a service station.

Anyway, I called and told him I had to go to Fayetteville, Arkansas, to go to school to learn how to be a writer and he met me in Vicksburg and drove me there. I made him wait outside the English Department while I went in to meet my professors. As I said, I always forgot who he was. I never thought of him as anything on earth but my lover. "Raine Matasick is outside in the car?" my professor said. "My God in heaven, tell him to come in."

III

His integrity was darkened by the lies he told to make me love him. One day at noon, at lunch somewhere, one of those expensive restaurants that come and go in Jackson like the tides, over Bloody Marys and lobster salad, in a booth, I think, not a table, although it may have been a table . . . what he said removed us from the rest of the room in such a way that it seems it must have been a booth, Dudley cheats at golf, he said. He moves the ball. He improves the lie. He couldn't look at me when he said it. It was something he had to say, something he had to unveil to me, for some reason, perhaps to ward off Dudley's telling me about his wife, that he wasn't separated from her, that she was pregnant, that when he left me, he went back to her house. Perhaps Dudley had threatened him, had said he would tell me. Perhaps my father told Dudley to put a stop to it. I can't play with him anymore, Raine said. People bet money on those games. If men stop trusting you, you're dead. I bowed my head. I was ashamed. I could believe anything of Dudley, the killer, the older brother, the one who always had the best of everything, the one my father loved the best, the one who had the power and the money. And one eye. A natural athlete who lost an eye. Yes, to make up for the handicap he might cheat. Because he has to win. He can't live if he can't win, can't be second in anything. Had been kicked out of college for letting his fraternity brothers copy off of him. Had lived his life to earn my father's love, which he could have had without lifting his finger. Because he looks like my father's father. So much like him the resemblence is uncanny. If you hold their photographs up against each other it is the same soft pretty spoiled face.

If it were true? If my brother cheated other men, what did that make me? It was a long time ago, nineteen sixty-three, I did not know you could leave, bail out, refuse to be part of such a family, a family that drank and cheated, whored around. Drank and lied and cheated, biblical sins. If I had known it, I could not have acted upon it. I had hostages, three sons, no money, no education. Three times I had escaped death by bearing them and still I was alive. I was twenty-six years old, then twenty-seven. I thought there was not much time left before it would be too late, before I would die from the deep dissatisfaction of my life. I had meant to be a writer, every moment of my life, since I was four or five or six years old, had counted myself a writer, had always written everything for everyone. Had always done it well, been praised for it, received the highest grades in English class.

But that was all consumed now, consumed in the men and the babies and this terrible wealth my father had acquired and let us waste in any way we chose. As long as we stayed out of his way so he could go on making money and as long as we acted like we were happy. As long as we acted like we would never be poor, never be frightened and poor as he had been for many years. That shadow on his life, that terrible fear of being poor.

I stayed because I had to stay and because my mother and father were still pure, did not lie or cheat or steal or drink. They were still the puritans they had had to be to make the money, to save, then multiply it into millions of dollars, enough to last us all forever, we thought. But my father did not think so, drove his old car, wore his old suits, stayed home at night, stayed sober.

I stayed to take advantage of their purity. Later, when I was pure again, had purged myself of evil, had stopped drinking, lying, cheating, then I could leave, could refuse to let anyone suck the hard-won goodness from me. But this was much, much later, after years of work, of writing and psychotherapy, after twenty years I was good again. I think I will remain that way. I do not think anything could pull me down again into that mire of pain.

You'll be alone, people warned me. Won't you be lonely?

I've never been lonely in my life, I answered. But I've been afraid.

I have tried to find a way to articulate what it was between Raine and me, the thing that passes between a man and a woman that is not words, that carves below the words and ignites them. Fire, the black people call it.

I pity lovers, caught in that consumption. From the word *consume*. When nature takes us back, which we call love. I had been practicing for Raine. Four unwanted pregnancies. He had four children and this new one on the way. This inconvenient child. This child who was my enemy because I was consumed in this unholy fire.

* * *

When we ran out of gasoline on the road between Dumas, Arkansas, and McGee I was listening to a tape of Willie Nelson singing "Stardust." Coming back from seeing Raine's dying sister. I had been talking for fifty miles about where we would spend the night. He did not answer me. He knew he was going to spend the night with his wife and children and he knew better than to tell me so. I would have stolen the car keys, torn him with my fingernails, jumped out of the car, done anything. It was of no importance to me if he had a family. He was my lover. No other Raine existed for me. Because I was in this consummation, was consumed by fire.

Why else down all these centuries have women lain down with men and died in childbirth? Lain down smiling, taken pleasure in it. It has nothing to do with freedom, tenderness, pity, love. *Tenderness, pity, love,* these are words we invented to forgive ourselves.

That cold December afternoon when we saw the flying saucer. Driving along the picked cotton fields, long flat fields to the east of Jackson, at dusk, just after the sun went down. The man beside me is Raine, the one who loved me so much he lied to keep me. It is the eve of Christmas Eve and in a while he will drop me off and leave me alone at Christmas. I had to escape that knowledge so much I saw an apparition, made him see it by the force of my will, gave him an apparition so we could both escape the pain inside that car. He always said he saw it. He told everyone he did. It flew along beside us, on the horizon, inside a long blue cloud.

Finally, we stopped the car and got out and stood along the highway watching it. Many years later, I saw a film about flying saucers and the people in the movie did exactly as we did. Got out of their cars and stood along the side of a road, in little groups of two and three, watching the apparition in the sky.

Perhaps we were holding hands, the tacky topaz ring he had given me upon my finger, a ring so big it would have cut into his hand if he had squeezed it. Later I gave it to a maid or lost it or threw it away. It disappeared within a year. We stood there watching the apparition, wrapped up in the lies he told me, the thing he had done to me in Chicago when he left me alone in the room and went to the banquet without me.

Soon after that I left him. Closed up the apartment, gave the furniture away, took a series of lovers, then married the wealthy Jewish lawyer, who should have known better, and moved away.

I was burned out for a while. When I recovered it was work that saved me. The work I had abandoned when the fire that made my sons consumed me.

What will you write? my mother asked me, terrified. The truth, I answered. Stories, poems, plays.

Going to Join the Poets

𝒫

RHODA LEFT THE HOUSE on Webster Street early in the morning on a November day. Teddy may have already left to go to school. Maybe the school bus had picked him up to take him to Metairie Park Country Day School and maybe it had not. She didn't mother him anymore. Eric mothered him. He was all that Eric had because she was almost never there. It was a marriage that had failed. She wouldn't have a child for Eric and he wouldn't fuck her anymore. Not that sex between them had ever made either of them happy. It had always been a tortured, patched-up affair. Because they didn't love each other. She loved his money and he loved her cousins getting them into the tennis club. He loved Faulkner. Had written his paper on Faulkner in undergraduate school. Now he was living Faulkner. He was in the middle of a Grecian Faulkner tragedy.

After Rhoda drove off in the new green car, the green Mercedes she had bought with the bonds her father gave her, Eric got Teddy up and made breakfast for him and walked with him to where he caught the bus.

"Your mother's going to be gone awhile," he said. "Let's have some fun while she's gone. Let's go out on the boat. Invite some of your friends."

"Sure." Teddy turned to his stepfather. Trying to decide how to make him feel better. Teddy felt responsible for Eric. "She'll be back, Eric. She always comes back."

"Yeah, I know. Look, there's Robert Skelton hanging out the window looking at you." Eric patted Teddy on the arm. They were the same height now. Every month Teddy grew another inch. He was fifteen years old. Had grown so tall, so sweet, such a sweet young man, such big brown eyes. Eric's heart melted when he looked into those eyes.

Teddy climbed aboard the bus and joined his friends. They waved to Eric. They all loved Eric. He was the best of the best. The best parent any of them had.

The bus drove off down Webster Street in a cloud of black exhaust. Eric walked back to the house to get the dogs and take them for a walk. Three Old English sheepdogs, an outrageous collection of dogs, an unbelievable problem on a fifty-by-one-hundred-foot lot in uptown New Orleans.

The day was cool and fresh. The dogs went crazy when they got outside the fence. They ran everywhere, jumping and turning, making their low muffled sheepdog barks. They overwhelmed Eric, licking him and jumping up beside him. They trembled, waiting to run to the park, in the cool of the morning, waiting to jump into the lagoon and swim out through the lily pads, chasing the geese and ducks.

Aboard the bus Teddy went to the back where the dealing was being done. Robert had a bottle of pills he had stolen from his physician father. David Altmont had a small amount of marijuana. Crazy Eddy had a bottle of whiskey in his lunch box. He was too crazy. He was going to get them all in trouble. Teddy had the sheet of Windowpane he had bought the day before at Benjamin Franklin. "I tried it last night. I want to save most of it for the weekend, but I'll sell ten hits. For cash. I'm not giving this stuff away and I'm not trading."

In the front of the bus the kids who weren't into dope yet looked straight ahead. They pretended not to notice what was going on behind them. "You kids sit down back there," the bus driver yelled. "Sit down and behave yourselves." Teddy took a seat next to his best friend, Robert. "We can go out on the boat this weekend if you want to," he said. "Eric's going to take me. Momma's gone."

"Where'd she go?" Robert liked Teddy's mother. She was always nice to him and talked to him about his father.

"To Arkansas. She's gone up there to find an apartment. She's going to be gone all winter."

"Where will you stay?"

"With Eric and grandmother."

"So where'd you get the Windowpane?"

"They made a batch at Benjamin Franklin last week. It's good. I had a good time last night." He pushed up the window of the bus and stuck his arm out to shoot the peace sign to some kids in a car. He was in a good mood. Nobody was going to bother him this week. The coach was letting him suit up for the game on Saturday morning. Ellie Marcus was going to let him see her Friday night. It was okay. If only he could stay away from his grandmother, he'd be all right.

Rhoda pulled out onto the Bonnet Carré Spillway and speeded up. Hammond, then Brookhaven, then Jackson, then Vicksburg, and Raine would be waiting to drive her up to Arkansas. Well, I'm not in love with him, she was thinking. I just want him to show me how to get there. Arkansas. My God! I don't even know where it is. And I won't feel guilty. It's Eric's fault, goddammit. He shouldn't have stopped fucking me. I can't have a baby. It would kill the children if I did that. It would kill me. She shuddered, thinking of it.

It didn't matter. It didn't matter. She had loved them with all her heart and they were breaking her heart. Especially the oldest, Malcolm, who was so beautiful it seemed the sun came out when he walked into a room. Now he was gone, God knows where. Walking like a god among the hippies. Her golden son, the one who was going to swim the channel for her. She tightened her mouth, speeded up, took a curve doing ninety. It didn't matter. To hell with them. She'd do it herself, would be a poet, would have her name everywhere. Fools' names and fools' faces, always seen in public places. But it wouldn't be like that. It would be like Anne Sexton. Women would weep when they read her poems, would be fused together and save themselves because of it. She slowed down. Tears were welling up in her eyes, the tears she shed every time she thought about the day she started writing. It had happened because of a poem she read. She had gone on her bike to the Tulane track to run. Then she had changed her mind and gone to the Maple Street Bookstore instead and bought a book of Anne Sexton's poems. A posthumous book. *45 Mercy Street.* She had ridden over to the track and sat down upon a bench and started reading. "I am torn in two, but I will conquer myself. I will take scissors and cut out the beggar. I will take a crowbar and pry out the broken pieces of God in me." Then she started crying.

She came around the last curve of the Bonnet Carré Spillway and out onto the long flat bridge across the marshes. Up ahead was the high span of the bridge at Pass Manchac, then the farmlands would begin, then Mississippi, her home. Then Vicksburg, and Raine would be waiting for her, her lover, her one and only love, the one who never stopped loving her no matter how long it was or what she did. Because she was as bad as he was. Because someday she would be as strong. Someday she would overpower him, but she did not know that yet. All she knew now was that he owed her favors and she was going to collect one.

She went to the motel where she had arranged to meet him and got a room and called him and sat down upon the bed to wait. Then he was there, with his exotic smell so terrible and real, so far away from the Chi Omega sorority and anything to do with modern poetry. It was a smell for Homer and the Greeks, for Odysseus, Julius Caesar, the Kha Khan. "How've you been?" she asked him.

"I've been great, baby. How about you?"

Then she took off her clothes and lay down upon the bed with him and tried to remember how to be his baby. Yes, she thought, I do not love him anymore but I will fuck him before I use him as a chauffeur.

Later she cried, because he could always make her cry. Maybe she really wanted to kill him. After they made love they went into the motel dining room and had dinner and then he left her and went back to his house and slept with his wife.

In the morning he came and got her and drove her up to Arkansas, to his state, past the small town where he had been a hero, past towns where he had fucked every other cheerleader, past plantations that belonged to men who paid to shake his hand, past Little Rock, where his sister had died in a dirty hospital, and on up to the northwest Arkansas hills, which did not belong to him or anyone, which were going to belong to Rhoda now, because that was what she wanted.

It was late in the afternoon when they found the campus of the University of Arkansas and parked outside the tall building that housed the English Department. She had been reading the poems to him. Reading some of them two or three times. They were in a blue loose-leaf notebook, more than a hundred of them. A hundred poems she had written that summer in a hundred days. "You stay here," she said, getting out of the car. "I won't be long. I just want to say hello and tell them that I'm here." She stood holding the door of the Lincoln. She was dressed in a black wool suit with a fur collar and black silk hose and high-heeled shoes. "I hate to leave you here."

"It's okay. I'll read the poems."

"Oh, good." She smiled. For a moment she stopped being scared.

She's scared to death, Raine thought. Poor baby, this is her big chance and she doesn't want to blow it. It's just a bunch of underpaid college professors but she doesn't know it. She thinks these guys can teach her something.

He smiled the smile he used for his Little League team. "Go knock 'em dead, baby. I'll be right here." She walked across the street and into the double glass doors of the building. It was growing dark. The swift dark that falls in November. Raine took a *Sporting News* out of the glove compartment and started reading it. Then he put it down and began to leaf through the poems. He liked the one about him. The one she had written years ago at Millsaps. "Pernicious sidewinder, coiled and waiting. Cold and free." She could do it. She was a winner. Well, he was pulling for her. He was on her side.

He had been a champion. He would never have to wait on jealousy, would never have to begrudge a moment's glory to another soul. He bowed his head. Raine paid obeisance to the gods of any place. He was a decent man. Most of the time he played fair and told the truth. He looked off into the west, between two buildings. What was left of the light was spreading out into the low blue clouds on the horizon. It was pretty country, no doubt about that. If she stayed up here it might be good for her.

"Raine." He looked back toward the building. She was hurrying his way with a big man beside her. "Come meet Randolph," she was saying. "He adores you. He had a fit when he found out you were with me."

Raine got out and shook the man's hand. "I'm honored," the man said. "I saw you play when I was a kid. I couldn't believe it when she told me you were sitting outside in the car."

Later, they all went over to the big man's house and the man's wife cooked dinner. Then they sat around the living room and some young people who were trying to learn to be writers came in and met them. Raine and Randolph talked about football. Rhoda and the young people talked about poetry. She acted as if she was happy. She thinks she knows what she is doing, Raine decided. She thinks this is going to save her.

The next day they drove around and found her an apartment to rent and gave a man a deposit on it and arranged for the heat and electricity to be turned on in her name the first of January. Then they went to the big man's office and told him good-bye and then they started driving home.

They stopped in Gould, Arkansas, and bought cheese and crackers and ate them in the car as they drove. It was the first thing she had eaten in days. "I'm glad to see you eat something, baby. You don't eat enough."

"Do you think they liked me? Did Randolph say anything to you?"

"They like you, baby. Hell, compared to those women that we met, I think that skinny blonde one is a lesbian. I'd watch out for her if I was you."

"She was strange, wasn't she? They said she was a good poet but I can't believe it. She's so ugly. I don't believe in ugly poets." She scooted over closer to him and let him put his arm around her. She dropped cracker crumbs on his pants, then brushed them off. She closed her eyes and lay her head down into the crook of his shoulder. It was over. It was done. She was going to join the poets. It was okay. On the second of January she would come up here to live. Nothing else mattered. Not Eric or Teddy or Malcolm or Jimmy. Nothing mattered but the poems. The poems she would write to make women cry and break them open. To have her name in lights, to be famous, lauded and beloved. She would make it happen. It had started. Nothing could stop her now.

II

The skinny blonde girl did turn out to be a part-time lesbian. She would be whatever her ambition needed her to be. She dug her nails into poetry and held on for dear life. Poison pen, Rhoda thought of her, and it would turn out to be true.

There was also a real poet, a sweet soft girl who was married to a carpenter. The Ally, Rhoda decided. The one I can trust. The night they met they had gotten drunk on gin and laughed until two in the morning.

There was a gorgeous preppie from New England. He recognized a blanket on her bed as coming from a store in Boston. My husband went to Harvard, Rhoda told him. So they formed a bond. He's the one I'll fuck, Rhoda thought. If I can get him.

There was a dope addict and a man who ate too much and a cynical graduate student who was going to make a career of going to school. And five or six more. It was nineteen seventy-six. Writing schools were new things on the horizon. Their staffs were small and made up of people who were still writing. The students were dedicated and poor. Some of them lived on welfare and food stamps. They didn't care if they had a car. They ate and drank and slept poetry and literature.

Strangely enough, a body of poetry was arising from this heat. There was a network of poets and writing schools across the United States. Men and women were writing morning, night, and noon. Some of it was very, very good. "Like a Diamondback in the Trunk of the Witness's Buick" was a title Rhoda loved, after the poet, Francis Alter, took over her education. After he took her away from the writing program and she only listened to him.

But on this first week, this ice-cold week in January, when Rhoda drove to Fayetteville alone and moved into her freezing cold, ugly, little ground-floor apartment, the main thing she had to do was keep warm. "I don't know if you can stand the freezing winters," the director of the program had told her. "It's hard up here in winter." Now she knew what he meant. The first night she slept in the apartment she piled all her clothes on the bed and slept beneath them. It was five above zero outside. It was ten above in the apartment. The next day she went to the office of the apartment building to complain. A gas pipe was broken, she was told. We'll have it fixed sometime today.

That afternoon she went out and rented a better apartment. One in a better neighborhood, which cost twice as much. Who am I fooling? she decided. Who am I trying to fool?

Later that afternoon she walked through the snow to the English department and found Randolph, and sat around and talked to him. Another man was there, a completely beautiful man of uncertain age. "Meet Francis Alter," Randolph said. "The best poet in the state."

Their eyes met. From that moment on they would be friends. Until the day he told her good-bye and left her and went home and shot himself, not a single moment would be cruel or jealous or untrue. Many years later she knew that even the days before he did it were not untrue. He kept saying things to her that she remembered later. Look, he would say, making her look at a revision he had suggested to a poem. Look at it, Rhoda. Really listen. I won't always be here to tell you this.

Good-bye, he had said, when he embraced her, on the day before he left New Orleans and went home and shot himself. Good-bye, remember this, remember me.

She had been so lucky. All the women who made love to him, who held him in the sleepless dark nights of his soul, had never had what she had from him. She had his friendship and his help with her work. It was a gift she had longed for all her life.

So there was that first afternoon and she had met Francis in Randolph's office and they had sat around and talked, the crazy talk that writers talk, talk that transcends the food stamps and old cars and cold apartments, talk that lifts the spirit out of the realm of houses or clothes or cars. "Farewell is a sword that has worn out its scabbard," Francis had written. "Men with names like water poured from stone jugs" was the kind of line they read and talked about and marveled over.

Poetry was alive in the United States in nineteen seventy-six. I read everything that's written, Francis said. So do I, Rhoda answered. I subscribe to forty magazines.

So that was the first night and the first day. Then the classes began and Rhoda was busy from morning to night, going to classes, writing poetry, making friends. She had the new apartment with a fireplace. She had the green Mercedes. She had enough money to pay for things. She was kind and wanted to be friends with everyone. The snow fell and people had to walk uphill on dangerous icy streets to get to classes. She never complained. She never worried about the ice. She got up at dawn and wrote poetry about everything in the world, everything she could see, every person that she met. Her soul unfolded like a lotus in the freezing cold January weather, in the little mountain town, with her young brilliant broke friends.

Only the thin blonde girl was mean-spirited and angry. Rhoda tried to stay away from her, but it was hard to do. She was married to the preppie, it turned out. So Rhoda gave up on him and fucked a fiction writer instead.

In New Orleans her family was getting along quite well, so they said. "I'm fine," Teddy said, when she called him. "Stay as long as you want."

A friend of Teddy's killed himself at a party in uptown New Orleans on a Saturday night. Shot himself in the head while sitting in a car outside his girlfriend's house. We don't know why he did it, Teddy told her. It's a mystery to me.

It was not a mystery. It was LSD. The sixteen-year-old children who knew it did not tell. It never made the papers. LSD was something Rhoda could not understand. It was inconceivable to her that anyone would do something that messed with their brain. She did not know alcohol was a drug. She was dumb as a post about the brain and the things that harm it. All she knew was poetry. All she knew was fantasy and escape.

Francis had that kind of imagination. Rhoda and Francis. They had learned to throw their minds like ventriloquists. And the language they shared came from the same place, from the Mississippi Delta, from the flat black bottom lands on the Mississippi and Yazoo rivers. Francis steals from black people, his detractors said. I think I'm part black, Francis told Rhoda several times. I have the body of the black people of the Delta, the tribes from western Africa. After he said it, Rhoda began to believe it. He did have that body, those huge hip muscles, the stout intense beauty of the football players in the line at Ole Miss. I wish I had some, she answered. But I don't think I do. They made the language, Francis went on. When Africa lent its drums to English, southern speech began. Listen to the drums in Faulkner, in García Marquez, who learned from Faulkner. Can't you hear it, can't you hear the heart, the beat.

The winter wore on. Rhoda sent hundreds of poems out in envelopes to magazines she read and liked. Francis told her of other magazines, gave her things to read, the names of editors, the addresses of small presses and magazines, and, slowly at first, and then faster, Rhoda's poems began to be published. Now she didn't have as many friends as she had had at first. Now only Francis and the sweet girl poet really loved her. And Eric began to call and tell her to come home. He was lonesome for her. He was worried about Teddy. He wanted to patch up the marriage and start again.

In April, before the semester was really over, she began to leave. She took her tests, won a poetry award that made some more people hate her, began to fly home to New Orleans on the weekends. She was saying farewell to this thing she had wanted so much and now was tired of. She was tired of acting like she was poor, tired of never getting dressed up in nice clothes. She was tired of the small, poor restaurants, tired of the skinny blonde girl saying arch jealous things to her.

At that time Rhoda always kept her word. Any promise, even if she made it when she was drunk, was treated as a sacred bond. She had not learned yet how to stop people from manipulating her, had not learned how to say, I reserve the right to change my mind. I will take back promises you curry from me in moments of weakness. She was many years away from that sort of wisdom. Which is how the skinny blonde girl ended up living in her apartment, wearing all her clothes, losing half her papers, and other hardly-to-be-spoken-of invasions.

It was the last day of classes and Rhoda was preparing to go home to New Orleans. She was keeping the apartment for the summer in case she might want to come back in the fall. The clothes she wore in Fayetteville were not anything she would wear in New Orleans so she left them in the drawers and closets. The worksheets of three hundred poems and five short stories were in the dresser with underwear and flannel gowns and heavy socks on top of them.

Rhoda woke up early and packed the car, meaning to begin driving at three o'clock. She left the car in the parking lot and walked to school. It was a lovely spring day, the trees were covered with small new leaves so delicate and clean they took Rhoda's breath away. She had been living in New Orleans for so many years she had forgotten how the seasons come and go. How one day there are buds, then fatter buds, then tiny leaves which grow and darken. There was a hickory tree behind her apartment that she had been watching with great delight. On this day, at the very first of May, the leaves were half the size of her hand and she marveled at them as she walked to school.

The preppie rode up beside her on his bicycle. When he was alone he was a lovely man. He got down off the bike and walked along beside her. "I really liked the story you put on the worksheet. The one that *Intro* took. It's really good, Rhoda. The best thing that's been written all year. I bet it made Ketch jealous."

"He's mad about it. He liked me as long as I stuck to poetry. You wouldn't believe what he did to me the other night. Well, who cares. Let him fuck his boring little wife. I'm going home."

"I wish you weren't leaving. We're having a party this afternoon. That's why I stopped. To ask you to join us. We're going to barbecue a goat. Wedge is bringing it from his mother's farm."

"You're going to sacrifice a goat?" She started laughing. The preppie laughed too.

"No, it's been in a freezer. I think it's an old goat."

"Who all is coming?"

"Randolph and his wife and Doctor Wheeler. We're going to have a symposium. Judy got some acid. Have you ever done it?"

"God, no. I couldn't do anything that changed my brain. I've only smoked marijuana once and then I got paranoid and almost went crazy. I stick to gin and vodka and I've about stopped that."

"You ought to try it. Everyone ought to try it once."

"Not me. I'm too afraid."

"Well, we're going to this afternoon. You can watch. If you decide to stay, come on out."

Understand this. Rhoda had no intention of going to the goat roast even if Randolph and Doctor Wheeler were going to be there. All she wanted to do was go to her last two classes, tell a few people good-bye, and start driving.

She went to her nine o'clock Form and Theory class. Then she wandered upstairs to see if she had any mail. She had three letters. A story had been accepted in the *Prairie Schooner*. A poem had been accepted by the *Paris Review*. Her mother had written to say she better hurry home.

She threw her mother's letter in the trash can and ran into Randolph's office to tell him about the poem and the story. "This demands a celebration," he said. "Are you coming out to Ron and Judy's this afternoon?"

"They're going to take LSD."

"No one told me that. Where'd you hear that?"

"I just did. Well, I meant to drive on home. But I might as well stay another night. I'd be too excited to drive. I can't believe it. They want the story."

"It's a good story. You can write fiction as well as poems."

"Oh, God. I can't believe it. It's too good to be true." She held the letter up in the air. She shimmered. She levitated. She left the earth and flew around the ceiling of Randolph's room. He was elated too. Students being published made them all look good, made the program defensible to the dean and the board of directors of the university.

"You better come on out there this afternoon and celebrate," he said. "Nothing's going to happen. They're just going to barbecue a goat, for Christ's sake."

So she went to the party. She took half an Antabuse so she couldn't drink and ate part of a sandwich she had made the night before. She hadn't learned how to be happy yet. She didn't even know how to feed herself or treat herself to the simple joys of life. All she knew how to do was to run from pathology and become ecstatic when someone in Nebraska, whom she'd never met, told her that her work was good. That's all most people ever learn. To see their reflections in other faces.

She ate her paltry little chicken sandwich and took a bath and changed her clothes and put on tennis shoes and socks and drove out to Markham's Hill. She went up a gravel road to a yellow mailbox and turned onto a dirt road that led to a pasture on the top of the hill. An old lady owned most of the houses on the hill. She imagined herself to be a patron of the arts and rented the various houses and shacks to painters and potters and writers. It was a little community, with an open-air hot tub built by hippies in the sixties that was said to be the place where twenty people got hepatitis one winter. Rhoda was fascinated and repelled by Markham's Hill, as she always was by squalor.

Not that anything seemed squalid to her that afternoon. She had sold a story and a poem. She was going home in glory. She had come and seen and conquered. If Judy and Ron were taking LSD, or dropping acid as they called it, it would be all right. Randolph would protect her and maybe later she could write about it. Nothing is ever lost on a writer, she told herself. Since today she believed she was one.

The barbecue pit was dug. The goat was roasting on the coals. Ketch was standing by the pit looking glum. He barely glanced up when she said hello to him. She shrugged it off and went over to the steps where the overeater poet was holding forth about hogscalds in the Ozark Mountains.

Judy came down the stairs wearing a cotton dress that made her look like a farm wife. "I sold a story and a poem," Rhoda couldn't resist saying.

"Who to?" Judy asked.

"The *Paris Review* and the *Prairie Schooner.*"

"You ought to send them to *Ironwood*. It would be better."

"Is Randolph here yet?"

"He's in the backyard, at the horseshoe pit." She motioned around the side of the house. Rhoda walked that way and found him pitching horseshoes with two of the students.

This afternoon was going to be a wash. That much was clear. This afternoon would waste the fine happiness of the morning, not to mention a day of driving time.

"Here's Rhoda," Randolph said. "She sold a story and a poem. Give her a drink, somebody. Come on, girl, you want to pitch horseshoes with us?"

"Not that I know of. I'll just watch. I just want a Coke, Tom. A Coke will be fine." The young man walked over to a tub of ice and reached down and retrieved a Coke and gave it to her. The preppie who was married to the skinny blonde bitch was behind him.

"I heard there was a hot tub that spread hepatitis from here to Maine," Rhoda said to the preppie. "Where is it? I'd like to see it."

"Come on. It isn't far. I'll walk you there." They set off down a path behind the house.

"Should you leave?" Rhoda asked. "What about the goat?"

"They'll take care of it. Wedge is doing it." He took her arm. They walked in silence for a hundred yards or so. When they were out of sight of the house, he pulled her to him and kissed her. "There," he said. "Sooner or later I had to do that."

"You're married to Judy," Rhoda said. "I'm swearing off married men."

"I married her when I was drunk. I'd leave today if I had anywhere to go. We live together because it's convenient. We don't fuck."

"Well, I don't want her mad at me. I'm scared to death of Judy." Rhoda stepped farther back.

"She's dropping acid. She wouldn't care if you fucked me by the barbecue pit."

"When is she going to do it?"

"She's doing it now. She did it this morning. Didn't you think she looked sweet? She gets sweet when she's high."

"Let's go back. I really want to go on back. I need to start driving. I need to get to Little Rock by midnight." Rhoda started back up the path. Judy was coming down the other way to meet them. Randolph was behind her. "I wanted to talk to you about something," Judy said, when the four of them met at a clearing in the path.

"Sure," Rhoda said.

"I was wondering. We're being evicted here in two weeks. I wonder if you'd let us sleep in your apartment for a few days while we wait to get our new apartment. I know it's an imposition, but Randolph said you were keeping it for the summer. It would be such a help. We have all this stuff and nowhere to put it."

"Sure," Rhoda said. "If it's only for a few days. But you have to take care of things. I left all my papers there. And I might come back at any time. I mean, I'm not going to be gone all summer. I have to come and get my mail."

"How could we get in?" Judy asked. She was beaming, standing in the shadow of divine Randolph, who was the most generous of men. Weighed down with Randolph's goodness and the triumph of the day and the need to escape and the shameful burden of her husband's money, Rhoda looked at the preppie, not at Judy, and said yes.

"You have to stay clear of my papers," she repeated. "I don't want anyone to even touch them."

"Of course," they said. So Rhoda took a key ring out of her pocketbook and removed a key and handed it over.

"Thanks so much," Judy exclaimed. "You don't know what this means to us."

Randolph was shaking his head from side to side. Randolph was not pleased.

By seven o'clock that night Rhoda was on the road. By ten she was in Little Rock. She stopped at a restaurant and called home and talked to her husband and Teddy. "I miss you so much," she told them and it was true. Then she called Raine and told him to come and meet her and he did. He got into a car and drove to Dumas, Arkansas, and met her there in the middle of the night and held her in his arms and made her cry. "Everything you said came true," she told him. "My work is being published everywhere. It terrifies me and I love it. I don't know what I'm doing. I have to go home and see what's wrong with Teddy. I have to mend my marriage. No one can live two lives at once. I'm schizophrenic from all this traveling. Now that bitch is going to stay in my apartment. I'm scared to death to have her in the same place as my papers. I'm paranoid and schizophrenic and I miss my sons."

"It's okay, baby," he said to her. "Go to sleep now. It will be better in the morning."

It was better. She spent the morning with Raine and took strength from him. She showed him the poems she had been writing. She sat beside him on a bed and ate breakfast on a tray and giggled and was happy. Then she dressed and drove home to New Orleans. It would be all right. The world was a goodly place. People could be trusted. There was time for everything.

In New Orleans Teddy and Eric were straightening up the house to get ready for her homecoming. They had been vacuuming for hours to get the dog hairs off the rugs and sofas. They had filled the refrigerator. Their mother was coming home.

In Fayetteville the skinny blonde poet and her husband and a lesbian friend were moving into Rhoda's apartment. They took all her clothes and papers out of the drawers and put them in boxes and lined them up against the wall. They brought in their typewriters and bicycles and the remains of the goat. They turned the air conditioning down to sixty-eight degrees. It was going to be a splendid summer. Living off the rich bitch from New Orleans. Off the fat of the land.

Rhoda walked into her house in New Orleans late that afternoon. Eric and Teddy were waiting for her. They had taken the sheepdogs to the vet to have them cleaned. They had put on clean shirts and combed their hair. They took her to the darkroom and showed her the photographs they had made of people in the park. After a while Teddy went down the street to a friend's house and Rhoda awkwardly made love to her husband. "I love you," she said, and she meant it. She did love Eric, his intelligence and goodness, his kindness and hope and gentle charm, his love for her child.

"We will start again," he said.

"Good," she answered. They both hoped it was so.

May went by and June and July. Rhoda took Teddy to a child psychiatrist. Teddy went to the psychiatrist on Monday and Wednesday and Friday. Eric and Rhoda talked to the psychiatrist on Thursdays. "You have to discipline him," the psychiatrist said. "He wants you to."

"Well, we aren't going to hit him." Rhoda laughed and looked at Eric. The psychiatrist was seventy years old. He was a friend of Eric's parents. Both of his children were doing all right. In a world of insane children, his children were married and sane. Rhoda and Eric had decided to take his advice.

"Be stronger than he is. Don't give him money."

"Is he taking dope?" They leaned toward the psychiatrist.

"I don't think so. But his friends are. Watch his friends. Keep him busy."

"He won't go to camp. He came home the first week last year. We wasted two thousand dollars on that camp."

"Get him a job."

"Okay. We'll try."

Teddy got himself a job. He got a job being a roadie for the Neville Brothers. He carried their instruments in and out of Tipitina's when they did their gigs.

Eric and Rhoda didn't know what to think about Teddy's job. They didn't know what was going on in the world enough to understand Tipitina's. Rhoda had seen the graduate students taking dope in Fayetteville but she didn't believe that applied to Teddy. Not sweet little Teddy with his sheepdogs and his camera and his bright red hair.

"I think it's a terrible idea," Eric said. "It's a bar."

"At least it's music," Rhoda answered. "At least it's art."

"We'll wait and see." Eric was in a quandary. He was so glad to have his wife back that he didn't want to queer it by being too suspicious of Teddy. He took Rhoda's arm. He smiled his Holden Caulfield smile. He was rewarded. She took him into the bedroom and made love to him.

In July Rhoda got an electric bill from Fayetteville for three hundred dollars. She got a phone bill for more than that. "I'd better go up there and see what's going on," she told Eric. "I want to get my mail. I have to kick those kids out of my apartment."

"Okay," he said. "If you have to. But don't stay too long. We need you here. Teddy needs you. I need you." He held his breath. He controlled his mind. He was a mensch.

"You're the sweetest man in the world," she said. She meant it. She knew that it was true.

That afternoon at Tipitina's one of the other roadies gave Teddy his first line of cocaine. He came home in a fabulous mood. He was so sweet to everyone. He went to the darkroom and developed film for two hours. He told his mother to go on and get her mail "Don't worry about anything," he told her. "I'll be with Eric. Stay as long as you want. We're just fine. I like my work. I'm learning so much. We have plenty to do."

In the morning Rhoda called her apartment and told the skinny blonde girl that she was coming to Fayetteville. "Be sure you're gone by then," she said. "I'm going to be real tired when I get there."

"Don't worry about the bills," the skinny blonde girl said. "We'll pay you back. I applied for a National Endowment grant. I'm pretty sure I'm going to get it."

"Just be sure you're out of my apartment, Judy."

"Oh, we will be. Don't worry about that. It was nice of you to let us stay."

Rhoda drove all afternoon and spent the night in Little Rock. The next morning she drove to Fayetteville and got there at noon. Judy and Ron were just getting up. The lesbian on the sofa was still asleep. They had had a party the night before.

"My God," Rhoda said. "I can't believe this. You promised me you'd be gone."

"Our place wasn't ready yet."

"Well, you have to get out of here. I mean right now." Rhoda stood in the living room trying not to look at the lesbian, who was a small, thin girl who only seemed to be along for the ride. Rhoda kept on standing there while Ron and Judy got dressed and packed some things and started taking them to the car. "I want all this stuff out of here right now," Rhoda said. "I mean it. My God, where are my things?"

"Calm down," Judy said. "You don't understand."

"I understand that this is my apartment and you said you were going to stay a few days and it's July. For Christ's sake. And you owe me
six hundred dollars for the phone and electric bill."

"You can afford it," Judy said. "Get your husband to pay for it."
She shifted the canvas bag to her other side. She waited.

"Get that typewriter off the dining room table. I mean it, Judy.
Get all this junk out of here by the time I get back. I'm going to see
Randolph."

"He knows we're staying here. We had him over one night to eat
supper."

"Oh, my God." Rhoda walked through the apartment opening
drawers and closets. The bedroom closets were stuffed with piles of
half-clean clothes. There were milk crates marked *Do Not Remove
From Premises*, filled with bric-a-brac.

Rhoda walked back into the living room and glared at Ron and
the lesbian and went out to her car and drove over to Wheeler Hall.

"I wondered what you'd think," Randolph said. "I should have
called you, but they said you knew. Christ, the suitors from Ulysses.
We went over there one night. Shannon was appalled. She told me to
call you. I should have done it."

"They'd better be gone when I get back."

"Good luck."

"I'll go get my mail."

"Why wouldn't you let us forward it?"

"I don't know. There's something about having a mailbox here.
It's important to me somehow. It feels lucky." She smiled. Her work.
Something of value that she alone had created. Her heart lifted, as it
often did in Randolph's presence. How did he have the bounty, the
largess, to go on giving and giving and giving. "I feel bad about being
so mean to them. After all, they're broke."

"They're grown people, Rhoda. Her parents are physicians in
Kansas City. She went to Duke. She's doing what she wants to do."

"Who's the lesbian?"

"Someone from Sassafras in Eureka Springs. They rescue housewives." He started laughing. Rhoda started laughing too. They wept

with laughter at the madness and divinity of humankind. Above Randolph's desk was a poster of Botticelli's *Primavera*. Rhoda laughed into the flowers on the heavenly woman's dress.

The day got better. There were five good letters in the stacks of mail. Two were acceptances of poems. Another was an encouraging letter from the *Atlantic Monthly*. One was an apology from Ketch. He was working in Washington, D.C., at the Library of Congress. He was reading the Christian Existentialists. He said he was sorry he had treated Rhoda as a Thou.

The fifth was from the *Prairie Schooner*. They were giving her a prize. A thousand-dollar prize for the story they were publishing in October.

Rhoda clasped the letters to her bosom. She was lucky again. Fayetteville was lucky for her. She was the luckiest woman on the earth. She went back over to the apartment and helped Ron and Judy pack up their things. She let them leave some of their stuff in the coat closet in the hall. She let them leave a whole closet full of musty half-clean clothes piled from floor to ceiling in the only storage closet in the house. She forgave them their debt. She offered to buy them dinner soon. She watched them drive away. She took an envelope the lesbian had given her into the house and wrote a check for fifty dollars to the place in Eureka Springs that saved the housewives and almost mailed it. She found the vacuum sweeper. She vacuumed the rugs. She called a housecleaning service and made a date with them for the following afternoon. She wiped off the table. She got her old Royal portable typewriter out of the pantry and set it on the table. She put a new ribbon in it. She found a ream of bond paper and set it on the table. She was a writer. In the morning she would begin to write.

She put on her old shoes and left the apartment and began to walk. She walked up to the campus and watched the sun go down. What the hell, this was her life as a writer. This crazy town that she had found that had nothing to do with any other life that she had ever led. She was here. She was back where she belonged. She could stay awhile. Maybe she would come back in the fall.

★　★　★

That night Eric called. She told him about the prize from the *Prairie Schooner*. She told him about the lesbian. She told him about the piles of dirty clothes. She laughed uproariously as she told it. "Fateville," she said. "Home of the Hogs and the Poets."

"Sounds like the suitors from Ulysses," Eric answered.

"That's what Randolph said. God, Eric, I forget how smart you are. How educated. I envy you your education. Listen, I won't stay long. Just a week or so. I need to clean this place up for the fall and answer all this mail. Is Teddy okay?"

"He's fine. You're going back in the fall? You definitely have to do that?" He sighed. He looked off into a bank of ferns growing in the dormer windows of his kitchen. His wifeless kitchen.

"Oh, please. Don't be mad about it. I have to have my turn. I never had a turn, Eric. All I had were babies."

"It's all right. But come home soon if you're going back in the fall."

"I'll fly home every weekend. I'll fix it so I don't have classes on Friday. I'll stay here from Monday to Thursday and be home every weekend. I thought about that driving up here. I figured it out. I love you, Eric. The happier I am, the more I love you. Don't you know that? Be happy for me. Let me have this. I have to have this. It's so important to me." She drew in her breath. She waited.

"Of course. Whatever you want, Rhoda. Whatever you have to have. But I miss you."

"I miss you. I love you. Take care of Teddy. It won't be long. Well, I better go now. I want to do some work."

She hung up the phone. Then she took it off the hook. Then she made a pot of coffee and went to her typewriter and decided to write all night. It was her one and only life. Her one and only chance. The best year of her life. The year her dreams might all come true.

snuffled

sniff